Unwanted Suspicion

A Teresa Da Silva novel, Volume 1

M J Dees and Michael Dees

Published by Michael Dees, 2022.

UNWANTED SUSPICION

First edition. June 21, 2022.

Copyright © 2022 M J Dees and Michael Dees.

ISBN: 979-8215633182

Written by M J Dees and Michael Dees.

Unwanted Suspicion
(Previously released as Living with Saci)

Set in the sprawling metropolis of Sao Paulo, Brazil, Unwanted Suspicion tells the story of Teresa da Silva, overweight, depressed, drink dependent, and her struggles in the city, estranged from her daughter who lives with her ex-husband in England. Teresa seems to be constantly dealt a bad hand, and she wonders whether the mischievous character from Brazilian folklore, Saci, might have something to do with it. Events seem to take a turn for the positive when she meets Felipe, who asks her to marry him, but when he disappears, Teresa finds she is the object of suspicion.

Chapter One - The Dentist – 11th January 2016

The building was as she remembered it. A private house before they had converted it into a dental practice. Large, beautiful faces with perfect teeth now obscured the front. Huge bubble letters spelt the words: 'Teeth U Like.' Teresa got her breath back from the short walk and reached up to press the entry phone button. She couldn't quite decipher the tinny voice which crackled through a small plastic speaker.

"I have an appointment?" She asked, unable to hear the reply before the device buzzed at her. She heard a metallic clunk, and the large gate opened an inch. Teresa pushed her way through and, with effort, closed the gate behind her.

"Name?" the receptionist asked between smiles.

"Teresa Da Silva. I'm early."

The receptionist was indifferent to Teresa's punctuality.

"Take a seat." she smiled.

Teresa flopped onto the only chair, a large sofa. She slumped down into its brown leather cushions and waited. Her phone vibrated. It was a text from her fiancé, Felipe, telling her he loved her and that he was sorry. She was about to text a reply when she heard her name.

"You can go through," said the receptionist.

"Through here?" Teresa pointed to the only door in the room other than the entrance.

"Yes." the receptionist sighed.

Teresa opened the door and walked into a white room filled with modern dental equipment. A man in a white medical coat was arranging utensils.

"Good afternoon, you can leave your bag here," the dentist turned and gesticulated to a chair.

Teresa had forgotten how good looking he was. She realised her phobia of dental work must have been huge to keep her away from that man for five years, but she could tolerate the pain in her jaw no longer. She climbed onto the examination chair.

"OK, let's have a look," he said.

Teresa imagined him leaning over and kissing her and then reminded herself she was still engaged to be married, even if her fiancé was a bastard. The dentist turned away, fiddling with something outside Teresa's vision. When he returned, he was wearing a surgical mask.

Teresa opened her mouth to expose her valuable collection of old fillings and complementary decay.

"Hmm," the dentist mused, peering inside.

Did dentists only date people with perfect teeth? What about bad breath? She tried to stop breathing for a while, but couldn't keep it up for long. She needed to swallow.

There was a bang and a loud metallic crash outside, then distant shouting.

"Excuse me." the charming dentist left to investigate.

Teresa lay still for a moment, her mouth wide open. She closed her stiff jaw.

More shouts. In the next room. A woman's scream.

Shit.

What should she do?

Teresa sat frozen in the chair until her amygdala allowed her frontal lobes to consider the problem. Before her frontal lobes made up their minds, a masked man burst through the door and pinned Teresa to the chair, knife in her face.

"Money!" ordered the knifeman.

Teresa kept her hand in clear view and pointed toward her handbag. Knifeman glanced at the bag and punched Teresa in the face.

Darkness.

*

Teresa's face hurt. She smelt burning. Her mouth, arms, and legs would not move. She was on a hard surface. She opened her eyes and recognised the white floor and white equipment.

She remembered what had happened and panicked. Wriggling and loosening what felt like tape binding her wrists, she twisted and turned, creating enough distance between her two chubby wrists to use her arms to prop herself up. From where was the burning coming? She looked around the room. It must be coming from outside. She listened, holding her breath.

Silence.

Where were the charming dentist and his receptionist? The robbers? Her handbag?

Teresa searched for something to cut the tape. The best she could find was the corner of a Formica cupboard door. Unable to stand up and search on the high surfaces, Teresa backed up to the cabinet and rubbed the tape up and down the Formica corner. She pulled her wrists further apart until the tape snapped and she was free to examine her wrists: red, sore and littered with shreds of tape that ripped the tiny bleached hairs off her arms when she tried to remove them. Leaving the remaining tape and turning her attention to her ankles, Teresa expected knifeman to burst in at any moment and was desperate to get free and get away. Teresa pulled at the bindings. Unable to tear the tape, she took a deep breath and, despite her heart almost beating itself out of her chest, somehow found the patience to locate the end and unwind it. Free of her bonds, Teresa stood, placed her ear against the door. Although she heard nothing, the smell of burning was stronger.

Teresa took a deep breath and eased the door open enough to peer through. She could see something smoking on the sofa. The same sofa she had been waiting on not so long ago. The sofa itself seemed to smoulder. A charred lump, spread out on it, was smoking. Teresa peered, trying to make out its shape, then fell back in horror as she realised the piece of smoking remains had hands.

Teresa retched, but nothing came out. She spat a mouthful of bile and wiped her mouth on her sleeve. What to do? She looked around the examination room for a phone. There wasn't one. She looked for an exit. None. Not even a window. The way out was through the reception past the smoking corpse. She took another deep breath, walked to the door, and pushed it open. There it was. She opened the door wide and looked around. No-one. No-one except the burnt remains on the sofa of the dentist or receptionist, she assumed. Teresa tried to give the corpse a wide berth, but, because of an overwhelming curiosity she could not control, she turned and looked. Looked at the two white round eyes staring back at her in desperation.

Darkness.

Chapter Two - The Fiancé – 12th January 2016

"What is your health plan?" the nurse asked.

"Banco São Paulo," Teresa answered.

The nurse frowned.

"We don't work with them," she said, handing Teresa another piece of paper.

"What's this?" Teresa asked.

"Your invoice," the nurse gesticulated to a cupboard in the corner. "Your clothes," she said, turning on her heels and leaving before Teresa could form any thoughts into sentences.

She looked at the paper.

Jesus!

What did they do to her? How long had she been in the hospital? They hadn't fixed her teeth. Her jaw ached worse than ever. She examined the paper, but none of it made sense except the large number at the bottom. This would swallow all the savings she had put aside to see her daughter.

Teresa opened the cupboard and discovered her clothes in a neat pile on the bottom shelf. She got dressed quickly and, leaving the room, found herself in a long white hospital corridor opposite the nurses' station.

"Excuse me," she said to the woman behind the counter, who seemed engrossed in paperwork.

"Excuse me." She repeated.

"One minute." The woman did not look up from her sea of forms.

Teresa waited. She shifted, coughed. She looked around. The woman looked up.

"Yes?" she asked.

"There's been some mistake," Teresa said, showing the woman the piece of paper. "I'm not sure how long I've been here but..."

"No mistake." the woman interrupted after the briefest of glances at the sheet.

"But it seems rather a lot." Teresa protested.

"You'll have to speak to your health plan for a reimbursement."

"How long have I been here? Did the police bring me here?" Teresa asked.

"I just got on." the woman answered, burying her head in her papers again, suggesting the conversation was over.

Teresa looked around and headed for the exit. Felipe, her fiancé, must be worried sick by now. She hadn't spoken to him since their argument or replied to his text before going to see the dentist. Teresa also wanted to ask him if he knew anything about Oliver, her missing cat. She thought she heard the nurse shouting something after her, but ignored her and continued to head for the exit, having to squeeze past two police officers who wanted to use the automatic sliding doors at the same time as her.

Teresa left the hospital car park and stepped out into the bright daylight of São Bernardo do Campo.

São Bernardo do Campo was much like any other satellite city of São Paulo. Grey concrete, broken tarmac, a tangle of black wires overhead strung from decaying concrete lampposts. Half-finished buildings rising out of every hill, their fragile brick facades shrouded with veils like virgins on their wedding days. Teresa understood the veils were to stop the bits falling off the buildings from killing anyone on the dirty streets below and Teresa considered the streets of São Bernardo do Campo to be filthier than most. Summer was well underway now, and the cockroaches were venturing out of the drains to escape the heat and feast on the detritus strewn around.

With no money, no cards, no phone, no idea of anyone's phone number and seeing as though the hospital hadn't mentioned that she was too ill to walk the 5km back to her house, she set off. In fact, the hospital said nothing about her condition. They didn't seem too worried. They offered her the use of their phone, but Teresa didn't remember any phone numbers. When she was younger, before mobile phones, she could remember at least a few: her parents' home phone, their work phones, her work phone, her home phone, her boyfriend's home and work phone (when she had a boyfriend, which was rare). Now the only number she remembered was her own.

What to do? She couldn't call anyone or pay for a bus or a taxi to get home. Then she remembered. Biometrics. She could use a cashpoint without her card by using her fingerprint. Brilliant. Now all she needed to do was find a bank. She looked up and down the street, recognised where she was and started walking towards where the city centre was.

A drop of water bounced off her cheek, and she looked up at the grey sky. Another droplet landed in her eye. She looked at the pavement as she walked and saw the light grey concrete become light and dark grey polka-dot with the dots becoming more plentiful.

'Bugger', she thought, recalling the moment she disposed of the latest broken umbrella in a street bin. Oh well. São Paulo needed the rain after months of drought and getting a little bit wet was not the worst thing to happen to her recently.

The rain wasn't heavy enough to soak her, only sufficient to make her damp as the droplets soaked into her blouse and made the material like a wet dishcloth.

By the time she reached the bank, she was more than damp and realised that she was dripping on the polished tile floor. To reach the cash machines during the day, she first needed to negotiate a revolving door that was also a metal detector which would refuse to turn at the slightest hint of guns, bombs, knives, keys, coins or mobile phones. She would need to empty the contents of her pockets into a small clear plastic tray built into the door designed to shield benign metal objects from the metal detecting door while making them visible to the security guard. Usually, Teresa carried so much metal that it was easier to deposit her handbag in a locker at the bank's entrance. Today, most of her metal objects had been stolen, so she only needed to drop her keys into the tray and, pushing at the door, she found it moved without objection.

At the cash machine, instead of inserting her card, Teresa touched the screen and, when prompted, placed her right index digit on the fingerprint reader. Happy with her identity, the machine asked what service Teresa would like it to perform. She asked for a modest amount of money so as not to venture too much further towards her already embarrassing overdraft limit. She heard the machine counting the notes. Teresa grabbed the cash and stuffed it into her pocket.

'At least I haven't lost my keys too', she thought as she reached home, fumbling for the one which unlocked the padlock on the gate. She twisted the key in the lock and shut the gate behind her, then opened the door leading straight into the kitchen, taking care lest her remaining cat escape.

There was no sign of Felipe anywhere, and it was only when she returned to the kitchen, she saw the folded piece of paper on the small metal kitchen table. She picked it up and read Felipe's handwriting.

I have gone to end it all. You will be happier without me.

Teresa slumped into a kitchen chair. Things were bad, but not this bad. At first, it seemed like some sick joke. Teresa tried to find her address book to get the number for her brother's wife. She was a police officer. She would understand what to do. Teresa preferred to speak to Selma than call Felipe's family.

As Teresa waited for Selma to arrive, she fed the remaining, now ravenous, cat, Ramsey. There was still no sight of Oliver, but as she searched the flat, opening every cupboard in case the moggy had trapped itself somewhere, she found Felipe's phone.

Teresa opened Felipe's messages. At the messages he'd sent her just before his disappearance, in the past hours and day, right up to the last SMS he'd sent her telling her he loved her just before she was called in to see the dentist. Skimming through them in reverse order was a bizarre rewind from desperation, anger, despair, recriminations, doubt, paranoia, entreaties, irritation, worry, questions and at first declarations of love.

Teresa panicked. The police would want to see his phone. What if they saw all these messages? They would question her involvement in his disappearance. Especially considering the content of some messages. Could this jeopardise her position at the school? What should she do? She couldn't risk anything that might lead to her losing her job. She couldn't delete all the messages, could she? The police were bound to be even more suspicious if there was no evidence of her boyfriend having texted her. Perhaps she should delete some of the worst messages. She tried not to look at his note on the table on the other side of the kitchen. Teresa could sense him staring at her from wherever he was. She went through his texts and deleted the most incriminating. What else?

She scanned through his other messages to his mum and dad and sister. The general collection of abbreviations that Teresa struggled to decipher. Why hadn't he gone to his family? That's what confused Teresa. Was his relationship with them as bad as he said? Why not go to them if he couldn't take things any longer? She made herself a large gin and tonic and felt guilty that she had been so selfish, thinking about herself when Felipe could be dead, not bearing to imagine what might have happened to him.

She heard a sound of clapping from outside and put down the phone, shut Ramsey in the living room and walked to the door, unlocking it. Selma stood at the other side of the gate. Teresa's brother's wife.

Teresa fumbled with the keys as she tried to open the gate, hugging Selma before her sister-in-law pushed past her and into the kitchen. Teresa closed the gate and door, then stood, feeling like a spare part as she watched Selma examine Felipe's note.

Selma pulled out her phone, dialled a number and, within a moment, was rattling on. Teresa struggled to understand Selma at the best of times because of her slang. Even when Selma was speaking to her slowly and directly, Teresa struggled to understand, so this conversation was impossible to follow, except for the occasional 'he' and 'her.'

Teresa gave up and sat on a kitchen chair, picking up Felipe's phone.

Selma hung up and turned to Teresa. She looked at the phone in Teresa's hands.

"Is that his?" she asked.

"Yes," Teresa replied and handed the phone over to Selma.

Selma tapped the screen and examined the contents for a moment before pocketing the device.

'Shit.' thought Teresa, but she'd always been intimidated by Selma and was not about to ask for the phone back.

Then came the questions, routine, Selma assured, asking where Felipe might have gone and whether the note meant what it seemed to say. The questioning seemed to Teresa to go on forever. Teresa remembered a conversation she'd once had with Felipe at the beach when he told her that his preferred method of suicide would be drowning and she described the location to her sister-in-law.

Selma several times invited Teresa to spend the night at her house, but each time Teresa refused.

"It's kind of you," said Teresa. "But I want to be left by myself to gather my thoughts."

After several more attempts to convince her and a protracted and awkward phone conversation with Teresa's brother, Selma prayed for her and left her alone.

Teresa was lonely in the empty house and yet she couldn't help the strange sensation that, at any moment, she might see Felipe round every corner. She let Ramsey out of the living room, made herself another large gin and tonic. She took it into the bedroom. Felipe was not there. She slipped off her clothes and crawled under the sheets. Ramsey, her remaining black cat, seemed aware of her distress, curled up close to her. Everything else could wait until tomorrow.

Teresa tried to sit up, unable to move. Someone seemed to have secured her somehow. Her hands were tied. She was back in the dentist's surgery, fastened to the chair. The dentist was there, his back to Teresa, but reached out a charred arm from which black, putrid skin fell away, revealing pink cooked flesh and bone.

The dentist turned his charred face to Teresa, and his bony hand removed his blood-stained surgical mask to reveal Felipe's tormented face.

"Water." Felipe's ghost pleaded with her. "Why did you let them bury me? I'm not dead."

Dead Felipe leant closer to kiss her, pieces of his decomposing nose falling onto her face.

Teresa opened her mouth to scream as loud as her lungs would allow, but a slither of burnt flesh dropped into her mouth, stifling all sound and causing Teresa to vomit.

She awoke, sitting upright. A pool of vomit soaking into the thin sheet which covered her lap and now stuck to her sweat and vomit covered thighs.

It was still dark. Teresa bundled up the wet sheet as best as she could and, trying her utmost not to drop any vomit on the carpet, carried the sheet into the bathroom and dumped it onto the cold tile floor.

Switching on the light, Teresa glanced at her pallid face in the mirror before dousing it with cold water.

She patted her face dry with the hand towel that smelt of Felipe. Anxiety was welling up inside her as she contemplated where he might have gone or what he might have done.

Teresa switched off the bathroom light, then hovered in the bedroom, deciding against going back to bed and choosing instead to go into the kitchen and make herself a drink.

The ice clinked as it tumbled into the glass and seemed to crackle with delight as Teresa poured in a generous helping of gin, a taste she developed during her years in England. This cheap brand she found on her return to Brazil. Even the tonic seemed to fizz with enthusiasm as it joined the mix.

'If Felipe were here now.' she thought. 'He'd be reminding me how gin causes depression.'

How ironic that seemed to her now as she took a large gulp of her cold fizzy drink that seemed the best thing she'd tasted in days or at least hours.

Teresa slumped on her makeshift sofa, a mattress on two piles of pallets, and listened to the rain falling outside. When she finished the glass, fatigue got the better of her, and she curled up where she was and dropped off to sleep once more.

Teresa woke, wondering where Felipe was, before her memory came flooding back to her, and she shivered in horror, wanting to go back to sleep and forget about it all, but it was too late. Her head was already full of the images of the dentist, and Ramsey decided it was time for Teresa to feed him. There was nothing more she could do but get up and face the day.

Teresa sat up and shuffled off the sofa. She wandered into the bathroom and realised how clean it was. The bedroom had been tidy too and, as Teresa walked through the rest of the house, she noticed that the living room and kitchen were also spotless. Why didn't she notice this yesterday? So, he'd tidied the house before he left.

Teresa felt even guiltier now. But there was no reason she could think of for not making coffee so, after feeding the hungry cat, she did that and sat down.

Teresa was on holiday. One benefit of working in her school was fifteen weeks off. It would be at least another two weeks before she would have to go back to work and explain anything to anyone. The trouble was she would have to spend those two weeks dealing with her family and Felipe's family and all the questions.

Teresa was listening to the coffee machine spitting its contents into the glass jug and Ramsey munching on his breakfast when a slow round of applause outside the gate caught her attention. Teresa shut Ramsey in the living room again and went to the door. Oh God, it was Selma.

'Bloody hell. What time is it?' thought Teresa. She tried to change her facial expression from annoyance to welcome as quickly as she could, but with little success.

"I've some news," said Selma, looking at Teresa in her dressing gown and slippers.

"What is it?" Teresa looked at Selma and realised it was not good.

"They've found his clothes," she said. "And his wallet."

Chapter Three - The Lover – 7th December 2008

Teresa lay on her back on the bed with her legs apart, looking at the bald patch of the doctor, who stared between her knees at her disappointing cervix. Between contractions, she looked at the man beside her and wondered how she had arrived at this point in her life.

He used to come into the coffee shop in Waterloo Station, where she worked. He spoke undecipherable sentences to her. She was sure they must have been delightful but, after only two weeks in the country, she could not understand a word he said. She was not the one taking the orders. One of her fellow Brazilians on the tills would hand her a cup and tell her what to make. She knew how to make the drinks because her friend Jose explained to her in Portuguese, but the conversations which went on between Jose on the till and the customers remained alien to her.

It must have been about six months, during which she began to understand his advances until, after rejecting him on at least three occasions, she agreed to go with him on a date. She learned how he had become addicted to caffeine to create opportunities to speak to her over the counter, that his name was William, and he was an environmentalist.

He invited her to visit his environmental collective, the Gaia community, where Teresa met a collection of people sporting hairstyles the likes of which she had never seen before, from blankets of dreadlocks collected up under knitwear to creatively shaved heads. She would visit William at the collective in-between her shifts at the coffee shop, occasional cleaning jobs and even more occasional visits to the language school, which was the reason for her visa. She even volunteered at the community.

William was a paid member of staff, paid through National Lottery funding, and he would joke on the rare occasion he bought a lottery ticket, he was paying himself.

Within another six months, Teresa moved out of her flat share in Harlesden and into William's flat in Stockwell where he proposed to her, and she accepted, and within six more, she discovered she was pregnant.

Still fearing the Catholicism of her parents, she arranged the wedding and executed it in extreme haste, so that the bump would not show. Less than six months later, Teresa found herself in an NHS ward being told by a balding man that her cervix was too stubborn to dilate enough and that they would have to do something.

Chapter Four - The Fiancé's Family – 13th January 2016

Teresa found the cemetery a dull place. They were all there. The sister, mother, father and brother. All teary. Some of them must have travelled through the night to be there. Teresa hugged them all and made all the right noises, but she was surprised to find she didn't want to cry in the slightest. It made her feel guilty, and with that sensation alone, she could maintain a solemn countenance. Her overriding emotion was one of embarrassment. She considered that Felipe's family might blame her for his demise, and this knowledge made her uncomfortable. She tried to stay out of the way as much as possible while seeking to look interested in proceedings, which she considered a pointless exercise and, in fact, a complete waste of everyone's time. Even though Teresa believed in the afterlife, she also believed that now he was dead, Felipe was only a fleshy sack of body parts. The Felipe that Teresa knew, loved and hated, had departed before she'd arrived home and this ceremony to bury a bag of molecules irritated Teresa as much as everything else in her world.

Teresa was suffering. But not from grief. She would suffer her grief on her own, away from these people. Felipe's mother, Lucretia, was bawling her eyes out like the drama queen she was. Teresa wondered whether Lucretia had displayed the same extremes of emotion earlier this morning when selecting the designer clothes to wear for the funeral.

Felipe's father, Jose, sat at the side, trying not to notice the antics of his wife. That he only had one eye, the other being a glass replacement for the eye he lost in a strange accident in the operating theatre, made the job of ignoring his wife easier. The freakishness of the situation was that he had been the surgeon operating, and the accident led to retirement and the opportunity for his wife and children to spend the results of his settlement claim, from the expensive private hospital, which did not want its valued clients to hear that faulty operating theatre equipment had almost blinded one of their leading surgeons. Teresa felt sorry for Jose, not least for having to live with Lucretia for so long. He was a broken man, long accustomed to his wife telling him what to do. Lucretia selected Jose's clothes too, judging by the uncomfortable manner in which he sat in them. Felipe's sister, Patricia, was doing her best to be a young Lucretia. Going through exaggerated motions of grief, embracing her mother and trying to make everyone aware that she cared.

'You didn't care much when he was alive.' thought Teresa.

Then there was Felipe's brother, who had selected a wife as ferocious as his mother so he could be as hen-pecked as his father. His wife, Izadora, sat at his side, critical. Just her expression, her half-closed eyes, told everyone that, had she been in charge today, she would have done things better.

Their child, Carlos, sat fiddling with his phone. Teresa remembered how much Felipe had loved this ungrateful slob of a teenager who texted his friends while Felipe waited to for burial as he lay in a wooden box.

Teresa looked at Carlos and thought about her own daughter, thousands of miles away, she remembered the circumstances that had separated them and felt guilty for criticising Felipe's relatives when the thought uppermost in her mind at that moment was whether she could get something to eat and drink.

Teresa knew there was a bakery across the street but was aware she could not leave.

She was waiting for it all to end. Everyone was polite to her, but she kept thinking about how they blamed her even though Teresa knew it wasn't all her fault and they had just as much a share in this as her.

While Lucretia was taking a break from her theatrics, Teresa felt she should spend some time at the coffin for appearance's sake, if nothing else. She approached the large box and looked over at Felipe. She'd been avoiding looking at him all this time. The undertakers had done their best to cover the marks where the fish had eaten him. The coffin was open, and Felipe lay with his arms folded across his chest and a crucifix, which Teresa knew he would have hated, placed over his hands. As she was leaning over to take a closer look, Felipe sat bolt upright. Teresa let out a yelp of terror, and the rest of the gathering gasped in unison.

"Water," Felipe said before slumping back in the coffin.

"He wants water. Get him some water." Teresa blurted.

"It's a miracle, praise the Lord." Felipe's mother declared, her arms raised as she rushed over to the coffin, pushing Teresa out of the way.

Jose handed Teresa a bottle of water, but Felipe was lying lifeless in the coffin, and no attempt Teresa or Lucretia made would revive him.

"Somebody get a doctor." Teresa pleaded, searching the astonished faces that surrounded her.

The doctor came but found no signs of life. Nor could he explain Felipe's apparent brief return to life.

After an afternoon of arguments, speculation and verification, they agreed Felipe was dead and that they should bury him without further disruption to the cemetery's already disturbed schedule.

Teresa stared at the coffin. Unable to process the events she had just witnessed. It was as if it had never happened. Trapped air, they told her was responsible. And the request for water was a fantasy devised by her already over-taxed brain.

But Teresa knew what she had witnessed and felt an overwhelming sense of frustration as they lowered the coffin into the family crypt.

Teresa wondered how much longer it would be before she could go home. She tried suggesting she could get a bus, but Selma was having none of it, and Teresa did not want to appear rude again.

As Selma walked to her car, Teresa stared back at the cemetery from the metal entrance gates.

"Teresa, Teresa," Selma shouted to her. "Teresa! Teresa!"

Selma was next to her, banging on the entrance gates, trying to get her attention.

Chapter Five - The Sister-in-law – 13th January 2016

"Teresa! Teresa!"

Banging on the security gate woke Teresa. She sat up, taking a moment to gather her wits. The banging continued.

"Okay, okay. I'm coming." Teresa shouted, taking care to shut Ramsey in the living room.

Opening the door, Teresa could see a furious-looking Selma glaring through the bars of the security gate in the rain.

"What the fuck is all this about?" Selma demanded, waving Felipe's phone at her.

"I can explain." Teresa pleaded as she opened the gate.

Selma dragged Teresa into the house, slammed the door, pulled a gun out of her trousers and waved it at Teresa.

"Give me one fucking good reason I shouldn't fucking-well shoot you in the fucking head right fucking now," Selma asked.

Teresa racked her brain for a good fucking reason.

"I... I..."

"Shut the fuck up!"

Teresa shut the fuck up. Selma waved the phone at her.

"Looks like you're not blameless in this."

"I can explain," said Teresa, forgetting to shut the fuck up.

"I said shut the fuck up." Selma reminded her.

Selma leant back on Teresa's makeshift sofa, dripping from the rain. On one leg, the hand holding the phone and on the other; the hand holding the gun. Selma was a woman who enjoyed the power offered her by a weapon.

"So, what do you have to say for yourself?" Selma asked, now in a more relaxed tone.

Teresa was confused, not knowing whether to shut the fuck up or tell Selma what she had to say for herself.

"Well?" Selma asked.

"Sorry Selma. It's just that you told me to shut the f..."

"Don't get fucking cocky with me," Selma shouted, waving the gun at Teresa afresh.

"No... er... no, of course not," Teresa sat down next to Selma. "It's just the gun makes me a little... er... you know. But Selma, there's nothing..."

Selma's face broke into a smile.

"No, I'm only fucking with you. You should have seen your face."

Selma laughed so loud she looked like she might lose control of her bladder at any moment. "Ah, it was priceless. I thought you might need a little diversion. You've got to laugh, haven't you?"

Teresa was not laughing.

"No. Don't take it so hard. I don't think you're involved," the smile disappeared from Selma's face, and she leant so close that Teresa could smell her minty breath. "Or do I?"

Selma glared at Teresa for a long time. Teresa swallowed her excess saliva. Then, as suddenly as it had vanished, Selma's smile returned.

"Hah! Had you again, didn't I? Come on, cheer up." said Selma, an inane grin plastered all over the face that Teresa wished she could punch.

"Teresa, I need to ask you something. You didn't tell me you spent the night in the hospital, or that you were involved in a robbery and murder at the dentist. That's what I came here for to..." Selma trailed off as she struggled to reinsert her gun into her trousers. "I just need to get this in..."

A deafening crack. Teresa watched in horror as Selma slipped off the sofa mattress to the floor in an ever-expanding pool of blood.

'Shit!' exclaimed Teresa, concerned about the blood on the floor but realising the fact that she needed to do something about Selma bleeding to death.

Teresa called the emergency services and tried to explain as best she could that they should come and get the bleeding police officer. She went over to Selma and, with some effort, rolled her onto her back and, locating the wound, tried to apply pressure until help arrived.

During what seemed like another very long time, Teresa tried talking to Selma in the vain hope that she might come round.

Chapter Six - The Ex-husband – 20th January 2014

"What you are saying is that she has a problem with alcohol?" the Judge said.

"Well, I didn't want to say so, but I guess, yes. After the incident. That's what it comes down to." William said with a smug smile, almost eclipsing the smugness of his smart suit.

'This is what it has come down to.' Teresa remembered picturing the man with whom, five years before, she thought she might spend the rest of her life. They had exchanged rings, exchanged bodily fluids. She had spent two days in a hospital trying to squeeze his offspring out of a hole that was not large enough until the British doctors arrived to cut her daughter out of her. Her daughter, whom she now loved more than anything in the world and whom he had stolen from her. The English cunts had taken Annabel, her angel, her darling, her reason for being.

Teresa contemplated 'the incident' as she sat in seat 24c on flight TP0351 to Lisbon, where she would change for another trip to Porto, where she would change yet again for another flight to São Paulo. 'The incident' hadn't been that bad. They made a big deal out of it, making it sound worse than it was. Yes, she enjoyed a drink or two. Yes, she should not have been in the car, but her daughter was hungry, and there was no food in the house.

She'd had a few drinks before she went to the airport, needing them to get through the ordeal, but had tried to judge it just right so that the flight attendants wouldn't think she was drunk. Teresa didn't enjoy taking off and landings. They were right up there with cockroaches and flapping birds' wings on her list of things to avoid.

This was the cheapest flight she could get out of this god-forsaken country with its pompous stuck-up Queen and its arrogant stuck-up people in their fancy suits and big offices who used big words to steal babies of mothers who were just going through a hard time. Cunts.

William had taught her that word. It was the only useful thing he did. The shit. Teresa wondered whether she had to wait until after the plane took off before she ordered a drink from the hostess.

She also questioned whether she had been too rash, buying a ticket to Brazil. She wasn't sure where she would get the money to fly back to England to visit her daughter, or where the money would come from to pay off the credit card she had used to buy her ticket to Brazil. She imagined calling Annabel via a video link on the Internet, but she couldn't help feeling that she had made a huge mistake and wondered, as the aeroplane began reversing away from the gate, whether it was too late to get off the flight.

She bought her ticket in a moment of anger with that bastard William for stealing her daughter and used her mother's illness as an excuse. But now, as the effects of several large gin and tonics wore off, and the fog settled, she thought through the implications of being stuck thousands of miles away from her daughter and she panicked. What could she do? Leap up and start shouting 'stop the plane'? She had lived in England long enough to have absorbed enough fear of embarrassment to prevent herself from causing a scene. But what else could she do? Once in Lisbon, she did not have sufficient funds to buy a ticket back to England. She wasn't even sure what her entry status would be if she attempted to return through immigration. What had she done?

She watched the terminal building shrinking outside the window. She was sweating.

"Don't worry." said the woman who sat next to her and Teresa realised she must be contorting her face with angst.

Teresa felt like a terrible mother. Abandoning her daughter, her asthmatic daughter who had so often been ill and whom Teresa had slept beside in the hospital during those long, breathless winter nights.

Teresa felt helpless and stupid. She smiled at the woman and stared outside, at Heathrow accelerating past the window, at England, home to her daughter, disappearing beneath the clouds below her.

Chapter Seven - The Doctor – 18th January 2016

The bus tossed Teresa around in her seat. The sun streamed through the window, toasting the seat next to her. As the bus gathered speed, a breeze would force its way into the open window and disappear as quickly as it came when the bus ground to a halt at each bus stop, traffic light or traffic queue.

Teresa's headphones compounded the uncomfortable heat. They kept the sounds of the world out of her ears, but they also had the unfortunate side effect of trapping the heat. Usually, Teresa would tolerate this, as the benefit of her music drowning out the surrounding noises of São Paulo compensated. At times, the noise still penetrated to her ears even when she listened to her music at full volume.

Today her headphones didn't seem to work, and the vocals sounded as if they had placed the singer in a tin bucket and dropped down a 300 foot well. This was disappointing for Teresa as she had downloaded Belle and Sebastian's new album to cheer herself up and was looking forward to listening to it. She listened to it anyway, played from the bottom of a pit.

'Even Belle and Sebastian playing at the bottom of a mineshaft was preferable to listening to the ambience of São Paulo,' thought Teresa.

Saci, the mischievous, one-legged character of Brazilian folklore, must have struck again. Teresa inherited the habit from her mother of blaming any minor misfortune on the red-capped, pipe smoking black boy. She had heard a striped cuckoo as she left the house that morning and, as her mother had often said, that was a clear sign that Saci, who could turn himself into the bird, was around and up to no good.

When the first bus she caught had broken down, her fears had been realised, and now she was travelling in the intense heat of the afternoon.

A teenager got on and sat next to her, cocooned in headphones. Teresa toyed with the idea of asking the teenager to listen to her Belle and Sebastian album or asking whether she could listen to the teenager's music to establish whether the fault was with Teresa's phone or her headphones, but the teenager didn't look approachable, so she didn't bother.

An electronic sign outside read 34°C. In the street, office workers were heading to or from lunch and didn't appear anywhere near as distressed by the heat as Teresa. As the bus turned a corner, the sun, which Teresa had been careful to avoid when she chose her seat, swung round and shone on her. Teresa was fair for a Brazilian and she would struggle to deal with this bombardment of UV for long, despite having drenched herself in sun cream that morning.

A woman ran for the bus; a bare-chested black man dragged a large sack of recycling, men wore suits. These made Teresa want to sweat even more. She passed air-conditioned shops, offices and banks, envious of their cool interiors.

The bus passed in front of a community, a slum, a favela, where the front of every tiny self-built house had been converted into a shop or bar, and over a river, which smelt a little less awful because of the rain the day before that washed away some of the filth.

Teresa felt guilty when someone older than her got on, wondering whether she should relinquish her seat, but opted instead to avoid eye contact, pretending she hadn't noticed them.

Car fumes blew in the open windows on the breeze and Teresa coughed.

It would be her daughter's birthday in a week, and Teresa knew that she would have to contact her ex-husband to organise a time to speak to her and explain why she wouldn't be coming to England. Felipe had proposed to her and agreed to take her to England on their honeymoon, but now the stupid bastard had vanished.

Teresa had put no money aside. She worked as an assistant in a school. Most of her salary went on rent and other bills, including the credit card debts she had racked up in the turbulent period following her petulant return to Brazil.

The driver pressed the accelerator pedal to the floor as the bus struggled to ascend a steep hill. Belle and Sebastian were no match for the engine, which howled its way past the headphones and filled Teresa's ears.

Teresa was middle-aged. There was no denying it. She was past forty, and its arrival was now a distant memory. She was also overweight. There was no denying that either, though she did her best to avoid scales. She didn't consider herself to be good looking, though she had got herself into relationships on some occasions and she thought this wasn't on the strength of her personality given that her personality was a major factor in some breakups.

She felt depressed, more depressed than usual. Given that she had been the victim of a violent robbery, her boyfriend probably just committed suicide, and her sister-in-law had shot herself in Teresa's living room, it was understandable that she should feel a little down.

She spent most of her waking hours in a constant state of irritation, by her situation, by the people around her, and this annoyance with everything that surrounded her often manifested itself in her voice whenever she spoke to people. The effect of this was to alienate most of the people she met.

This was not her intention. She, like most people, had an innate desire for people to like her, but she had a manner that rubbed people up the wrong way, and so far, she seemed powerless to do anything about it.

Teresa detested her life since she returned to São Paulo; she craved to be back in England, that stupid, pompous, arrogant England where she would be near her daughter. Her deepest fear was that her present situation would form the rest of her life and that she would never escape and maybe never see her daughter again. At least not for a very long time, by which time the maternal bond which she was worried might slip away, and could be lost forever.

The bus arrived at the metro and Teresa alighted and followed the crowds into the station, down the escalators and onto the packed platform.

The train pulled into the station and Teresa squeezed her way into the carriage past indifferent commuters unable to decide whether they should disembark. She negotiated as far inside as she could until a man reading Basic Biomechanics, a book whose size matched the man's stature, blocked progress. She peered over his shoulder, or rather, around his arm, and noted he was engrossed in a chapter on photosynthesis.

'Fascinating.' Teresa's sarcastic brain kicked in.

At that moment, Belle and Sebastian gave up, and Simple Minds took over, promising Teresa a miracle. She long yearned for a miracle. Teresa tried her hand at many things: a cleaner, a waiter, a lover, an environmentalist, a wife, a mother. She hadn't stuck at any of them and achieved no real success, most painfully with regards the last.

'So who am I?' she often mused. This question plagued her even more after the events of the previous week.

She listened to Jim Kerr singing: 'Promises, Promises'.

Most song lyrics she could match with an embarrassing memory. This song now had two such associations. The first was an inebriated night in a karaoke bar when, during a shouted performance of the song, she pissed her pants. The second was more recent and more painful.

Teresa realised the train had already arrived at Consolação and it was time to change. She shuffled along the moving walkway, which wasn't moving. It never worked in the mornings, never, but now it decided not to work in the afternoon as well. The shuffled journey along the walkway reminded Teresa of the near-fatal motorway journeys she sometimes made from the city to the coast and back. Always waiting for an opportunity to move into a gap, in this case, to walk past the man with a weird limp in both legs, holding up the other commuters like an aged truck belching black smoke with a queue of cars trailing him up the hill. Teresa saw the big 'biomechanics' man in a parallel queue, which seemed to move quicker than the human caterpillar of which she was a part - the commuting equivalent of the post office queue.

Teresa exited the air-conditioned metro onto the street, where the evening summer heat was oppressive. Even the slight breeze felt like someone was following her around, pointing a hair dryer at her. The next bus she jumped on had no air conditioning, so no respite from the heat. At least she could get a seat. *Bat Out of Hell* filled her ears, but the full volume and the enclosing headphones still didn't help her forget where she was.

She had the courtesy to wear proper headphones that kept the sound near her ears, she thought, and not the cheap type that just sat in the hole in the middle of the ear and allowed everyone within a two-metre radius to share the tinny ghost of the baseline. Teresa thought back to some occasions when she was on a bus, and she could hear the music of a person from at least four metres away as if they were holding a pair of speakers. Goodness knows what damage they were doing to their eardrums.

It was not surprising she was in a bad mood, a worse mood than usual. She felt over the hill. 43. She'd always felt old. Even when she was young, she felt older than her peers. She was listening to The Beatles while her friends were listening to Gal Costa, Kim Carnes, Dalto and Ritchie. She hated those songs at the time: Menina Veneno, Muito Estranho, Bette Davis Eyes, Balancê. Now she was older, she would sing along to them in a karaoke bar with the rest of them.

She used to read old classics like Tolstoy or Dostoevsky because she imagined they made her look intelligent, but now she couldn't for the life of her remember the plots to any of the stories. Teresa drank the distilled sugar cane, pinga, long after her friends switched to vodka and she kept drinking long after they stopped altogether.

She was on her way to her doctor, to be told off for drinking too much and eating badly, but she feared she would be late - even by Brazilian standards.

She arrived, out of breath, into the delicious, air-conditioned waiting room ten minutes late.

"The traffic was terrible," she explained, but the receptionist was not in the slightest bit interested. Ten minutes? Most of the patients paid little regard for the appointment system and turned up when they felt like it. The receptionist understood this well, and she allocated the appointment times to accommodate the fact. She took Teresa's medical card and asked her to take a seat. Teresa knew she was in for a long wait. They held appointments in low regard and never happened at their appointed time.

Twenty minutes after Teresa's scheduled appointment time, just ten minutes after her arrival, they called Amanda. Amanda had been the other person in the waiting room when Teresa arrived, and she had speculated about the reason for Amanda's visit. Amanda looked like a church type, hair tied back in a ponytail with unnatural tightness, plain clothes that showed off the fact that Amanda had a body in better shape than Teresa's.

'Sexually transmitted diseases.' Teresa concluded.

She calculated that Amanda might have, say, a ten-minute consultation. Teresa thought the doctor might even see her by 5:20 pm. A ten-minute consultation for herself and she could be out of the surgery by half past and back on the bus to Consolação. She would make it to the kebab shop before the two for one offer ended at 7 pm. Teresa's mouth responded in a Pavlovian fashion.

She reached for her phone to text Felipe before she remembered he had gone. 'Get your arse in gear' would have been the sort of thing she would have suggested, and he would have replied 'ok, love you xxx'. She told herself it had been the bang on the head that caused his depression and reassured herself that he had loved her in his way, but it was becoming difficult to convince herself.

Amanda emerged from the consultation room clutching a prescription.

'For some vaginal ointment designed for sexual deviants masquerading as devout Christians,' Teresa speculated.

Amanda's consultation lasted nine minutes. Teresa timed it. Now the Doctor seemed to be on the telephone. No matter. He wouldn't be long, would he? In her hand, Teresa clutched the results of her blood tests, for which she had waited an entire morning in a clinic, without breakfast or coffee. Once the nurse had removed the blood into tiny tubes, the nurse warned Teresa not to lift anything and said she could go. Teresa hadn't considered the weight of her paper bag to be of any consequence, so she held it with the forbidden arm just long enough to put the appointment paper away, but that was enough to send a tiny river of blood trickling down her skin and onto the floor of the clinic. Teresa pretended she hadn't noticed, slapped a tissue against the source of the egress and hurried away. Collecting the results had been easier; she downloaded them off the Internet and used a printer at the school.

Teresa felt a sudden panic. What if the doctor had wanted her to send the results in advance? Maybe he needed time to look through them before the appointment. The doctor could scan through them in about thirty seconds. Couldn't he?

And so he did.

"Your cholesterol is high," he said, not lifting his head from the paper.

'Here we go.' thought Teresa.

"Your liver function is okay."

Yes! Triumph. No questions asked about alcohol consumption.

"How much do you drink?"

Bollocks.

"Oh, not much, maybe a small drink in the evening," she lied.

"Hmm," he considered her response with the contempt it deserved. "I recommend you make some changes to your diet. Eat more foods with Omega-3. Oil, nuts, red wine."

Teresa smiled.

"Tuna is a wonderful source of Omega-3." he continued.

'Yeah, and mercury and other heavy metals.' Teresa remembered from her brief foray into environmentalism.

"Jump up here," he said, getting up and pointing to an examination table in the room's corner, where he prodded Teresa with a stethoscope and blood pressure equipment, scribbling notes until he was satisfied. He sat down at his desk while he waited for Teresa to join him.

"Do some exercise? Get some new blood tests at the end of February, or the beginning of March, and come back and see me."

'Exercise?' thought Teresa, returning to the chair.

"If the cholesterol is better, fair enough. If not, we'll put you on statins. Are you still getting spots of blood in your urine?"

"A little," Teresa admitted.

"Hmm," the doctor furrowed his brow. "Well, the tests have revealed nothing. No pain when you wee, you said?"

Teresa nodded. The doctor paused in thought.

"I'll have to refer you for an examination, I'm afraid," he said, scribbling. "We'll see what that turns up. Anything else?"

Teresa took a deep breath.

"My boyfriend disappeared," she just came out and said it. There was no other way to say it. The doctor was giving her the concerned doctor expression he had spent hours in front of the mirror perfecting in medical school. "He left a note and his phone and just left. The police found his clothes and wallet on the beach but no body. They think he's committed suicide."

The doctor now changed his facial features to grave sympathy and leant forward.

"I've been feeling depressed," Teresa confessed.

Reaching a satisfactory conclusion, the doctor sat upright once more, plucked his prescription pad from his side and scribbled in a business-like manner.

"Get yourself along to a psychologist," he said. "Tell them all about it and come back and see me if you have any more problems."

He tore off the top sheet and thrust it toward Teresa who, bemused, took it and held it with the other sheets he had given her.

"Thank you," she said, not sure that this was what she had expected.

By 6 pm Teresa was sitting in the Kebab restaurant with the first of her two for one kebabs.

'I'll start my diet tomorrow,' she told herself, contemplating the bottle of wine she would buy on the way home, on doctor's orders.

Teresa sat just inside the restaurant, whose large windows opened so that nothing stood between her and the street where they had arranged more tables and chairs on the pavement. As she ate, she watched a girl with short hair chatting to a blonde with tattoos.

'Not a natural blonde,' she surmised.

When Teresa had been in England, people had always been delighted to hear that she was from Brazil. Teresa imagined they pictured her living on the beach sipping caipirinhas. They could not imagine the decaying streets of São Paulo covered with tags, graffiti and litter. Why would they? Football, beaches, samba and rainforests were all anyone talked about when they talked about Brazil.

Teresa noticed a woman crossing the road. She used this as further evidence to support her argument that São Paulo was not the paradise that her fellow staff at the Spondooley traditional bar and grill, Vauxhall Bridge Road, Stockwell, London or the staff at Gaia environmental collective, Hercules Road, Lambeth North, London, thought it was.

On this day of the month, Teresa was only halfway through her overdraft limit, and she was feeling flush, even though she had maxed out both of her credit cards. Hence the kebabs. Besides, she kept telling herself that she needed cheering up, but so far no amount of kebabs, chocolate or gin seemed to make much difference. She should have been trying to save her money to go back to England to see her daughter. That made her feel even worse.

Teresa finished her second kebab, paid, and walked up Augusta past the shop selling trendy tat she liked to browse. Having reminded herself that she should save money and not spending it on tat, she felt poor again and kept walking up the hill in the way someone does when they have eaten one too many kebabs.

She decided not to enter the metro straight away but to go for a browse of the bookshop first. It was a Monday and Teresa knew there would be a book signing which meant there would be lots of people not interested in looking at books, taking up space, impeding the shelves, eating nibbles and drinking glasses of wine that Teresa herself wouldn't mind drinking. The books they were launching were never the intellectual literature that Teresa always prided herself on reading. They were more the trashy books of the kind her ex-husband would like: *How to make a Million Dollars with Little or no Effort* or *Cooking Spectacular Meals with Little or No Effort.*

Teresa couldn't arouse interest in any of the books like she did, so she left. In fact, she had lost interest in just about everything. At work, she felt demotivated. Her students, who must have sensed this, were bored too. She became irritated by both students and staff, and couldn't find the patience to deal with anyone in the way she should.

The icing on the cake was an email she had received from her ex-husband in England. It regarded her daughter. The daughter she'd left behind, that she couldn't afford to visit, who suffered from asthma and pneumonia and who now, in the middle of the British winter, had, according to the email, been admitted to hospital again. Just before her seventh birthday, too.

The wind messed with Teresa's hair, hair that she should have cut at least three weeks ago. It also threatened to blow off her headphones. Headphones that her students broke and were now held together by sticky tape. Perhaps that accounted for the tinny sound. It was a warm evening, and she sweated from the exercise of negotiating the metro and walking to the bus stop. She squinted to see through the old scratched, dirty, cracked screen of her smartphone, which had been the cheapest in the shop three years ago and was now, by modern standards, something of an antique. The bus arrived, and she found a seat in which she could sweat even more.

Teresa received some cryptic messages from her ex about going to the doctor, but that was par for the course. Annabel had been to and from the doctor with her chest since she was six months old but nothing anyone did seemed to make any difference.

Chapter Eight - The Psychologist – 19th January 2016

"Murellies," Teresa told the security guard, who asked for her ID card, checked a list and dialled a number.

"Teresa Da Silva," he said into the telephone, replacing it straight away. "Tenth floor."

Teresa took her ID card and followed the guard's gesticulation to a door beside him that led to a set of lifts.

When the doors slid open on the tenth floor, a middle-aged woman stood waiting.

"Teresa?" she asked. "Dr Murellies."

"Pleased to meet you," Teresa said, shaking the doctor's hand.

"This way," the doctor gestured to an open door at the end of the corridor. Teresa stepped inside and waited while the doctor followed her in and closed the door.

"This way please," the doctor showed Teresa through to a large room with two chairs placed quite some distance apart. The doctor pointed towards the nearest chair. "Please take a seat."

The doctor waited for Teresa to seat herself before she seated herself in the other chair.

"So, Teresa," the doctor began in a slow, reflective tone. "What brings you here today?"

Teresa swallowed.

"My boyfriend disappeared. The police think he committed suicide."

The doctor nodded to show her understanding.

"And I've been feeling down," Teresa continued. "I went to my doctor, and he suggested I come and see you."

"OK," said Dr Murellies. "Why don't you tell me all about your boyfriend?"

The psychologist listened as Teresa told her the story of how she met Felipe, how they were planning to get married, planned to go to England on their honeymoon, and then he vanished or killed himself. She told the doctor all about her failed relationship in England. The divorce, her daughter, the fact that her mother died the previous year. She told her about her missing cat. She even told her about her fears that Saci might be following her around, breaking things.

"Well, our session is ending," the doctor said when Teresa finished her story. "What I do is I work a lot with dreams because dreams often reflect what is happening inside us. Why don't you try to keep a small notebook by your bed for you to write any dreams you have and in our next session, we can discuss a dream. Is that a deal?"

Teresa nodded.

"You may find that keeping a journal may help you with all the negative feelings you have been having. At the end of each day, try to make a list of all the positive things that have happened during the day. You'll be surprised how long the list is."

Teresa nodded again.

"Well, thank you, Teresa," the doctor's tone changed to suggest that the session was now concluding. "If you are happy with this time, we could meet at the same time next week."

Teresa and the doctor stood. Teresa nodded again.

"Yes, that would be fine," she confirmed. "I'll try to write down some dreams."

"Great. Well, it has been nice to meet you. Can you find your way downstairs?" the doctor asked, showing Teresa the door.

Chapter Nine - The Journal – 19th January 2016

Teresa wrote in the journal her psychologist suggested would be good for her. She wrote her name, her age, her nationality and the fact that she lived in São Bernardo do Campo in São Paulo, that she was a mother, though her daughter was with her ex-husband in England and she hadn't seen her for over almost two years, about how her ex-husband had married again and how much it pained her to think of that bitch raising her daughter.

I guess that's one reason I'm seeing a psychologist. That and the fact that my boyfriend vanished or killed himself and my sister-in-law shot herself, and I was held hostage while they murdered a dentist.

My family doesn't talk to me. My boss hates me. But I'm writing positive things so... It's sunny today. I left my flat to buy and post a present for my daughter. It's her birthday in two weeks. She'll be seven.

What else? Did some laundry? Washed the dishes. At least the house is clean. It's my holidays at the moment, so I've got plenty of time to keep on top of the chores. I work as a teaching assistant in a school.

To be honest, I'm not looking forward to going back. Oops, that wasn't positive. I'm trying to get my teaching qualification so I can earn more money. Now that my boyfriend is dead.

Is it still right to call him my boyfriend? Should I call him my ex-boyfriend? Or my late boyfriend? Late boyfriend sounds like I'm waiting for him. Dead boyfriend sounds like I keep his rotting body in a cupboard. The man who used to be my boyfriend until the stupid bastard killed himself or ran away or whatever. How about that?

Oh, God. I hope my psychologist doesn't ask to see this journal. Or the dream journal she's also asked me to keep. The first dream I had after she asked me to write them down was one in which I was having sex with my boyfriend, and my mother walked in on us. My psychologist would have a field day with that one. The one I've remembered so far is one where I was trying to play the guitar with the Beatles on the roof of Abbey Road, but I didn't know any of the chords, and no matter how much they tried to teach it to me I couldn't get it right. Because I know three chords in real life.

Positive things. My house is tidy. Except for the bloodstain on the floor where Selma shot herself. The stupid cow. Positive things. I still have a week of holiday left. Can't think of anything else right now. Will try harder tomorrow.

Here's a positive thing. Although not very positive, I found writing today's journal therapeutic so to hell with the positivity and sod the psychologist. I'm going to write what I want. Get it all out there. Where to start. My father, my dead father, that is. Drank himself to death, which might be why I drink now. God, I'm turning into my dad. I don't want to pretend that I had an unhappy childhood. When I say it was the drink that killed him, that's half true. He was drunk when he stepped off the kerb, but it was when the truck from the brewery hit him. That did it - an irony that did not escape my mother, who was not sad to see the back of him.

Teresa put her pen down and exhaled a deep sigh. It was true she felt a little better, and she resolved to write more the next day.

Chapter Ten - Another Dream – 20th January 2016

Teresa dreamt she was in England. It was the day of the Grand National horse race, and people were watching the race on the streets in television showrooms. An old friend asked her to put a bet on for her even though Teresa knew the friend would have already put bets on of her own. She used her phone and bet on every horse, even though the stake was much greater than any winnings could be. Unless a horse came in at 100/1, which, even at the National, was unlikely. Halfway through the race, some jockeys had a muddy brawl, like some bad-tempered Sunday pub league football match that her ex-husband used to drag her along too. The camera zoomed in on two of the jockeys, one of whom she could see was Captain Mainwaring from Dad's Army, a programme that her ex-husband loved and made her watch even though she hated it.

She woke up, turned on her iPad and opened Facebook. 99 notifications because she hadn't dared look at it since Felipe disappeared.

Swiping down the list of notifications, she realised she'd forgotten her sister's birthday. What a terrible sister Teresa felt she was, and a terrible mother, a terrible girlfriend, a terrible teaching assistant, a terrible daughter.

She would have to send her a message now and acknowledge that she'd forgotten.

On another bus. Before 9 am and it was already almost 30°C. The traffic crawled into the city in snakes of single-occupant cars and vans through which wove convoys of reckless motorcycles. The occasional patch of hill or woodland suggested that the area must have been beautiful when the first colonial settlers arrived, before São Paulo's concrete tentacles reached out, devoured the beauty and excreted the dull grey effluence that now covered every surface, breeding the ubiquitous mould, which thrived in the humidity. Teresa was already sweating. She had begun to sweat almost as soon as she'd stepped out of the shower. Her ex would have reminded her that ladies don't sweat, they perspire. She thought about her daughter, and then her thoughts returned to Felipe. She blamed herself to some extent for Felipe's death, but her guilt revolved around her motivation for being with him. If she were honest with herself, she would admit that she had entered the relationship because she saw him as a potential way to get her back to the UK and closer to her daughter, even if for a holiday. Usually, they granted custody to the mother, but after the incident, her ex-husband didn't need expensive lawyers to establish that she was unfit to look after her daughter.

'What complete and utter bollocks,' she thought.

They cited her fondness for a drink or two. Bastards. She'd stayed off the stuff since she came back to Brazil. She hadn't mentioned drink to her psychologist. It hadn't come up. It hadn't been a problem. Now she was counting down the days until she went back to work. Five more sleeps. Could she get away mentioning none of this to anyone? Not only did Teresa doubt she could handle the conversations, but she feared that any perception of emotional or psychological instability might be the last excuse her boss needed to convince herself to fire her. She glanced out the window of the bus as it passed an electronic display that declared the air quality was terrible next to a bright red square designed to illustrate, through colour, the level of badness.

She took out her dream diary and wrote what she remembered of that morning's dream.

Chapter Eleven - The Headteacher - 21st January 2015

Teresa tried her best to smile while everyone shared their holiday stories.

When it was Teresa's turn, she answered: "Ah, not much, stayed in São Paulo."

No-one seemed to care. Teresa exchanged a grunted hello with the headteacher, Catarina Sidebottom, a formidable-looking woman with a mono-brow to rival Frida Kahlo, who would not have looked out of place as the headteacher of a Victorian girls' school but who embraced the modern methods of education, and that was it. Back to stapling coloured paper to display boards, organising books, pencils, rulers, rubbers. Teresa avoided the protracted conversations that typified this stage of the school year, but she could not avoid the assistants' meeting. She followed the conversation as best she could. Trying her best to concentrate. Just as she grasped the subject and felt she had something to contribute, the conversation had moved on, so she remained silent. This did not escape the headteacher.

"What do you think, Teresa?" she asked while Teresa's brain was still assimilating the conversation that had just taken place regarding the new policy for lunch and break duty.

There was a long pause while Teresa absorbed the discussion that had taken place among the others. This was one of the few subjects in the meeting about which she had no opinion.

"I'm happy with whatever the majority decides," she said, at last, giving the impression she hadn't been following the conversation.

"Well, that was worth the wait," said the headteacher.

As the meeting ended, Teresa tried to retreat to the class without becoming embroiled in conversation with the rest of the assistants. Before she could get away, Mariana stopped her.

"Teresa," her voice was too enthusiastic for Teresa to bear. "A few of us are going for a drink after work if you'd like to join us."

"That sounds great," Teresa lied. "I've got something I'm meant to do, but I'll try to get out of it," she lied again.

"Great, we'll come and get you," said Mariana.

"Why don't I meet you there?"

"OK," said Mariana. Concern was creeping into her voice. "Is everything OK?"

"Yeah, fine," Teresa lied a third time, expecting to hear a cock-crow. "A little busy. That's all."

"Yeah, there's always so much to do, eh? Oh well, see you later," Mariana smiled. Teresa smiled back, and they went their separate ways.

On the way home, Teresa wondered what she had done all day. She'd kept herself busy but couldn't remember what she'd done as if she was working on auto-pilot.

The metro made her anxious, and she was glad when she was home behind a locked door in her living room.

Teresa poured herself a large gin and slumped on the makeshift sofa, staring at the television, which was pumping out the usual soap opera. A sudden terrible fear that perhaps she'd forgotten to lock the door shook Teresa from her reverie. She rushed over and checked it. Locked. Through the frosted glass, she could also see that she had padlocked the security gate. Despite the evening heat, she closed the windows and checked she had fastened them. This eliminated any possibility of a cooling breeze from entering the flat, let alone an intruder. She slumped back on the sofa, breathed a sigh, took a large swig of her gin, and sweated.

The combination of heat and gin made her sleep poorly that night. She awoke tired, hungover and unprepared to face the terrible ordeal of bus and metro, followed by school, followed by metro, followed by a bus.

As she showered, Teresa rehearsed the conversation she would need to have with the chirpy Mariana about what a great time the girls had last night and what a terrible shame it was that she hadn't been able to go. Teresa wondered how Mariana managed to be so happy all the time and tried to recollect a time when she had experienced such gaiety herself but could not identify a single period in her life when she hadn't felt even a bit miserable. She wondered whether she would ever reach the point where she was happy, like Mariana. Why couldn't she be more positive? What was wrong with her? Did she lack self-discipline? Maybe she didn't have what it took to be like Mariana.

Teresa rushed into the class, five minutes late. Thank goodness that this was preparation week and that the children wouldn't be here for another two days.

"Cheer up, it can't be that bad," said Brenda, seeing the dark look on her face as she entered the class. Brenda was a large gringo, the teacher whom Teresa assisted.

Teresa forced a smile.

"Sorry," Teresa was used to apologising for her mood.

"Catarina was looking for you earlier," said Brenda. "She didn't say what it was about."

'Shit,' thought Teresa. 'The head knows I was late. I'm in for a right bollocking now.'

"Is everything OK?" Catarina, the formidable headteacher, asked. Teresa took a seat facing her desk. "Did you have a pleasant holiday?"

"Yeah fine," Teresa lied. "And you?"

"Well, I spent most of the holiday in England," said Catarina.

'Bitch,' thought Teresa, jealous that she wasn't the one that had spent five weeks in England.

"You seemed a little distracted at yesterday's meeting,"

Teresa struggled to find an answer. Catarina took her silence as an admission of guilt.

"We had our little discussion at the end of the last term, didn't we, Teresa?" Catarina spoke as if she was addressing a naughty child. She waited for a response. Teresa nodded.

"I hoped we wouldn't need any pep talks this term. Hmm?" Catarina raised her mono-brow. All Teresa managed was a weak smile.

"Whatever it is, Teresa, you're going to need to snap out of it." Teresa wanted to slap her boss.

Teresa emerged from the meeting feeling guiltier than ever. She didn't understand how to snap out of it, feeling guilty that she seemed to ruin the lives of anyone with whom she came into contact, appearing to be the kiss of death.

"Everything okay?" Brenda asked when she returned to the classroom.

Oh God, Teresa didn't want to embroil Brenda in all her problems. Brenda had enough of her own as a full-time teacher, let alone trying to raise a disabled child at the same time.

"Yeah." lying was becoming a habit for Teresa.

"What did Catarina want?"

Why was she so nosey? Teresa thought for a moment.

"Oh, she wanted to talk about yesterday's meeting. About the rota."

Brenda raised her eyebrows with boredom. Teresa returned to cutting out name tags and hoped the conversation was over.

After a moment, Teresa looked up again and saw Brenda busy typing away on her computer. It was almost as if Teresa wasn't there, as if she was observing a play or a television soap opera.

At break time, Teresa tried to sneak down to the lunchroom for a quiet coffee alone, but chirpy Mariana dropped into the seat next to her.

"Hey, how was last night?" Teresa tried to be polite. "Sorry, I couldn't make it." Another lie.

"It was incredible. We all missed you. You should have come."

Teresa offered an apologetic smile which said "yeah, sorry" while saying "yeah, right."

"No. We missed you," said Mariana, seeming to divine Teresa's true feelings. "Is everything okay?"

Teresa wasn't sure for how long she could maintain the deception.

Mariana persisted with a manner so endearing that Teresa felt it was difficult to resist her charms.

"I've been going through a rough time," Teresa admitted.

"Would you like to talk about it?"

Teresa looked around the filling lunchroom, fearing another assistant might join them at any moment.

"Not right now," she said. "But thank you."

Mariana smiled.

"Remember, I'm always here if you need me."

The next morning was sunny. Teresa tried to remember this as she entered the metro. In her head, she had already imagined an aggressive argument with an imaginary fellow passenger and had to remind herself that this was a daydream and took some deep breaths to calm herself as she reached for her travel card.

06:50, the clock read as the already full train pulled into the station. Teresa positioned herself in the middle of a carriage so she was in a suitable position to occupy a vacated seat should any of the seated passengers alight. However, by Paraiso, which she knew was her best opportunity to get a seat, she was still standing and so resigned herself to the fact she would be on her feet the entire journey. Her legs were already tired.

A man pushed past her to access the other half of the carriage.

'Why didn't he use the other door,' Teresa thought with annoyance.

At Paraiso, the carriage filled, and women of dubious age, disability or pregnancy occupied even the preferential seats.

Teresa always wondered why they included obese people on the list for preferential seats. Standing would help them burn a few calories and do them good.

At Trianon MASP, the stop before hers, she moved from the centre of the carriage toward the doors.

'If everyone did this,' she thought. 'There wouldn't be any need to push past people blocking the doors.'

Changing lines at Consolação involved a long walk and crossing the paths of many people whose intention was to go in another direction. Teresa hated having to judge how fast or slow the other commuters were walking to avoid a collision. In Teresa's mind, the Paulistas seemed to walk how they drove - aggressively. By the time she reached the yellow line platform, she was a nervous wreck.

Teresa did her best to go unnoticed while entering her classroom. After exchanging half a dozen forced smiles, she managed it. The list of to-dos on her desk didn't seem to get any smaller day by day. Cutting display paper, fixing it to the walls, preparing reading journals, homework, there was always something to do, and in a couple of days the children would come back to school, and there would be break and lunch duty, library sessions, taking them to and from classes.

Teresa knew she wasn't good at what she did but did her best in her opinion and if her best wasn't good enough, then what else could she do?

Chapter Twelve – Carl Dixon - 26th January 2015

Hollywood star Carl Dixon placed the Native American headdress on his head.

Hallucinations flashed in the mirror.

He removed the headdress, having to catch his breath from the devastating effects of its power.

This effect had not happened when Dixon tried on the same headdress in Wyoming. Perhaps the stories he heard were true; the results varied not according to the user but according to the place of use.

Dixon placed the headdress on his head a second time and this time he removed his hands.

Hallucinations flickered in the mirror once more and this time resolved themselves into precise forms. A collection of silver implements lay before him and in the centre, a large silver knife of the type found in the kitchens of professional chefs.

Dixon reached out and touched the knife. He felt its cold steel. He wrapped his fingers around the handle and, tightening his grip, found he could hold and lift the object.

Dixon twisted the blade in front of his eyes and watched the artificial light reflecting off its surface.

The door opened, and the security guard rushed in, followed by the other hotel guests that had witnessed Dixon's rant in the bar earlier.

The guard halted in his tracks when he saw the knife, stretching out his arms as a warning to those following him that Dixon was armed.

In an instant, Dixon plunged the blade deep into the guard's chest and was wrestling with the hotel guests, trying to pull him off the guard's twitching body.

Van Helsing who, until this point had been an observer in the whole affair, reached into the affray and plucked the headdress from atop of Dixon at which point the latter collapsed onto the guard's bleeding corpse causing the entire mass of struggling bodies to fall in on itself like a bloody rugby scrum.

Chapter Thirteen - Back to school - 26th January 2015

The day the children were due to come back to school, Teresa was more anxious than usual. Perhaps it was the nightmare about the headdress, from which she had just awoken, or perhaps it was because her head was sore from the gin the night before. Maybe it was because on the way to the bus stop she heard a striped cuckoo.

Every day, the same bus seemed to pass her on the same stretch of road. Teresa imagined she must travel to work with the same groups of people every day, although she didn't recognise any of them.

In her mind, she was going over an annoying email she received from her husband and her even more annoyed reply, which she now regretted.

Teresa knew she wasn't in a positive frame of mind for work, but felt helpless to do anything about it. She didn't feel sad about anything that had happened, her father's death, his abuse. She didn't feel angry; she felt nothing, and she had to stand on the metro again.

As she walked along the stationary, because it was broken, moving-walkway, she ran her hand along the handrail until she imagined how many germs coated its surface and pulled her hand away.

At the school, Mariana met Teresa almost as soon as she walked through the door.

"Hey," she bubbled. "How are things? A few of us are going to play volleyball after school tomorrow. I thought you might like to join us."

Teresa forced a smile. It sounded awful.

"Great, I'll try to remember to bring my kit."

Teresa's headache stayed with her the whole day. It was a hot day and to make matters worse at 09:00, in the middle of some photocopying, the lights flickered and the power went off. That meant no air conditioning. Twenty-four hot children in a hot classroom with no lights, no computers, no projector. She cursed Saci and remembered the striped cuckoo. It was a long, long morning. At lunch, in the staff canteen, she had to eat in the dark, and all day she could not quench her terrible thirst because the water from the communal fountains had a strange taste. People said it was because the water in the reservoir had got so low that now the tap water contained all sorts of heavy metals. She would have bought bottled water if she had enough money to spare.

At the end of the day, Teresa trundled back onto the metro with the rest of the tired-looking commuters. Again, she had to stand in the middle of the carriage. The strap of her bag, she filled it with stuff she never used, cut into Teresa's shoulder. She always promised herself she would have a clean-up and get rid of all her junk, but she never did.

Sometimes she would buy herself a new bag, and that would resolve the issue for a while, but in her current financial position, that was not an issue. It was still a week and a half to payday, and she wasn't sure whether she had enough money on her travel card to get her to work until then. She'd have to manage with whatever food was in the cupboards. She'd have to be pretty creative. Another month in which she failed to put anything aside for her savings fund to buy her tickets to go back and visit Annabel.

At home, she opened the rice container. Unseen eggs had hatched into tiny insects. She couldn't afford to throw the rice away. She tried washing the rice to get rid of anything that didn't look like rice. The trouble was, it all looked like rice, so she washed it as best she could, cooked what she hoped was rice and crossed her fingers.

In the evenings, the water company had already stopped supplies to save the dwindling levels in the reservoirs, and so the washing-up would mount up in the sink and tiny fruit flies buzzed around the sticky remains. Teresa had been saving buckets of water from the washing machine as it emptied and collected this to flush the toilet. The used detergent smelt terrible as it decomposed. Every week there were heavy storms that made slight work of São Paulo's older trees. The irony was that the rain that fell in torrents in massive electrical storms disappeared via the drains into the river Tiete, too polluted to treat, and went on its way through the interior of Brazil, finding its way in-between Argentina and Uruguay into the Atlantic.

It was hard to sleep in the heat and to make matters worse, the neighbours on one side arrived home in the early hours, and the neighbour's at the other side left their dog outside so it whined for hours in the rain. It made sleep all but impossible.

By the morning, Teresa's bed sheets were a wet puddle of sweat, and she felt more tired than when she had gone to bed.

She stood all the way on the metro again, and the offer of a seated passenger to hold her bag did nothing to lift her mood.

Teresa had remembered to forget her trainers, providing herself with the perfect excuse not to join the game of volleyball that she knew would have done her good.

During the morning, she had to take a group for reading, and two boys in her group insisted on chatting through her instructions despite several attempts at shutting them up. Teresa wanted to take them over her knee and give them a good spanking like her mother would have done to her, but she knew that it was more than her job was worth. She remembered when she was their age the teachers didn't use to think twice about hitting their students and Teresa's parents had made a point of telling the school that they were in support of any level of physical violence the teachers cared to inflict on their daughter.

Now things were different and children, rather than having facts beaten into them, absorbed knowledge through a series of 'learning experiences.'

It was on the weekends Teresa felt loneliest. In some ways, she preferred being alone. When there was money, Teresa was free to do whatever, whenever. She longed to be with her daughter, but saving the money to return to the UK was proving impossible. Teresa missed playing with her, comforting her, sharing her life with her and sometimes wished she could at least have someone in Brazil with whom she could share things.

On Saturday, she slept late. Catching up on the week's sleepless nights. She made herself a large coffee, resolving that this would be her last and that from now on she would drink nothing except green tea. She didn't have any green tea. That would have to wait until she got paid next week, but at least the right intention was there.

She ate a bowl of muesli with soya milk and flicked through the hundreds of cable channels, but nothing interested her. She heard that muesli was good for her heart and for the same reason would drink red wine whenever the opportunity presented itself. Fiscal restrictions meant that the opportunity did not present itself often and so she resorted to working her way through the leftovers in the various bottles of spirits she had accumulated. Gin, cachaça, rum, port, brandy, even a bottle of single malt whisky that seemed to have sat there forever. She was working her way through them and intended to buy more as soon as she got paid. Even whisky, which she used to hate and would drown in as much dolly cola as possible, now seemed palatable. She consoled herself that by drinking spirits, she was saving water and contributing to the common interest.

On Saturdays, when she had money, she would go to 25 de Março where the streets and stores were as crammed full of shoppers as they were cheap Chinese-made tat. Teresa loved all the tat. Rows and rows of useless items made of plastic from halfway around the world. Once she found a tin box with a picture of the Eiffel tower under the words 'Welcome to London'. She was so excited at finding it, she bought every one she could find and gave them away as presents.

There would be no shopping trip today. Teresa would have to wait another week before her salary arrived in her bank account. She put her breakfast bowl aside. Put her feet up on her black velvet poof and sighed.

Chapter Fourteen - The Cat - 1st February 2015

Sunday began as a repeat of Saturday. A lay-in followed by breakfast and TV. Then the phone rang.

"Teresinha?" a voice asked. It was her sister whom she hadn't spoken to since her mother's funeral. She seemed cheery despite the recent loss of a parent.

"Would you like a cat? I have two adorable little kittens, and one has your name on it. Oh, they're so adorable, sis," Teresa hated when anyone called her Sis or Teresinha. "Come on, sis; they're gorgeous."

"But I don't have the money to look after a cat."

"I've got everything here that you need, bowls, tray, I've even got a little scratching post for you."

Teresa was confused. Why was her sister trying to be nice to her? Maybe her mother's death had left her unhinged?

"He needs one vaccine a year, and I've a friend who's a vet, and she said she would do a deal on the castration," she continued. "Look, I've sent you a picture. He's so lovely."

As Teresa's sister spoke about the cat, her voice increased in pitch until she became a soprano.

Teresa was feeling lonely. A cat might just be what she needed. But she was struggling with the rent, and she couldn't move to a cheaper flat. Her contract wouldn't expire for another year.

"Well?" her sister asked.

"OK, I'll take him," Teresa said, throwing caution to the wind.

"Great. I'll bring him round now," her sister hung up.

Teresa looked around at the mess that seemed to creep in on all sides of her and realised she had quite a bit of tidying up to do before her sister arrived with her critical comments.

She chucked sweet wrappers, random pieces of paper, junk mail, old receipts and a variety of other debris into plastic bags and stuffed them into drawers. Next, she circled the flat, recovering the contents of the cutlery and crockery cupboards and reuniting them with their filthy colleagues next to and in the already full kitchen sink.

She hurried into the bedroom and changed, collecting all the dirty clothes that littered the floor and depositing them in the, also full, laundry basket.

The bathroom was a necessity, so she collected all the hair from the floor of the shower and deposited it in the small bin overflowing with used toilet paper. Emptying its smelly contents, she replaced the bag with a new one, took the old bulging sack of shit, and dumped it by the front door.

The kitchen bin was next. A mountain of packaging and orange peel propped the lid up. Teresa had long given up trying to keep the contents inside. When she eased the bag from its plastic retainer, putrid liquid dripped from the underside of the bag into a pool which had already collected in the bin's bottom. A swarm of fruit flies hovered; investigating what sticky, rotting delights might be in store.

Teresa barely had the house in a half-decent state when she heard her sister outside.

"Teresinha, Sis!" her sister shouted.

Teresa unlocked both locks on the door and the padlock on the security gate and let in her sister and the cat.

"Look. Didn't I tell you he was adorable?" Teresa's sister said in an 'I told you so' voice as she let the tiny black lump of fluff out of the travel box.

Teresa's heart melted as she saw the little kitten, too small for its fur that stuck out in all directions. Its head seemed large, and its small grey eyes seemed to get lost in its black face. The kitten was black except for a napkin of white under his chin, like a lost diner in search of his table.

'Ah great,' thought Teresa. 'A black cat. All I need is more bad luck.'

The tiny kitten was so cute, and Teresa felt a smile crack her face for the first time in as long as she could remember as she watched the little animal become surprised by almost everything which surrounded him.

"Isn't he gorgeous?" her sister asked, seeing the tears well up in Teresa's eyes.

Teresa nodded, unable to speak as she held back the tears. She sensed all the emotions that she had bottled up inside since the death of her father welling up to the surface and couldn't repress it anymore. The floodgates opened.

"Hey, that's what sisters are for." said her sister, thinking it was all about her. She put an arm around Teresa.

"Thank you." Teresa blurted through the sobs.

She called the cat Oliver after the TV chef whose programmes she enjoyed while she was in London. The shows kept her company during her long days at home with Annabel while William was at work.

Teresa spent all day, after her sister left, playing with Oliver. Periods of frenetic activity among the cat toys Teresa's sister had brought alternated with resting on Teresa's lap, being stroked, tickled and pampered.

When Teresa decided it was time to go to bed, Oliver was entering a phase of frenetic activity, and Teresa waited until she wore out the tiny creature before lifting him into his box and disappear off to bed herself.

That night she slept. If she dreamt her typical anxiety dreams, she couldn't remember them. When her alarm went off, instead of pressing snooze, as usual, she rushed out of bed to see whether Oliver was awake.

He was in his box, peering out at Teresa's face, grinning back at him.

While Teresa made coffee, she chatted with Oliver. Asking him what kind of night he had. Whether he slept well, did a wee, ate any food.

As the last drops of coffee dripped into the jug, the machine gurgled and spat, making Oliver jump backwards in alarm.

Knowing she couldn't put off the fact that she still had to go to work. Teresa went into the bathroom and looked at herself in the mirror. She contemplated how she had become so fat. As she dressed, she struggled to squeeze into her clothes, but even if Teresa had the money; she didn't want to buy new clothes for a body this fat.

When it came time to leave, Teresa shut Oliver in the living room, at which point he cried dramatically. Each of his tiny, high-pitched, weak meows cut deep into Teresa, and it was all that she could do to close the front door and leave him in the house alone.

The journey to work seemed a little more bearable. Rather than getting annoyed by the other commuters, Teresa wondered what Oliver was doing and whether he had enough to amuse himself.

Even at Paraiso, where people forced themselves into the carriage as if they were cattle on the way to slaughter and then forced themselves out of doors on the other side at Brigadeiro, like the opening of the January sales. Even this herd of pushers and shovers didn't upset Teresa.

She was still tired, but it was a good tired.

At the school, she met Mariana getting a coffee in the lunchroom.

"How's it going?" Mariana asked. Teresa told her all about Oliver and how guilty she felt about leaving him alone.

"Get another cat," Mariana suggested.

"What do you mean?"

"They can keep each other company

Teresa thought about it. What would the difference in cost between one cat and two be? Would it be double?

Teresa sent a text to her sister asking if there were any more kittens available and her sister replied that Oliver's brother had yet to find a home. Did she want him?

Did she want him? Two cats to look after. Oliver must be so lonely stuck in the kitchen all by himself.

She texted her sister saying that she would take the other cat. Her sister replied that she would bring him around that night.

Chapter Fifteen - The Beach - 3rd February 2015

"We get paid on Friday. I'm going to the beach," said Mariana, in-between sips of sweet lunchroom coffee. "Why don't you come with me?"

"But what about the cats?" Teresa racked her brain for more excuses.

"They'll look after each other. Make sure they've got enough food."

Teresa couldn't think of any plausible reasons not to go.

"Okay," she agreed. "I'll come."

Mariana smiled.

"Great. Bring your bag; we'll go straight from work."

The journey from São Paulo to the beach should only take an hour and a half, but on weekends during the summer cars, filled with luggage, clogged the lanes.

"What time is it now?" Mariana asked."

"Eight," said Teresa, glancing at the pink, cheap, plastic Hello Kitty watch that she'd won at a fairground and ended up using every day.

"And what time did we leave?"

"Four?"

Mariana stared at the dent in the car's bumper in front.

"Four hours and we're still not at the bottom of the serra yet," she said.

"If it's like this now. Imagine what it will be like during Carnival," said Teresa.

"Forget about it. It'll be a mess."

They sighed in unison.

Two hours later, they pulled up in front of an eight-foot wall topped with electric fencing broken by an eight-foot-high gate which swung open when Mariana pressed a button on a small plastic device clipped to the sun visor. Teresa heard dogs bark. It reminded her of Oliver, and Ramsey stuck at home with a mountain of dried cat food and each other for company.

When Mariana's mother opened the gate, Teresa realised from whom Mariana inherited her personality.

"Girls!" she shouted at the top of her lungs, cackling like a banshee even though it was past ten at night.

Teresa eyed the dark, tree-lined street to see whether there were any neighbours about to complain, but save for a few dried leaves and a couple of small branches, which must have come down in the last storm, there was nothing.

Mariana's mother led them through the decorated house and sat them in an expensive-looking kitchen where she produced cakes from nowhere.

"Mum! I told you I'm on a diet." Mariana complained.

"Nonsense," protested her Mother. "You get this stuff down you. There's plenty more where these came from."

Teresa wondered where they had come from and whether she could live there, wherever there was, but she was also conscious of the fact that she was struggling to get into her clothes as it was. She helped herself to some of the smaller slices of the cakes that looked the least fattening - carrot and coconut. What she wanted, though, was a large gin and tonic.

Despite consuming sugar, Teresa felt herself struggling to keep her head upright and her eyelids open, so when Mariana suggested it was time for bed, she agreed with relief.

That night she dreamt she was back in England on the hen night to which they subjected her in the run-up to the sham of a marriage. This time, she was not touring the bars of the freezing northern town of Newcastle, filled with bikini-wearing teenagers whose slim, toned bodies made Teresa ashamed of her own. She was in the hills of Malvern where her ex, William, took her on the only holiday they had together where she was happy, felt she was part of a couple.

She walked along the main street with the rest of the girls. Other hen parties were checking into hotels they passed on their way. In their hotel, there was a party and William was there, but he was angry with Teresa and drank large quantities of vermouth while Teresa thanked the departing guests for coming. It could have been a rerun of their wedding if it had been her drinking the vermouth. Then she was back in the street on her way back to the train station with the rest of the girls. It snowed, and everyone began singing White Christmas. Then she woke.

She turned over and drifted into space between awake and sleep. There, she had another dream. She was at the school, and her students were falling asleep. She couldn't remember any of their names, so she couldn't call them to wake them up. Instead, she showed a video that she hoped might engage them more. She turned on the projector and clicked on a link. A window popped up, and the video played. The students raised their heads to gaze in half interest at the moving images on the screen.

Another window popped up and another, but instead of an engaging educational documentary, these pop-ups contained videos of an explicit sexual nature. Naked bottoms, an erect penis, vaginas, tongues caressing and massaging large breasts.

Try as she might, Teresa seemed helpless to close the windows. No sooner did she click on the small red square in the corner to close a window showing a well-endowed woman masturbating, than another would pop up with a well-endowed naked blonde fellating a horse.

By clicking on small red squares like a frantic electronic version of splat the rat, Teresa was able to close all the wanking, sucking, fucking, slapping and licking images but by this time pandemonium had broken out in the classroom. Children were screaming, banging desks, throwing chairs, and generally losing it. Teresa restored order to the classroom, which now resembled the scene of looting, with papers and chairs scattered this way and that. Even after the chaos abated and some of the more conscientious students picked up some of the debris, one student, who was new to the school, picked up a chair and threw it into the middle of the class.

"What's your name?" asked Teresa.

"Fernando Enrique." came the confident reply.

"What are you doing? You'll clean all this up." Teresa attempted to give him a hard stare.

"No, I won't," Fernando Enrique replied with astonishing defiance. "You'll have to clean all this up yourself, anyway."

Teresa was speechless. It amazed her that the boy possessed the temerity to be so rude, but she also knew that he was right, that she would never get the class to tidy up the mess before the bell went and they rushed out of the door without her permission. She would have to tidy up during the break so that the other staff didn't think she couldn't control them. Teresa knew she would waste half of the rest of the morning if she tried to get the students to tidy the room themselves.

She woke up sweating and looked around the strange room in a panic. It was a few moments before she realised she was in Mariana's mother's house and could sink back into her pillow with a sigh of relief.

Teresa turned the stainless steel dial, and the hot water stopped cascading out of the showerhead and dripped off her hair and body. Sometimes she felt more hungover in the mornings after she hadn't drunk. She struggled into the swimming costume and beachwear she had set aside found her way back to the kitchen, where Mariana and her mother were already dipping into an enormous breakfast spread that covered the vast table.

"Here's the sleepyhead." chirped Mariana's mother, looking at the clock that Teresa realised it was almost ten thirty.

"You must have been tired," commented Mariana. She gestured to the seat next to her. "Come and sit here. Coffee?"

Teresa nodded, smiled, and sat down. The same selection of cakes and buns as the previous night covered the table, plus French bread, ham, cheese, jam, hazelnut spread and peanut butter. Teresa wondered how many people they were feeding.

"I went for a run this morning," Mariana boasted. "I've just got back and had a shower."

Teresa raised her eyebrows in amazement. It was already hot, and it was still only ten thirty in the morning.

"How far did you go?" asked Teresa, not wanting to hear the answer.

"To the end of the beach and back. I guess that's about twelve kilometres."

Teresa thought she might start to hate Mariana.

"I don't know how you do it," she said.

"Well, it's a question of habit. You build up the distances. I did the São Paulo marathon last year."

Now Teresa was confident she was going to hate Mariana. How could she eat all these cakes and still run those distances?

"Eating after exercise is the best time to eat," Mariana advised. "The body burns all the calories."

"What about this water shortage?" Mariana's mum asked.

"Teresa has it worse than me," said Mariana.

"Yes," Teresa admitted. "I don't have water in the evenings. It makes it tough to do the washing-up. It's a good excuse."

Neither Mariana nor her mother understood her little joke.

"Don't you have a tank?" Mariana's mother asked, still not grasping why anyone would not want to do the washing-up.

"Yes," Teresa replied." But it only supplies water to the bathroom. So, showers are okay, and I can flush the toilet, but I've got no water in the kitchen. I have to fill the kettle in the bathroom and boil the water. I've been saving the water from the washing machine and using that to flush the toilet."

Mariana and her mother wrinkle their noses in disgust.

"Would you like to go to the beach?" Mariana changed the subject.

"Yes. It's sweltering, isn't it?"

"That's okay, we have shade."

Even with the shade, the beach was like a frying pan in which Teresa was the sausage. The sand reflected the heat onto Teresa, who sat and panted like a dog while Mariana ran to and from the sea. Then she saw it, stood at the edge of the beach where the sand gave way to long grass. At the brink of the long grass, a striped cuckoo stood there and looked at Teresa. Teresa stared back, and they looked into each other's eyes for what seemed like an age.

"Come on," Mariana pleaded, breaking Teresa's trance. "The water will cool you down."

Teresa waved to Mariana, agreeing, and looked back to the striped cuckoo, but it had already gone.

The water at first seemed cold, but once she was inside, letting the cool waves lap over her back, Teresa felt good. She noticed how beautiful the mountains were with their blanket of green trees. It seemed like there were no clouds in the sky, but when Teresa looked about, she saw some small fluffy ones here and there. Teresa thought Annabel would love the beach. She had taken her to the Isle of Wight one summer, but the water was cold, and the sun didn't seem to warm her. Not like in Brazil.

The tide was a long way out, and there was a large band of flat wet sand that met the dry sand about twenty metres from the kiosks that were stationed every hundred metres as far as the eye could see and served cold drinks, hot food and ice cream.

As Teresa soaked in the salty ocean, she observed a range of plastic detritus float by. Bottles, cups, bags, straws. More stranded rubbish showed where the high tide left it. Cigarettes, bottles and discarded polystyrene food trays littered the area where Teresa and Mariana placed their seats and towels, though it was cleaner than the high tide mark.

Teresa stared at the distant mountains, spared from the deforestation that dispensed with nearly all the Atlantic Forest, She imagined what the country must have looked like to the colonists when all the land was covered in these beautiful shades of dark green, right up to the beach. What must life have been like for the Tupi who lived in these forests before the Europeans arrived with their influenza and smallpox?

"What a mess we have made!" Teresa thought aloud.

"That's not one of ours," Mariana replied, watching an empty can of coke float away.

"Yes, I know."

The sea and beach were always filthy after the New Year and Carnival. Thinking about the pre-lent celebration reminded Teresa of the date. It would have been her wedding anniversary had she still been married.

Chapter Sixteen - Unlucky for some - 7th February 2015

The shower felt good, and Teresa's skin tingled the way it did when she failed to apply enough sunscreen. Still, it was nice under her clean, albeit tight, clothes and she wandered to the kitchen with the hunger that always followed a day on the beach.

"You caught the sun," said Mariana's mum as soon as she laid eyes on Teresa's skin, which was growing pinker by the minute.

It was already getting dark by the time Teresa and Mariana waved goodbye to her mother and headed off back towards São Paulo. The streets were still full of people coming back from the beach in their swimming costumes.

Teresa always found it amusing that the international media always filmed shots of beautiful women in Copacabana for their news segments. She thought it would be much more interesting if they came down to the coast south of São Paulo and filmed all the saggy bellies on the sunburnt middle-aged uglies.

The motorway wasn't too busy, and both Mariana and Teresa felt they'd made the right decision to go back early.

There was a sudden bang followed by the shattering of glass. Teresa held her face and, without intending to, screamed.

"Christ!" Mariana accelerated.

Teresa felt a dull throb in her head; she seemed to be clutching a handful of sand against her face, wind rushed through the window. Liquid trickled down Teresa's nose.

Teresa tried to piece reality back together. Something must have entered the window and struck her on the forehead.

"Let me see," Mariana ordered as she drove at breakneck speed.

Teresa turned toward Mariana and lifted her hand from her face to get her opinion.

"OK," Mariana said.

"There's a police checkpoint up here. We'll stop there and ask the cops where the nearest A&E is."

Teresa placed her glass-filled palm back onto her bleeding forehead.

"What happened?" she shouted to Mariana over the roar of the wind rushing through the open window. Shattered glass sat on Teresa's lap.

"Criminals," Mariana shouted back. "They wanted to rob us."

Teresa heard stories of people dropping bricks onto cars from overpasses, only to rob the driver stopped to examine the damage.

Mariana screeched to a halt at the police checkpoint. Teresa heard Mariana was explaining something to the police officer, but her head was too much of a fuzz to comprehend.

The police officer leapt into his car, turned on the lights and siren before pulling into the centre of the road, stopping all the traffic. Another police officer removed the barrier across the central reservation, and Mariana followed the speeding police car onto the opposite carriageway in the direction they had come.

They followed the police officer only a short distance before he pulled off the motorway and onto a side road and pulled up in front of a public medical centre.

Mariana thanked the police officer and parked before rushing round to the passenger side to help Teresa out of the car.

"You OK?" Mariana asked, cringing at the stupidity of the question.

Teresa did her best to nod without rubbing her handful of glass further into her face.

Mariana led Teresa into a waiting room filled with bored-looking individuals, clutching various parts of their anatomy with bits of cloth. People, who had stood on broken bottles on the beach, were a popular feature of accident and emergency rooms at this time of year, and, as a result, there were people hopping in all directions.

Teresa's sudden appearance seemed to provide a significant source of entertainment for the injured multitude who turned their gaze from the television hanging on the wall, which they had been watching for hours, and redirected it towards Teresa as Mariana led her over to the nurses' station.

Nurses directed Teresa to sit and used water to wash as much blood and glass as possible away from her eyes.

Comments from the nurses like "Oh, that's a big one" and "That'll scar" did nothing to reassure Teresa.

Mariana fished through Teresa's handbag for her medical card.

Her face washed, Teresa opened her eyes. She held one hand on the wound, although now she was pushing a surgical dressing against her forehead rather than a handful of glass.

Before long, the nurses led Teresa through to a treatment room where the doctor reminded Teresa of a famous black American actor. The doctor looked as if either he had been taking his own medication or he hadn't slept for a week, or both.

"What have we got here?" he asked, removing the dressing. "My, it looks like you've been in the wars, doesn't it? You'll need a few stitches, I'm afraid."

He took care to make sure the wound was free of glass and dirt.

"Will I have a scar?" Teresa asked.

The doctor looked at the wound and thought for a moment.

"It's quite a big one. I'll do my best, but there is quite a significant chance you will end up with a scar, I'm afraid."

Teresa sighed.

"Have you got any oil?" the Doctor asked.

"Oil?"

"Yes, when the stitches come out, rub oil on twice a day. It'll help reduce the scarring."

"Thank you," said Teresa, but she was still very disappointed she would have a scar at all. The size of it seemed secondary.

"Now this might hurt a bit." said the doctor as he started injecting a local anaesthetic into the skin along the wound.

Teresa observed him prepare his needle and thread on a small silver tray. She took a deep breath as he made ready to sew her skin back together.

"Here you are," said Mariana, bursting into the room. "Well, that's all the paperwork sorted." She gave a big smile as she saw the doctor and sat on the other side of Teresa.

"Hello, I'm Mariana," she said to the doctor

The doctor looked at Mariana between stitches and smiled.

"Pleased to meet you, Mariana," he said, pushing the needle through Teresa's flesh and pulling the thread.

"It must be absorbing being a doctor." Mariana continued.

Teresa would have rolled her eyes at Mariana's shameless attempt to flirt were it not for the fact that she considered any movement of eyebrow or forehead to be inadvisable, so she kept her reproach to herself.

"It has its moments," smiled the doctor, inserting a new stitch.

"Do you live in Praia Grande?" asked Mariana.

"I do, yes."

"Married?"

"No."

"Attached?"

He smiled again.

"Nope."

Mariana's grin was as wide as the Cheshire Cat's.

Teresa could not believe her friend was trying to get off with the person sewing up her forehead. There must be some etiquette in situations like these.

"And what do you do Mariana?" asked the doctor.

"I'm a teaching assistant," Mariana replied.

"Teaching, a caring profession."

Teresa couldn't believe it. Now the doctor was flirting with Mariana.

"There you go," he said, snipping the last thread. "The nurse here will apply a dressing. When you've finished here, come to my office."

He took off his gloves as he walked to the door with what Teresa perceived was a definite limp.

"We won't be long," said Mariana

Teresa wished she could throw up, but she felt trapped in Mariana's blind date.

Mariana applied makeup while the nurse applied Teresa's dressing and, as soon as the latter finished, Mariana whisked her off to see the doctor.

"Careful," Teresa complained, being dragged along the corridor.

"Sorry," said Mariana, who didn't slacken her pace.

Mariana made them hover in the grim corridor outside the doctor's room until he finished with a patient, a dirty looking old man in a vest hopping on one leg and with a fresh white bandage around the other.

"Come in," said the doctor as Mariana sat down and Teresa took the seat next to her. "Well, there doesn't seem to be anything broken," he said, slipping an x-ray of Teresa's head onto a light-box on the wall.

Teresa marvelled at the image of the inside of her head. Technology never ceased to amaze her.

"We'll give you a shot of antibiotics now and a course to take at home to make sure there's no infection. If you have any problems, here's my card."

In an instant, Mariana took the card, leaving Teresa wondering to whom the doctor had been talking.

"Now, if you'd like to step behind this screen."

The doctor limped to the back of the room, pulled back a screen and waited for Teresa, who still sat motionless in her chair.

"Who? Me?" Teresa said, at last awakening from her daze.

"You silly," scolded Mariana. "You didn't think he was inviting me behind the screen, did you?" she leant over and whispered in Teresa's ear. "I wouldn't mind if he did."

Teresa ignored her and did what the doctor told her to do.

"Now I need to give you an injection in your buttock," he informed her. "So I need you to lift your skirt at the back for me. Unless you'd like me to call a nurse to give you the injection."

Teresa shook her head to show that would not be necessary and lifted her skirt, thanking the heavens she'd put on a decent pair of knickers today and not the industrial strength enormous brown pants she wore during her periods.

The doctor took the largest needle Teresa had ever seen and filled it with an antibiotic. The sight of the needle left Teresa feeling a little faint, and she steadied herself by holding onto the back of a chair.

"Now you might feel a little prick," he said, but Teresa wasn't in the mood for making a joke out of it and anyway, before she could prepare a decent response, he had already pushed the needle into her buttock.

"I'll give you a letter," the doctor said, returning to his desk. "So you won't have to work for two days and a prescription for some antibiotics. Any problems, call me."

"I will," said Mariana.

Teresa and Mariana sat in the car, contemplating the rest of the journey to São Paulo.

"He was nice, wasn't he?" Mariana commented.

Teresa was about to raise her eyebrows but thought better of it.

"He was looking after me," Teresa complained.

"And?"

"And you're trying to get off with him all the time. It's so embarrassing." Mariana laughed.

"Sorry about that. But you've got to seize the moment, haven't you?"

Teresa didn't think she'd ever seized the moment. Moments seized her.

Mariana started the car, pulled out of the car park, and re-joined the motorway toward São Paulo.

"You're still going to stay at mine tonight, right?" said Mariana. "There's a 24-hour pharmacy nearby where we can get your drugs. No drinking for a while, eh?"

What was Mariana suggesting? Did she think she had a problem with drinking? Teresa sat in silence.

"Don't worry," Mariana said after a while. "Everything will be fine."

Teresa snapped.

"It's OK for you to say that. You'll marry the doctor and live in a big house and have lots of children and live happily ever after. I'm middle-aged with a scar on my forehead. Who'll marry me now?"

She cried.

"Look. Teresa. I'm... Jesus!"

A car wheel lying in the middle of the motorway appeared in the headlights. There were cars in both lanes on either side. There was not the time to swerve aside without rolling the car, so Mariana had no choice but grip the steering wheel as tight as she could and hope for the best.

Teresa imagined it was the end.

The car struck the wheel and leapt over it. Mariana struggled with the steering wheel, somehow kept the vehicle on the road, and steered it over to the hard shoulder where they sat breathing for a moment until, after a second or two, Teresa began laughing aloud.

Mariana looked at her as if she had gone mad and then her mouth cracked into a smile, and she, too, started laughing.

"Phew," said Mariana, at last, trying to catch her breath. "I tell you what. You've cheated death twice this evening. Do you still think you're unlucky?"

Teresa thought about it.

"Oh my God," she said. "Have you heard that phrase 'bad things always come in threes'? We have to think of something else bad that has already happened, otherwise a third bad thing will happen."

"It's not threes; it's pairs. Bad things always come in pairs. So we've had our bad things now so we can relax."

Once she got her breath back, Mariana set off again, and the rest of the journey went without incident.

They stopped at a 24-hour pharmacy where Teresa bought her antibiotics and then drove on to Mariana's house, which, to Teresa, seemed huge. Three bedrooms, two bathrooms and, what Teresa considered to be a beautiful kitchen, as expensive looking as Mariana's mother's but more trendy.

"How can you afford to live in a house like this?" Teresa asked.

"It belongs to my parents," Mariana laughed. "When they moved to the coast, I had it all to myself

"It's gone midnight," said Mariana. "Let me show you to the spare bedroom."

Teresa followed Mariana up a spiral staircase.

"Here's the bathroom," she said, showing a door on the left. "And this is your room."

Mariana led Teresa into a spacious, well-decorated bedroom with a large double bed covered with white sheets, large pillows, and at least a dozen cushions. At one end of the room, a thin white curtain was riding a breeze that was entering through the half-open French windows.

"Oh no, I didn't close the windows. I hope there are no mosquitoes." Mariana rushed over to close them.

"So there you are," she said, waving her arm towards the bed. "You'll find fresh towels in the cupboard. Would you like some water?"

"Yes, please."

"I'll get some. If you need anything in the night, I'll be in the room at the end of the hall."

While Mariana fetched some water, Teresa found a towel and went to the bathroom opposite for a shower. It was the first time she had seen her face in a mirror since the accident. She looked terrible. A large dressing covered almost half her forehead, and black rings circled her eyes. Teresa sighed. She turned on the shower and undressed. Blood on her dress.

Small pieces of glass dropped out of it and onto the floor. Teresa stepped into the icy stream of water. More glass that had stuck to the sweat on her body now washed off and edged its way to the drain.

She soaked up the water for a while, taking care not to get her dressing wet, patting herself dry in case any glass somehow still clung to her.

When she returned to the bedroom, there was a jug of water and a glass on the bedside table, but Mariana was nowhere in sight.

Teresa climbed into bed; Mariana had already moved the cushions to a white wicker sofa, which sat on the opposite side of the room.

The sheets were soft, and Teresa soon drifted into slumber.

A buzz which brushed her ear woke her.

Mosquito?

Knowing she could never sleep while the predator was tormenting her, she turned on the bedside lamp and began searching for her nemesis.

She caught a glimpse as it made a pass across the bed, but it wasn't close enough or slow enough for capture or assassination.

Teresa sat up and scanned the air. There it was again. She grasped for it, but it was beyond reach.

Buzz. It flew past her left ear, taunting her with its agility.

"Bastard," she muttered, becoming more determined that the insect would die.

Teresa looked around. She spied the creature against the duvet and lunged for it. She eyed her clenched fist. Was the beast inside? She unclenched her fist and out flew the mosquito, unhurt. She lunged again. Did she have it? She ground her fist to guarantee the insect's mortality. Once more she opened her hand, but her palm was clean, no bug. She spied, in-between her middle and index fingers, a black smudge. She spread her fingers and saw the crumpled and crushed remains of her enemy. For a moment she eyed the entomological corpse as a victor salutes a worthy adversary and flicked it onto the floor, turned off the light and went back to sleep.

Teresa had no way of knowing how long she slept. This time it was the sound, not of a mosquito, but of more than one mosquito.

Her immediate reaction was that the mosquitoes saw what she had done to their friend and had now come for revenge

She switched the light on again and hunted for the insects; she saw several, all beyond reach. How could she hope to murder them all? Perhaps there were hundreds.

She decided her bed sheets would protect her, turned off the light and hid beneath the covers, but it soon began to get scalding, and she was sure she could feel one of them attacking her leg through the sheet.

She sat up and turned the light on again. There was a fan on the ceiling. Perhaps if she turned it on, the mosquitoes wouldn't be able to land on her. There seemed to be a controller as part of the light switch on the wall, so she got up and fiddled with the controls until the blades of the fan whirred into action. She returned to bed and, trying not to listen to the occasional buzz, she closed her eyes and attempted to get back to sleep. After a long time, fatigue overcame the fear of being bitten, and she slept.

When she awoke, it was daylight, and she felt an overwhelming desire to itch her ankle, her arm, her leg. Still tired, she lay in bed and listened for sounds of activity in the house.

After a while, she heard what sounded like Mariana in the kitchen, so decided she should get up and dragged herself into the bathroom.

After a wee, she observed herself in the mirror with horror. An army of red blotches had joined the big white dressing and black eyes.

'Oh Brilliant,' she thought. 'Things are just getting better and better'.

Once showered and dressed, avoiding any disruption to her dressing, she wandered down to the kitchen to see what Mariana was doing.

As she rounded the kitchen door, an old woman seemed to leap out and scream at her. Teresa shouted back.

"My God!" exclaimed the old woman, placing her hand on her chest.

"Jesus! You scared me." Teresa responded, doing likewise.

The old woman found a nearby stool and sat on it.

"I'm Teresa," Teresa said after a long pause and held out her hand, which the woman ignored.

Mariana rushed in.

"What happened?" she asked, breathless from her race down the stairs.

The old woman and Teresa observed Mariana.

"Jesus! What happened to you?" Mariana asked Teresa, staring at her pockmarked skin.

"Mosquitoes."

"Oh my God, are you OK?"

"Never mind her. I almost had a heart attack," the old woman snapped.

"Sorry Nanny."

Nanny?

"This is Teresa. Teresa, this is Nanny."

"You have a nanny?"

"Well, Nanny was my nanny when I was growing up, but now she still helps around the house."

"Cooks cleans, does the dishes, the laundry, and takes the dog for a walk." Nanny elaborated.

"Dog?"

Teresa felt a sudden urge to be alone, to be at home with her cats without human interference. She had been aware for some time that when with other people, she often desired solitude, but when she was alone, Teresa felt lonely and longed for the company of others. There was no pleasing her. She used to get frustrated with her daughter not doing as she was told and long for someone to take her off her hands for a while so she could have a break but they only had to be separated for five minutes and Teresa would miss her and long to get back to her.

Sat there in Mariana's kitchen, she longed to be far away, not least because she had a growing sensation that soon she would need to do a giant fart.

"Would you excuse me for a moment?" she asked and headed straight for the bathroom.

Teresa sat on the toilet. She felt bloated. She tried to poo, but only the smallest of farts escaped. Reaching for the toilet paper, her arm brushed against her breast, which felt tender, a sign that her period was on its way.

When Teresa returned to the kitchen, the old woman had gone, but not before she had laid out breakfast on the large white kitchen table. Teresa wondered whether everything in the house was white.

"Is everything in the house white?" she asked.

"No," Mariana answered, confused.

Teresa accepted some coffee and some bread, which she dressed with slices of cheese.

"I know we were going to hang out together." Teresa began.

"Oh, don't worry," Mariana interrupted. "You want to get home, don't you?"

"Well..." Teresa smiled.

"It's fine. After breakfast, I'll run you home. Give me a chance to have a quick shower first."

"Thank you, Ma. You've been excellent to me. I can't thank you enough."

"Don't mention it," said Mariana. "I feel responsible. If I hadn't invited you to the beach, none of this would have happened."

"It's not your fault."

Mariana smiled.

"At least I met an excellent doctor," she said.

Teresa laughed and then winced.

"I better not laugh," said Teresa. "It hurts my head."

Mariana laughed for both of them.

"Have a cake," she said, pointing to a spread almost as large as the one Mariana's mum had offered. "Dotty makes these. They're better than mum's."

"Thanks," said Teresa. "But I'll stick with the cheese."

After breakfast, Mariana had a shower while Teresa brushed her teeth and collected her belongings.

Teresa felt a little guilty to be abandoning Mariana on what looked to be turning into a beautiful Sunday, but she was glad to be going home. She was in no state to face the public.

"Do you want to come in?" Teresa offered as Mariana pulled up outside her house.

"Thanks, but I'll leave you to it. Have a good rest, and I'll see you in a few days."

"Thanks."

Teresa got out of the car and leant down to close the door.

"Thanks again," she said. "See you at school."

At the front door, Teresa was about to place her key in the lock when a sound made her stop. She listened. There it was again. That bird. Another striped cuckoo. She'd never seen one in years, or at least not paid attention to them, and now, here they were, popping up all over the place. The Saci bird.

In the house, Oliver and Ramsey rushed to see her. Oblivious to the state of her face, they brushed up against her in excitement.

Teresa dropped her bag on the floor and walked into the kitchen. Stray tiny balls of cat food crunched under her feet. The cats' bowls were almost empty.

"Good job I came home when I did," she said to them as they brushed around her legs.

She took the bag of cat food out of the cupboard and put a handful in each of their bowls, which they devoured.

Teresa went to wash the dusty cat food residue off her hands and wondered whether there would be any water in the tap. There was. Teresa was ambivalent about the current supply of water. On the one hand, it meant the water tank would refill. She could refill the ice cube dispensers and all the plastic bottles she'd collected to store water and also fill the kettle without going to the bathroom. The downside of having a supply of water was that she had no excuse for not doing the washing-up that had been accumulating in the sink, and now sat there festering under a small cloud of fruit flies. She decided there was plenty of time to do the washing-up and decided instead to put the kettle on for a cup of tea. Tea was another taste she gained during her time in England, along with salt and vinegar crisps, brown sauce, chocolate buttons, Polo mints, jelly babies and shortbread, none of which were available in São Paulo.

To put the kettle on, she had to unplug the microwave. Some years ago, Brazil changed the type of electrical plug and socket it used. None of the plugs, even the ones that worked, were the right size for any of her appliances, and adapters and extension cables littered the house. Also, even the new type of electrical plug seemed to have two kinds, fat and thin, so that some plugs would only fit in some adapters she purchased. This led to a shortage of holes for her large plugs. Both the kettle and the microwave bore large plugs, and because they also shared the same area of the kitchen, there was not enough big plug capacity, and she could only use one at a time. So, every time she wanted to use the microwave, she would need to unplug the kettle, and every time Teresa needed the kettle, she would need to unplug the microwave. Teresa found it tough to source the correct adapter. So far, she had bought five, but she had deployed these at the ends of various devices and appliances around the house. She would put the kettle on and realise five minutes later that it wasn't plugged in. Today was no exception. Five minutes later, she unplugged the microwave and sat back down to wait a second time for the kettle to boil.

The cats fussed around her, punctuating attacks on her feet with attacks on each other. When the kettle boiled and she walked into the kitchen, a ball of black fur darted between her feet and she was in grave danger of being tripped.

Opening the fridge door for the milk, she noticed a remarkable absence of coldness. She smelt the milk. It was off. She checked the plug. It was plugged in. She checked the lights on the fridge door. The lights showed the fridge was running at maximum power. It wasn't. She checked the freezer. That seemed to be OK. Teresa pressed a few buttons, then left the festering milk next to the festering washing-up and resolved to drink her tea black on this occasion.

She sat back down and pointed the remote at the TV, pressing the small red button. Nothing. She pressed it again. Still nothing. She considered the possibility that the power company had cut off the electricity or that there had been a power cut, but the boiling water in her cup and the small red light on the television disproved this theory. What could have caused the simultaneous failure or her TV and fridge? Neither was under guarantee.

It would have to be music then. Teresa put on the iPod. Belle and Sebastian started on the shuffle; *I'm a Cuckoo*. She could relax and kicked off her shoes.

When Teresa awoke, it was dark, and she had a splitting headache and a damp sensation in her knickers. She got up from the sofa, but there it was. A small red spot of blood on the couch/mattress.

"Bollocks," she said out loud pulling the sheet off to reveal a stain on the mattress below.

Teresa rushed into the kitchen and grabbed a pinch of salt and a damp cloth. Thank God, she had water. Teresa rushed back to the mattress and rubbed the salt on the spot. Her mother had told her it was good for removing blood stains when she tried to wash the blood out of her sheets when she'd lost her virginity to her childhood boyfriend, Guillermo.

She padded the stain with the damp cloth, covered it with kitchen towels and sat two heavy books on top, a dictionary and Learn How to Paint, to soak up the stain while she went for a shower. The cats chased her, but she rushed to close the bathroom door before they could squeeze in.

Clean, dry and wearing a fresh pair of clothes protected by super strength tampon and maxi-strength sanitary pads, she led the cats into the living room and observed the damage on the mattress. The tissues had lifted most of the stain, so, following a rub with a clean damp cloth, she laid new tissues and replaced the books.

Teresa tried the TV again, but it still didn't work, so she tried the fridge, but it still wasn't cold. She emailed the Head, explaining why she wouldn't be in school for the next three days.

Chapter Seventeen - The Car - 9th February 2015

The metallic rattle of the front gate roused Teresa. She shuffled in her slippers to the door and opened the small window in the middle, but there was no-one there. She noticed a piece of paper wedged into the gate. The electricity bill.

Checking that the cats weren't close enough to escape, she opened the door, grabbed the bill and closed the door again. Oliver and Ramsey sat on the opposite side of the room, wondering what all the fuss was.

Teresa sat back down and opened the bill.

"Ninety?" she said aloud as she read the total. She couldn't understand how this was possible. Flipping the bill over, she saw a whole panel explaining the new traffic light system, based on the level of water in the state's hydroelectricity generating reservoirs. The power company charged their usual tariff when the levels in the lake were high. However, when levels were low, the status would switch to amber, and they would add a cost of R$1.50 per so many units of electricity. An additional R$3 would be added per so many units when levels were low, as they were now, and that, it seemed, was the reason that Teresa's bill was such a shock.

She breathed a sigh of frustration and put the bill down on the sofa beside her, knowing that she would need to do some budgeting if she was going to make it to the end of the month.

The cats jumped onto the sofa next to her as if they sensed she required some consolation.

Her head throbbed and her stomach cramped. She treated herself to more painkillers and another cup of tea. The TV still wasn't working, so she made herself a hot water bottle and listen to music in bed. It was too hot for a hot water bottle, but it eased her pain, so she opted to sweat.

Teresa decided Benny Goodman might be the answer. It was cheerful music, which made her feel better, and the fact that it was jazz made her feel a little cultured.

Teresa had an old-fashioned turntable for playing vinyl. She bought it not long after she moved into the flat when she found a pile of old vinyl records in the back of a dusty cupboard. Since then, Teresa visited second-hand stores to rummage through the vinyl, and Benny Goodman had been one of her greatest discoveries. A ten-inch album. She slid the shiny black disc out of its sleeve and placed it on the turntable. Lifting the needle arm, she moved it first to the right, which engaged the motor and started the turntable spinning at 33 1/3 revolutions per minute, then moved it left and lowered it onto the edge of the black disc. There was a moment of crackling and hissing before the sound of trumpets burst through the speakers and filled the room.

Although the TV was not working, the Internet was. So, Teresa pressed the 'on' button of her, now aged, laptop and waited for it to start-up.

When the computer had gone through all the checks it needed, it paused twice, giving Teresa the impression it had crashed. It concluded the start-up process with a message assuring her it started 12% faster than it did before she installed the Power Tools Performance Enhancer 2.1 utility. She was not impressed, and double clicked on the Internet browser icon before going to make another cup of tea, which she knew she could do before the application would open itself and be ready for use.

The browser was ready, and she wandered through sites, clicking on any links which seemed of interest. The first side of Benny Goodman finished, but she couldn't be bothered to get up and turn the record over. She saw an advert that caught her eye.

'The secret to health and happiness without effort.'

Teresa snorted with derision but still followed the link to a website with a video, which kept talking about interesting facts about the secret to being slim and happy but which never seemed to get to the point. The presenter was a beautiful, happy and slender woman wearing a white doctor's coat which flapped open to reveal how healthy and happy she was. Every time she seemed to be about to reveal the secret to the perfect body and the key to unbridled happiness, the secret that THEY don't want you to know, she would start talking about another compelling piece of research THEY have tried to keep secret to stop you from finding out the secret to real fitness and unparalleled delirium with no effort.

After about ten minutes of compelling research presented delightfully by the woman with the most beautiful body on the planet, she told Teresa that all she needed to do was order a pack which contained everything she needed including two types of herbal pills which the Chinese have sworn by for centuries but which THEY don't want you to know about.

The price seemed reasonable. Teresa glanced at the bill sat next to her on the mattress sofa and thought about how one expenditure or another accounted for every centavo of her salary. She closed the laptop, set it aside, laying her head on a cushion, she drifted off into a deep sleep.

Teresa awoke in the middle of the night, still lying on the sofa with a splitting headache. She got up for a glass of water to wash down her painkillers. The cats followed her into the kitchen. She tried the tap before she remembered that there was no water at night and instead looked inside the fridge for a bottle. There was nothing in the fridge, and as she surveyed the line of empty bottles by the kitchen sink, she realised she had forgotten to refill them all. Teresa turned to the kettle which had a small amount in the bottom together with a collection of limescale residue. She poured it into a small glass and unwrapped her medicine from its packaging. The cats took it in turns to investigate their litter tray, food bowls, water bowl and scratching post. Teresa smiled a weary smile at them, dropped a tablet on her tongue and drank the water, wincing as the small pieces of limescale joined the tablet on the way down her oesophagus.

Waking up late on a weekday was always enjoyable for Teresa and staying at home knowing that everyone else was working was a nice sensation. She felt a little guilty that someone at the school had to cover her lessons, but the delight of not having to leave the house but being able to enjoy being at home with the cats offset this. It would be perfect if she didn't have a splitting headache and stomach cramps, but if she weren't ill, she'd have to be at work taking abuse off ten-year-olds who thought they were better than she was.

Teresa decided that since she was forced to stay at home, she would try to sort her life out. She opened her laptop again and started with her finances. She checked her bank balance and opened a spreadsheet to list all the expenses she would have this month. Rent, bills, credit card payments, store card payments, the fee to the University for the distance course she was doing. The result was more disappointing than she had realised. Once she added up all her outgoings, Teresa discovered that her salary did not cover everything.

She knew she would have to do something she had been trying to avoid for a long time. She would have to sell her car. That would give her enough money to pay the bills and pay off some of her cards and overdraft. She didn't use the car that often anyway; she travelled to work by bus and Metro and she would also save on tax, insurance, maintenance and petrol. Teresa decided she would strike while the iron was hot. She would get dressed, clean the car and take it to a car dealership to see what they would give her. R$13,000 seemed a reasonable amount.

She felt like she had a mission. A purpose. She felt things would improve.

Her mood changed at the car showroom.

"R$6,000? But it's worth at least twice that," she complained.

"Sorry darling, but the market is depressed at the moment." said the gorilla with whom she had just been trying to negotiate.

'No kidding,' she thought, feeling depressed herself.

"That's the best offer I can give you." he continued.

"It's okay," she answered. "I'll have a look around."

"You won't get a better offer than that," he warned.

He was right. After a day of traipsing around the showrooms of half a dozen almost identical gorillas, six thousand was by far the best, and she returned to the gorilla and accepted his offer.

Chapter Eighteen - The Bus - 10th February 2015

"Sorry."

Not that she didn't have any money, she had R$6,000 in her backpack. It was just that she had financial problems of her own. At least she wasn't begging on the street to buy nappies, if that's why he wanted the money.

"Do you know how expensive nappies are?" he asked.

"No."

"A pack of eighteen nappies costs R$25. And my three-year-old needs three packs a week."

Teresa raised her eyebrows but thought it unlikely that a three-year-old would need 54 nappies a week. Teresa couldn't quite do the maths, but it was over seven a day. One every three and a bit hours. She supposed it was possible. Annabel would get through 6 to 8 a day, she remembered, but because she was trying to be an environmentalist; she washed them all.

"This is all I have," she said, pulling all the loose change out of her pocket.

The bus came, and she could escape her intimidating new friend.

The bus was a brand new air-conditioned bendy bus, and when Teresa climbed on board, there were few passengers inside. She went in, past the bendy bit, and sat on one of the cushioned seats. A marked improvement on the hard plastic seats to which she was accustomed.

At the next stop, the bus filled up. Teresa turned her head toward the window, hoping no-one would look at the dressing on her forehead and that no-one outside the bus would bother to look in.

"Excuse me." someone said as they sat in the seat beside Teresa, but Teresa kept her head down and gazed at a bendy bus outside that her bus had started to overtake.

She considered whether it might have been quicker to take the metro, but that would have involved changes and lots of walking whereas, with the bus, Teresa could sit down and ignore people until she arrived at her destination.

The bus crawled through traffic, weaving its way around cars that ground to a halt trying to change lane. It turned between tall glass towers in which Teresa imagined well-dressed executives were working unsociable hours to justify enormous salaries. She tried not to dwell on her financial difficulties or the ridiculous offer she had accepted for her car, the car she had grown attached to, grown to love despite its scratches and bumps and occasional mechanical issues.

At the next bus stop, even more people got on until they stood in the aisle and by the doors.

In a tooth cavity, Teresa could feel a piece of bread that had been stuck in there since breakfast. Teresa tried to brush it out before she left but it seemed well lodged, and she feared to be too aggressive in her attempts to remove it in case the tooth caused her pain again. She needed to go to the dentist to get it fixed.

At the next stop, even more, people got on the bus, and now all the standing space was solid too. There was a delay at every stop as new passengers got on. Nobody seemed to get off. Teresa didn't mind the delay. She was not in a hurry to get home. The cats would wait for her. They wouldn't love her any less if she arrived a bit later.

After accommodating what looked like an impossible number of passengers at the next stop, the bus moved on around a square in the centre of which stood towering palms, a small grass area and some chipped stone furniture which all looked like it might be pleasant to sit in to read a book and eat a Brie baguette with a bottle of chilled Pinot Grigio if it were not for the plethora of discarded beer cans and other detritus which littered the place.

'Such a shame people don't look after the places where they live,' Teresa lamented to herself.

The bus turned the corner of Avenida Brasil, and Brigadeiro and the monument on the corner of Ibirapuera Park looked beautiful, illuminated in the enclosing darkness.

The bus climbed Brigadeiro, past more litter, graffiti-tagged walls, piles of rubbish sacks, a dirty-looking hotel with a single doorway through which Teresa could see a young man and woman checking in, in front of a beaded curtain.

Business people climbed uphill toward the metro. Joggers ran downhill. At every bus stop, fat women with their hair tied back in tight ponytails, bags over their shoulders and hands resting on their bellies stared into the distance awaiting their full bus which they would have to squeeze onto and complain about the terrible state of public transport in Brazil.

Weary commuters took a break from their journeys to buy soggy sandwiches, bars of chocolate, and a variety of salt or sugar-filled snacks.

A man in a second-hand bookshop surveyed the stream of pedestrians walking past, ignoring his goods.

Near the top of Brigadeiro, where it meets Avenida Paulista, half the bus passengers alighted for the metro. It had already taken Teresa almost an hour to get this far, but she was enjoying her seat.

Commuters filled the pavements of Paulista, most of whom wore the ubiquitous small backpack. Customers filled tables in front of cages, enjoying a beer after work even though it was still early in the week.

As Paulista turned into Vergueiro, the class of establishment, the bus passed became less classy. Paraiso looked anything but a paradise. Dirty looking men sat against graffiti-stained walls smoking cigarettes. Every available surface seemed to have a tag sprayed on it.

As Paraiso became Ana Rosa, which became Vila Mariana, the walls became duller and the overhead electrical wiring more anarchic. At the station, the bus population halved temporarily as those who alighted were replaced with new fodder.

Vila Mariana reminded Teresa of the time a pigeon defecated on her head. It seemed like poo; it was white like bird poo is, but it was runny.

The shops in the backstreets of Vila Mariana became more budget, and the bars catered less for trendy professionals and more for aged alcoholics older than her.

An old man in a combat jacket leant against the entrance to a car park. A grandmother pulled a young girl in a ballet uniform along the street. Cars stopped at petrol stations to fill up while their drivers complained about the price of fuel. On every other corner stood a pharmacy with shelves filled with coloured packs of nappies. Teresa felt a little guilty. But not very.

Strawberry cream cakes rotated at the entrances of bakers. An empty Lebanese restaurant advertised for a chef. Cars negotiated each other in supermarket car parks. Neon lights flashed the word Hotel on the front of an establishment that charged by the hour.

Teresa had lost her bearings a little. It didn't matter, though. Her stop was the last one. They named the streets after revolutionary heroes. Even the pharmacies sported independence-themed names.

The flame burned at the foot of the Independence monument in Ipiranga, where the placid margins smelled of the polluted drain running alongside.

When she reached home, another bus ride from the Sacomã Terminal, Teresa contemplated her options. Her car sale did little to ease her financial difficulties, and she was regretting it.

As she stared at the figures on the spreadsheet, trying to find some way to make them work, an idea occurred to her. She set the laptop down on the sofa, being careful not to place it on top of a cat, and walked over to the bookshelf. She scanned the volumes and selected The Alchemist by Paulo Coelho. Opening its pages, she pulled out a small white envelope and, opening the envelope; she removed a gold band and a second gold ring with a solitaire diamond, the remains of her marriage. Neither summoned happy memories.

Turning back to the laptop, Teresa googled the price of gold, £24 per gramme. Then she googled the exchange rate and almost dropped the computer. One pound could now buy 4.68 Reals; the rate had been 2.7 when she returned to Brazil over three years ago. Another web search told her that an air ticket which might have cost R$1500 was now over R$4000. Her dreams of going back to England to visit Annabel were now very much in tatters.

There was a noise at the door, another letter, another bill. This time the rental insurance R$2,400 split into four instalments. Teresa sat back down on the sofa, unable to think about how she could even start to get herself out of this situation.

Maybe she could apply for another credit card. Maybe she could get some tax back. She had all the documents she needed to do her return. She went to the Receita Federal website and started downloading the application. Rushing off to her pile of papers, she found the tax statement the school had given her. When she returned to the laptop, the application had already downloaded, so she installed it and started typing in the details. She completed the quick and straightforward form and pressed calculate. The application thought about it and announced that Teresa owed Receita Federal R$1,800. How was this possible? She opened the form requiring more specific details and entered all the fields relevant to her. Teresa took a deep breath and pressed calculate once more. The application thought about it for longer and announced that Teresa owed the Receita Federal R$8. It was much better than before, but it would solve none of her financial problems. Maybe she should start teaching English lessons after school again, as Mariana did. She didn't understand why Mariana taught private lessons; she didn't need the money. Teresa made another cup of tea.

Chapter Nineteen - The Doctor - 11th February 2015

Wednesday rained all night, and by the time Teresa got up, drops of water were collecting on the bathroom ceiling and taking it in turns to dive into an expanding puddle on the floor. Teresa called the property management company, who apologised that the earliest they could get someone round to look at it would be Saturday. Teresa left a bucket collecting the water.

The fridge was still not working, and the limited contents were smelling. Teresa searched online for someone nearby who might come and look at it.

"Saturday." declared the telephonist. Saturday it would have to be, and Teresa consented.

By the time Thursday came. Teresa was bored with life without television and was relieved to get back to the school. After three days, it felt strange crowding on the bus and metro with all the other commuters. She didn't get a seat. Most of those with seats seemed to be sleeping, trying to sleep or pretending to sleep so they would not have to relinquish their seat to anyone older, more infirm or more pregnant than themselves.

Questions bombarded Teresa from the moment she walked through the door of the school. Both from staff and students. About what had happened to her head, how she felt, and what could anyone do to help?

Teresa rolled off her stock answers and tried to find a corner to hide in, which was impossible.

Thursday morning was always school assembly. Classes would take it in turns to present what they had been learning in class. This week it was the turn of a class to present what they had learned about explorers.

Children in Columbus costumes, like ships, as the first explorers, to arrive in Brazil, as natives who seemed happy to accept smallpox and influenza of the conquistadors in return for gold. The class had a mix of confident performers who would deliver their lines at full volume accompanied by exaggerated gestures and children who looked like they might urinate themselves if someone in the back row whispered 'boo'.

The performance was the usual mix of monotone lines delivered at lightning speed or languid torpidity, with the enthusiasm of the minority as usual far outweighing the apathy of the majority. The cute factor of nine-year-olds trying to remember their lines or arguing with each other over who should say what and when ensured that, as usual, the assembly was an unmitigated success.

On the way back to class, Teresa bumped into Mariana, who thrust a present into her hands.

"I saw this and thought of you," she said. "I hope you like it."

"Thanks." Teresa started to say, but Mariana had already gone.

At break time, she unwrapped the present. It was a book. *Wreck this Journal* by Keri Smith. Teresa was expecting it to be a novel but when she opened it, most of the pages were blank except for random instructions such as 'attach your shopping list here' or 'compost this page'. Teresa turned back to the introduction and read. The book was a kind of creativity development workbook with lots of interesting and creative ways to destroy the book.

"Do you like it?" Mariana asked during the morning break, dropping into the seat opposite Teresa.

"It's great. But you don't have to buy me presents." Teresa protested.

"But I wanted to," Mariana said, applying cream cheese to the cracker on her plate.

Brenda joined them, sighing as she slumped into the seat next to Teresa.

"Mind if I join you?" she asked.

Teresa shook her head. It was too late, if she minded.

"Hey, are you coming to the protest on Sunday?" Mariana asked Teresa.

"Protest?"

"Yeah, at Paulista. There'll be a protest against Dilma. You coming?"

"I'm not political," Teresa admitted. "I'm not for or against Dilma."

"But what about the corruption?" Mariana argued. "President Dilma and her cronies are robbing the country."

"All politicians are corrupt," Brenda joined in without being asked for her opinion.

"So, who do you vote for?" Mariana asked.

"The Green Party," Brenda admitted.

Teresa would not admit that in the second round of the presidential election in October, she had voted for Dilma.

"If all the politicians are going to mess things up, you may as well have someone messing things up with a chance of a little benefit to the planet," said Brenda.

"You know the Green Party has no chance of being elected. It's a wasted vote," said Mariana.

"When faced with the same corrupt leaders, it is always best to vote for the candidate on the left because, no matter what else goes on, the poor might benefit," Brenda continued. "However, voting for the right means that, no matter how wonderful the economy becomes, the people that will benefit are the rich. The same corruption goes on, but under a different name, meanwhile they cut social programmes, the poor get poorer, and the rich get richer."

Teresa didn't want to join in.

"Dilma and her party are robbing the country." Mariana continued.

"You have to admit, though, that over the last ten years, they have lifted millions of Brazilians out of poverty," Brenda argued.

"Those Brazilians would have been lifted out of poverty anyway," countered Mariana. "It was Cardoso who introduced the family allowance benefit system before Lula, and his Workers Party were ever in power. Lula enjoyed the economic success that Cardoso started."

Brenda had no answer for Mariana.

Teresa was fed up with the news programmes, filled with stories about corruption and the struggling economy. But what made her angry was the state of the currency, the Real, which was at a shocking low against the dollar. This meant that a trip to England to see her daughter was beyond her reach.

"Come on Sunday," Mariana pleaded. "I've invited someone and told them you'd be there."

"Who?"

"You remember the doctor who sewed up your head?"

"What?" Teresa was astounded.

Brenda raised her eyebrows.

"Come on Teresa. You have to come."

Teresa was feeling like a bit of a protest against the government, and she had nothing better to do on Sunday, so she agreed to go.

"Thank you, thank you, thank you," Mariana blubbed. "I owe you."

That evening, on the way back to the Faria Lima metro station, Teresa passed three students performing what looked like some protest art. One student held aloft a piece of cardboard with 'body in change' written in large letters. A second student, dressed in washer women's clothes, stood by a large bowl of soapy water in which she had soaked a large São Paulo state flag which she was slapping on the paving stones like a washerwoman beating clothes on rocks by a river. A third student sat looking bored next to a large bottle of water and an assortment of bags which Teresa imagined might contain their supplies of snacks – even radical students never devolve themselves from consumerism. Teresa wasn't sure of the exact meaning of the art, but she liked it. She felt her creativity workbook in her bag and promised herself to be creative as soon as she got home.

Teresa had great fun scribbling all over her book, stamping on it, dropping it from a great height, cutting pieces out of the pages, writing bad words, drawing dirty pictures. She found the experience liberating, started feeling creative, something she hadn't felt for a long time. Not since she had sat down with Annabel and created messy arts and crafts. She recalled one occasion on which she had become angry with Annabel for making a mess, and now the memory filled her with guilt.

During Friday's journey to work, the usual standing in public transport, she got a seat on the metro a few stops from her destination and when she sat down, her legs tingled with relief.

'I must do some exercise,' she thought, and vowed to join Mariana and the other girls to play volleyball on Wednesday.

As she dismissed the children, the grey clouds that had lingered all day decided they'd had enough and emptied their contents over the school. Teresa had no appetite for attempting the walk to the metro station, but she did not relish the prospect of hanging around at the school until the rains stopped.

She grabbed her umbrella and headed for the exit. In Teresa's experience, the rain in São Paulo reached an intensity which rendered the use of an umbrella pointless as the huge drops of water would bounce off the ground with such force and rapidity that, even if the umbrella user's head remained dry, the rest of their body would not.

In Teresa's opinion, the rain was not falling with such ferocity, and she could make her way to the metro station in a state of relative dryness. The other reason she wanted to leave the school on time was that at quarter to four, the hour they expected her to work until, there were fewer people on the metro and buses than, say, six o'clock when people filled the platforms and carriages. Even at this time, the subway was busy, and there were long queues for the bus but two hours later and the trains were like tins of sardines and getting a seat on a bus would involve joining another queue for the second bus to arrive.

Teresa arrived early enough at Sacomã bus station to get a seat on the quarter to five bus, although, by the second bus stop after the station, all the seats were full and the aisle was filling. Teresa gave a tentative glance up at the standing passengers in case any of them were old, disabled, or pregnant. Two passengers were borderline old, so she kept her head down and pretended to be asleep.

At home, as she waited for her cup of tea to cool down, she played with the television remote, and the screen burst into life. Teresa screamed with elation at the opening credits of the news on Globo. William Bonner, the anchor, was as dashing as usual, his greying hair adding a touch of class to his handsome features. Sometimes Teresa enjoyed watching him read the news so much that she could lose track of the subject of the news story.

Today, however, knowing that she would be a political activist on Sunday, she tried to pay less attention to Bonner's bright smile and more to the content of the reports, which interrupted her enjoyment of him.

As usual, the news revolved around the Petrobras scandal in which over 50 politicians, including an ex-president, were being investigated for receiving money from the national oil company. The water shortage came next, with floods on the border, with Peru coming in third.

There had been pro-Government protests in the afternoon, and Facebook was full of stories about how the incumbent Workers Party paid protesters R$35 and a ham and cheese sandwich to attend. Teresa wondered how anyone who worked would take their Friday off to support Dilma. There was one story about an immigrant from Guyana who didn't speak Portuguese, did not understand why he was there but attended for the money and the sandwich.

It had been a while since Teresa had a drink because of the antibiotics the doctor prescribed her, and she needed to use all her strength not to make herself a large gin and tonic as a nightcap. Instead, she turned the television off, hoping it would turn on again the next day, and called the cats to follow her to bed.

On Saturday, Teresa was up early because the man who was repairing the fridge was due to arrive at 8 am and the person to look at the roof at 9 am. The cats had already woken her up at 6 am. They did not understand there was such a thing as a weekend and would ignore it even if they did. She made herself coffee in the kitchen, which was now full of fruit flies hovering over the dirty dishes again.

Teresa sat in front of the TV which had stopped working again. Now that she had no car, she had no means of getting the TV to the repair shop. Her phone rang. She answered it.

"Sorry, did I wake you?" asked Mariana.

"No, that's OK. I was already awake." This was a kind of lie because even though Teresa had fed the cats and made coffee, she didn't feel ready to classify herself as awake yet.

"Good," Mariana continued. "A few of us are getting together later at House of Europe if you want to come along. It's an Italian place in Jardims. If you want to come, I'll text you the details."

Teresa didn't have the money to be going to Italian restaurants in Jardims, but she thought, if she was careful, that she might squeeze it on her credit card.

She waited all morning, and part of the afternoon, but neither the fridge nor the roof repairers appeared. Following two angry phone calls to unsympathetic telephonists, who could not promise more than an uncertain appointment the following week, she felt something moving on her leg.

She looked down and saw a tiny black dot. She grabbed it and squeezed it between her thumb and index finger. Examining the now dead black dot, she realised, to her horror, that the black dot was a flea. She looked at Oliver and Ramsey, who were both scratching. How much would it cost to rid her two kittens of fleas? She could do without yet another expense.

Teresa decided she would cut her losses and go for a meal with Mariana. She took the last of her antibiotics and promised herself a large glass of wine as soon as she arrived at the restaurant.

When she arrived at the House of Europe, Mariana was already there with some of her friends. She went around the table and introduced her. There was a guy with a friendly smile whom Teresa was convinced was gay, a young-looking boy who gave Teresa the creeps with his 'Hello darling don't you think I'm the one you've been waiting for all your life' smile. There was a girl who was also very smiley but appeared a little possessive over the man who gave Teresa the creeps and another girl who seemed indifferent to her. Mariana told her all their names, but Teresa didn't remember any of them a moment later, partly because she had a terrible memory for names, but also because of the last guest. He had his back to her at first, but Teresa knew something was strange by the huge grin on Mariana's face as she began the introduction.

"And this..." she began. "Is..."

Teresa missed the rest of the sentence because at that moment the man turned around and she found the doctor staring back at her.

"Aha, I see the bruising is coming down," he said to Teresa's open-mouthed face.

"You..." Teresa faltered. "You came."

"Isn't it fantastic?" said Mariana, throwing her arms around the doctor, whom Teresa perceived to be a little uncomfortable with the physical contact.

"I pride myself on the aftercare I offer my patients," he said at last, after Mariana released her embrace.

"And he's coming to the protest with us tomorrow," Mariana announced.

The doctor raised his eyebrows as if to acknowledge that what Mariana was telling her was true.

"Where are you staying?" asked Teresa.

"With a friend."

The waiter arrived and asked Teresa if she would like something to drink. Teresa said she would like to look at the menu. This waiter exhibited an expression of deep dissatisfaction but did a half pirouette and fetched the menu anyway. Teresa scanned through the list of drinks on the menu. Bottles of wine were R$92.

"What are you drinking?" She asked Mariana, who had returned to trying to engage the doctor in conversation.

"We're on the wine," she said, pointing towards a bottle of wine in an ice bucket, which was almost empty. "You're welcome to join us."

Teresa knew that drinking R$92 bottles of wine would be a dangerous move, but she fancied wine.

"Shall I bring Madam another glass?" the waiter asked in a tone which suggested he was wasting his life with this bunch of losers who couldn't decide what they wanted to drink.

Teresa nodded.

The waiter brought another glass for Teresa and emptied the remains of the bottle into it.

"Another?" he asked.

Teresa nodded. She sat observing the conversations which went on around her. Mariana was deep in conversation with the doctor, who kept glancing over at Teresa. Mariana's other friends were deep in conversation with each other. Teresa sipped her wine and smiled at anyone who looked at her, which, most of the time, was the doctor.

"What do you think, Teresa?" the doctor said, leaning over the table towards her, much to the annoyance of Mariana. "Mariana here argued that Brazil was better off under the military dictatorship and that we might be better off with a military intervention."

Teresa glanced at Mariana, who wasn't happy about more people joining her conversation.

"Well, I don't think going back to a system where people tell you what music to listen to is a good thing," Teresa said at last.

"Good point well made." said the doctor, receiving a fiery look from Mariana.

"Shall we order?" announced Mariana, changing the subject.

"Good idea." said the doctor who requested a menu from the waiter who, outraged at being disturbed, nevertheless delivered a pile of menus.

Teresa scanned the range of dishes, which seemed pricey, so she selected the cheapest main dish which sounded edible.

"What are you going to have?" the doctor asked her.

She looked back at the menu and spotted pasta with mushrooms, which was a little more expensive than the one on which she had settled.

"I'll have the Fettucini with mushrooms. It's not everywhere you see mushrooms, is it?" As soon as she had spoken, Teresa got a distinct impression that although the restaurants she frequented did not serve mushrooms, the restaurants to which Mariana and the doctor were accustomed, did.

"A wise choice," commented the doctor. "I'll have that too." Another fierce stare from Mariana.

Teresa wasn't sure what to make of all this. What was he doing stalking her food choices and antagonising Mariana by focusing his attention on her? Teresa was nervous and downed the rest of her wine. No sooner had she rested it back on the table than the doctor was refilling it. Teresa became even more nervous, but she smiled a thank you past Mariana's glass, which was being held out for a top up.

"What team do you support, Teresa?" The doctor asked.

"Well, my father was obsessed with Santos, so that made the whole family Santistas, but I don't follow football, I'm afraid."

"No kidding," exclaimed the doctor. "I'm a fish too."

'Oh no.' thought Teresa. Mariana supports São Paulo. At that moment, Mariana was busy discussing the benefits of prawns with her friend, so Teresa smiled again.

"Are you always this quiet?" The doctor was leaning over the table towards her. This caught the attention of Mariana, who abandoned the prawns discussion to defend her territory.

"Right. Have we all decided?" She asked in her best schoolmistress voice.

Teresa nodded like a naughty schoolgirl. The doctor smiled.

For the rest of the meal, Mariana ensured she monopolised the doctor. Teresa had a brief chat with some of Mariana's other friends, but as neither she nor they were interested in maintaining the conversations, they withered and died. Instead, Teresa focused on drinking her wine, which the waiter always seemed to top up, and by the time the reluctant waiter brought the dessert menus, Teresa was already more than a little tipsy.

The dessert menu offered a conundrum. Tiramisu or chocolate browny?

"Have you chosen a dessert?" the doctor asked while Mariana was distracted.

Teresa confessed her dilemma.

"Well, why don't you order the tiramisu? I'll order the chocolate browny, and we can have half and half each," he suggested.

This seemed to Teresa like a brilliant suggestion.

"Okay," she smiled. A genuine smile.

The desserts arrived, and Teresa and the doctor as agreed consumed half of each. Mariana eyed the exchange. Her eyes followed the plates as they exchanged places across the table.

"What's this?" she asked, as if she had caught Teresa and the doctor cheating on a spelling test.

"Would you like some?" asked the doctor, offering Mariana Teresa's half-eaten tiramisu. The effects of the wine were taking hold of Teresa, and she could not suppress a giggle.

"No thank you," Mariana replied, as if someone had offered her a piece of second-hand chewing gum.

"Suit yourself." mumbled the doctor, getting stuck into the part two of his dessert course.

Chapter Twenty - The Judge – 7th January 2014

Teresa surveyed the judge with incredulity. Who was she to separate a mother from her baby? She didn't know Teresa. She hadn't the slightest conception of the love Teresa felt for her daughter.

Her mother had always told Teresa that honesty was the best policy. That, no matter what other transgression she made, she should always be honest and would offer Teresa leniency when she confessed her childhood crimes.

It was this belief which led her to admit that she drank. She knew that a small amount of perjury would have helped her keep her child, but she only admitted the facts and said nothing she felt showed she was incapable of looking after her daughter. The judge awarded custody to her husband, or rather ex-husband, and the opportunity to visit was all she had left.

William had the evidence of her conviction in his favour. After 'The Incident', she received a three-year driving ban, a twelve-month order for alcohol rehabilitation, a £50 fine for resisting police and £170 in costs. Her admission had not been that she had never drunk. That was obvious. She admitted that in the twelve months since the incident, twelve months in which she attended a 'rehabilitation programme', in which her husband slipped from her grasp and in which even her ability to care for her daughter came into question. She could not give up the drink.

The judge's comments in awarding custody hurt her. Her husband, ex-husband, the judge said, was better placed to raise her daughter and that it was in the best interests of the child that she should live with him. With him and the bitch, with whom he was shacked up.

And now Teresa had to be content with only seeing her daughter at weekends. At weekends. Not tucking her into bed, reading her a bedtime story, she wouldn't be the one to take her or pick her up from school, comfort her when she woke with a bad dream. That would be William and that bitch of his. They would raise Annabel.

Teresa felt down. Not just about the court decision. She already had a slight hangover from the previous night's commiserating. And she was getting a cold.

Her nose was blocked, her throat sore and judging by the chill she felt, and she suspected she might be running a temperature. She did what she always did in England on these occasions, which was to run a hot bath and sit in it for a long time with a large glass of wine. The issue was that she had no wine. She had vodka, but no tonic. However, she had a carton of orange juice which was getting on a bit in age now, so she sniffed the contents but satisfied herself that it was drinkable, once she had mixed it with a decent helping of alcohol.

Chapter Twenty-One - The Stalker – 14th February 2015

All the reluctance seemed to have vanished from the waiter when it came time to deliver the bill. It shocked Teresa when she discovered the extent of her share and had no choice but to use the diminishing line of credit on her card.

"Who would like to come back to ours for champagne?" Asked one of Mariana's friends.

"Are you going?" the doctor asked Teresa.

"I don't know," admitted Teresa.

"Are you coming?" Mariana's friend asked as they were leaving the restaurant.

"I'll go if you go," said the doctor.

"Okay," said Teresa.

The flat where Mariana's friend lived was tiny, but had a tremendous view of the São Paulo skyline.

Teresa sat on the balcony and drank champagne out of a fluted glass while she surveyed the twinkling lights of the city ahead and the passing people and cars below. This moment seemed a million miles from her real life, her life of bills, broken fridges and televisions, leaking roofs and flea-bitten cats. She imagined what it would be like to have money, to live in an apartment overlooking the city, to have champagne in the fridge just in case she invited friends round after a meal in an expensive restaurant in Jardims. She was wondering what she could do, apart from buying a lottery ticket, to afford the lifestyle she dreamt of when the doctor arrived and sat beside her.

"A centavo for your thoughts," he said

"I was thinking about what a beautiful view it is," she said, embarrassed by her true thoughts.

"Yes, it is beautiful, isn't it? Almost as beautiful as the company."

This took Teresa by surprise, and she didn't know what to say, so she just laughed and tried to convince herself that he was referring to the gathering as a whole.

"Where's Mariana?" Teresa asked.

"Not sure," the doctor answered. "In the bathroom?"

There followed an awkward silence which neither party knew how to break.

"I love comfortable silences, don't you?" The doctor said at last.

Teresa mumbled an affirmation when, in reality, the last few moments had been anything but comfortable.

"Here you are," Mariana said, bursting onto the balcony. "I've been looking for you everywhere."

Teresa sensed a look of disappointment in the doctor's eyes when Mariana appeared.

"More to drink?" he asked, getting to his feet.

"Yes, please," replied Teresa, offering her glass.

"I'll come and help you," Mariana said, eyeing Teresa with suspicion.

Teresa returned to looking at the view and decided this next drink should be her last. The energy in the party was flagging, and Teresa knew she had to get to the bus station before the last bus left.

"I better go," she announced to Mariana when she finished the contents of the next glass.

"Oh no," Mariana feigned disappointment.

"I need to go too," said the doctor. "I'll walk you to the metro."

Teresa shot a glance at the shocked face of Mariana, back at the doctor, then back at Mariana.

"Don't worry," said Teresa. "The metro station isn't far."

"It's okay," said the doctor. "I need to go, anyway. My friend will wonder where I am."

He deposited a polite kiss on Mariana's cheek and went to get his bag.

"Okay," Mariana put on a brave face. "I'll see you at the protest."

She turned to Teresa to give her a polite kiss and whispered in her ear.

"Behave yourself."

Teresa hasn't been thinking of getting up to anything, but now that he planted the thought, she observed the doctor in a new light.

"Let's go?" the doctor asked Teresa, as he returned with his bag. "See you tomorrow," he said to Mariana and, having already said his other goodbyes, he was limping out of the door, leaving Teresa to wave goodbye to everyone as she left.

"I was thinking we would never get out of there." the doctor confided to Teresa in the lift.

"You seemed to have a good time," she suggested.

"Just being polite."

As they stepped outside, Teresa felt a light drizzle. The doctor pulled an umbrella from his bag and, putting it up; he pulled Teresa close to share its shelter. Teresa was a little taken aback by the forwardness of the doctor, but his advances weren't unwelcome, so she enjoyed the moment while it lasted for the short walk to the metro station.

"Where are you going?" The doctor asked.

"Sacomã. I need to get a bus to São Bernardo."

"Really?" The doctor sounded surprised. "I'm going that way too. Where do you live in São Bernardo?"

"Assuncão."

"You are kidding." the doctor continued. "That's where my friend lives. Whereabouts in Assuncão?"

"Do you know the Joanin supermarket?"

"Yes."

"Near there."

"What a small world. My friend lives close to Joanin too. What is the best bus to get there?"

"Did your friend not say?" Teresa asked.

"No." the doctor answered.

Teresa looked at him. He looked like butter wouldn't melt in his mouth, but she didn't trust him one bit.

"Where does this friend of yours live?" Teresa asked.

"Near the Joanin supermarket," he answered.

"On the side near the McDonald's or the Pizza Hut side?" She probed, knowing there was no McDonald's or Pizza Hut in Assuncão.

"There is no McDonald's near Joanin," he said without missing a beat.

"On the Pizza Hut side?" She continued.

"There is no Pizza Hut either," he replied.

Teresa thought for a moment. Either he was telling the truth, was good at guessing, or he'd been stalking her, and that was why he knew Assuncão, which nobody would go to unless they had to. She thought the latter option was unlikely, so either he was telling the truth, or he was good at lying.

An underground train rattled up to the platform, and they took seats in the almost empty carriage. Teresa eyed him.

"So what bus do you think I should get?" He asked again.

"Well," began Teresa, thinking that there was little she would gain from withholding information about bus routes. "Depends on which comes first. I get the 152 or the 004. Both of them go to Area Verde, and I walk from there. Do you know your way from Area Verde?"

"If you can get me near Joanin, I'm sure I'll be fine."

Teresa was uncomfortable to have to be nice and polite to the doctor all the way on the metro and for the entire bus journey, and now the walk from Area Verde. She would take him down the main road from Area Verde and then he wouldn't know where she lived, in case he was a psychopathic stalker.

They changed at Paulista, and Teresa led him through the underground corridors, up the escalator and over the moving walkways onto the green line platform at Consolação, which was busy. She led him to the platform until a train arrived. The carriage they boarded only had light blue preferential seats available, so they stood.

"Tell me about yourself," he asked.

"Not much to tell," Teresa began. "I'm a teaching assistant at the same school as Mariana, live in Assuncão, have two cats. I earn nowhere near enough money. How about you?"

"I'm sure there's more to you than that." he protested.

"What about you? I've told you about myself. Now you need to tell me about yourself. That's fair, don't you think?"

"Okay," he acknowledged. "Well, I'm a doctor. I live in Praia Grande. I have no cats, no dogs, and no pets at all. And I have more money than I can spend."

This last point seemed the most interesting to Teresa.

"Is that it?" She asked.

"My turn," he said. "Just cats, no romantic interest?"

Teresa laughed.

"No romantic interest, no," she said. "How about you?"

"Nothing at the moment, although I'm working on it," he said. "So it's my turn, right?"

Teresa nodded.

"What is a beautiful girl like you doing being single? You're not a lesbian, are you?"

"No," Teresa laughed.

"Then why?" the doctor persisted.

"I guess I haven't found the right man yet," the old cliché leapt to her aid.

"Is the male population of São Paulo that bad?"

Teresa thought about it for a moment and then nodded.

"Oh dear, well, we'll have to do something about that, won't we?"

Teresa imagined he was trying to be suggestive.

"My turn," she said. "Why did you agree to come and meet Mariana this weekend? Do you always travel halfway across the state to meet women you've just met?"

Teresa could tell by his expression that he had been waiting for this question and was ready for it.

"To be honest with you, Teresa," he said. "I didn't come all this way to see Mariana. I came to see you."

"What?" Teresa blurted. "Me? So you travel halfway across the state to meet someone you've met once, and that was when you were sewing her head up, and you didn't know if she was attached. Are you mad?"

"Never say that," the doctor snapped and then, on seeing the surprise on Teresa's face, he laughed. "I hope not."

"I don't even know what your name is."

"It's Felipe," the doctor said, being more sensitive now to the clear agitation in Teresa's voice.

The train arrived at Sacomã station, and they got off. Felipe followed Teresa towards the escalator when she turned around to face him.

"You don't even have a friend in Assuncão, do you?" she confronted him.

"I hope I do," he said.

"Okay," she challenged him. "What's the name of your friend in Assuncão?"

"Teresa?" He said.

"Oh no," she replied. "You don't think I'm going to invite you into my home, you crazy lunatic?"

"Don't say that," he said, a little annoyed, and then softened again. "Why not?"

"Why not? You think I'm going to take you home and let you fuck me because you sewed up my fucking head?"

"Who said anything about fucking anyone?"

"I don't know you from Adam, you crazy... Do you think I'm going to let a nut like you in my house?"

"I'm not a nut," he insisted and reached out to her.

"Don't touch me," she snapped. "Do you find following women home often works?"

"I've never tried it before," he admitted.

Teresa looked around for some answer and found none.

"Look, I've got to go, or I'll miss my bus. I'm not sure what you're going to do, but you can't come with me. Okay?"

She turned and walked away.

"Okay. I'm sorry," Felipe said and watched Teresa leave.

She got as far as the foot of the escalator before she turned and stomped back to him.

"What are you going to do now?" she asked.

"Find somewhere to sleep, I guess."

"Mariana would have been happy for you to stay at hers. Would you like me to call her? I'm sure it's not too late to get back there."

"No, thanks."

"Okay." Teresa turned to leave again. Felipe stood motionless, looking sorry for himself. Like one of her cats when she'd caught it doing something naughty.

Teresa sighed in frustration.

"Look. It's not my fault you followed me here. You could have been fucking Mariana right now, if you'd wanted," she said.

"I'm sorry," he said. "Don't worry; I'll be fine."

Teresa sighed an enormous sigh.

"I can't believe this," she said to herself. "Okay, come on. You can sleep on the sofa. But try anything, and I'm calling the police. Got it?"

"You don't have to, Teresa. I'll be fine. Don't worry."

"I don't have to, but what are you going to do? Sleep on the street? Come on. Let's go, or we'll miss the bus."

Teresa turned once more and headed for the escalator. Felipe followed like one of her naughty kittens.

The bus was on the platform, about to leave by the time they reached the terminal, so they had to run to get in the doors before the driver closed them. Teresa placed her travel card on the reader, and with a click, it unlocked the huge turnstile in the centre of the bus, and she pushed her way through to the rear. Felipe, however, was struggling to convince the driver to accept a R$20 note, so Teresa got out her travel card again and released the barrier for Felipe.

"I can't believe that not only am I letting a stalker into my house," she said as they sat down. "But I have to pay for their bus ticket, too."

"Sorry." said an embarrassed Felipe.

"What have I done to deserve all this?" She asked aloud.

Felipe said nothing, but just stared at his trousers. Teresa simmered for a while and then cooled down.

"Admit that this is not normal," she said at last.

"What is normal?" Felipe asked.

"I don't know," Teresa admitted. "But not this."

Silence resumed as much as it can on what must be one of the noisiest models of bus in the world. With little traffic, the bus sped as fast as it could, and its engine screamed with effort. Teresa looked out the window at cars weaving in and out of lanes, their drivers full of beer, or worse.

"I came because you are the most beautiful woman I have ever met," Felipe said at last.

"Oh, shut up."

"And I had to take whatever opportunity I could," he said, not shutting up. "To spend time with you. However, I could. And if that meant being a little economical with the truth with Mariana and not being straightforward with you ..."

"Straightforward?" Teresa interrupted. "Is that what you call following someone home? Downright creepy is what I call it."

"Okay, I admit," he continued. "I might not have handled things the right way."

"You can say that again."

"I might not have handled things in the right way," he examined her for a smile, but she was not in the right mood. "But I want you to understand that I've never done this before and that I was so afraid of not getting another opportunity that I couldn't let it go. I had to take the chance. And okay, maybe that chance backfired, but at least I gave it a go, and you can't blame me for trying."

Teresa wasn't sure how to answer this. It was probably just another load of bullshit, but he looked, and sounded, genuine.

"Couldn't you have just got my email or something?"

"Would you have answered it?"

"Maybe."

"Would Mariana have given it to me?"

"Maybe not?"

Teresa thought of Mariana and screwed up her face in mock pain.

"Oh God, Mariana," she said. "She'll kill me when she finds out you stayed at my place. She'll never believe that nothing happened. "

"Well, if she'll not believe..."

"Nothing will happen."

"Right."

Teresa fixed Felipe with a stare usually reserved for the cats or for children at school she had identified as being at risk of imminent naughtiness.

"Don't tell her," he said, trying his best to avoid her imminent naughtiness prevention stare.

"I can't do that. Mariana's my friend."

"Tell her my accommodation fell through last minute and so you offered to let me use your sofa."

"She'll never believe me."

"She will if she's your friend. And besides, it's almost the truth."

"Except that you had no accommodation."

"OK, but that's not your fault. I could have lied and said it fell through."

"You were going to, right?"

"No, I never planned to lie to you."

"But you would lie to Mariana?"

"For you, yes."

"Hang on a minute," said Teresa, remembering something. "You said you had more money than you could spend. Why don't you check into a hotel?"

"I can do that. Know any good hotels?"

"The kind you pay for by the hour."

"That's okay."

Teresa looked at him to see if he was serious. He appeared to be.

"If it makes you more comfortable," he added.

'Ooh, that was clever,' she thought. Now if Felipe stayed alone in a love hotel, it would be her choice. He was trying to make her feel guilty.

"Okay. I'll show you where there's a hotel." Teresa bluffed.

"Okay," he said.

Now what? The bus turned off the main road onto a side road at a pace so terrifying that Teresa wondered why the buses didn't turn over more often. The centrifugal force shoved her into Filipe.

"Sorry."

Felipe didn't appear to mind at all.

The bus careered up a side road.

"Come on, we'll have to get off in a minute," she warned him.

The bus shot past a bus stop, and Teresa struggled to stay upright to press the request stop button. As the bus tore along the road, Teresa moved from pole to pole, like a monkey reaching from branch to branch. As the bus approached the stop, it halted with such force that Teresa could traverse the last five metres to the door with ease, grabbing a pole to stop herself from being catapulted back through the turnstile. Felipe seemed to fare rather better, more like a hiker negotiating a hurricane. The bus arrived at a complete and abrupt standstill, and the two of them jumped down to the pavement to gather their bearings as the bus sped off again into the night.

"This way," Teresa instructed Felipe, who was looking around at the mix of building sites, slums and government-funded housing which lined the road.

He followed her across the road and into a side street which divided the building site from the slum. Closed shops lined the street, except for a pizza delivery place, outside of which a group of motorcycles stood. The owners were inside talking about something that neither Teresa nor Felipe could discern because the language was so thick with slang and expletives. They may have just been practising their swear words because Teresa couldn't make out a single noun or verb in any of their sentences. Teresa thought she would find few of the adjectives the owners used in a standard dictionary.

The road climbed a steep hill, and Teresa walked upward with Felipe limping as fast as he could to keep up, until they reached a small green area with steps leading up to a dark-looking street at the top of the hill.

"Are you sure it's safe around here?" Felipe asked.

"Are you having second thoughts?"

"Of course not."

They climbed the stairs and once at the top, to Felipe's clear relief, the street looked respectable if a little dark.

The multilevel pavement they were negotiating was a series of entrances to the garage rather than a pavement. They rounded the corner into another street at the other end of which gathered a group of young men, chatting and joking.

"What are they doing?" Felipe asked.

"Are you a man or a mouse?" said Teresa.

"Squeak," he replied.

The group of youths seemed to be having a loud street party. Felipe patted his pocket to verify the presence of his wallet even though the youths were a good fifty metres away.

"Come on," said Teresa, turning into another, an even smaller street which was both dark and deserted. It was now Felipe and not Teresa who looked like he thought that his following her to Assuncão might have been an error in judgement.

Not far into the street, Teresa stopped at the front of her house and opened the gate. Felipe hesitated for a moment before Teresa beckoned him through. She led him through a door which led into her kitchen, being careful to make sure that Oliver and Ramsey could not escape. As he followed her, she locked the gate.

They stood in silence in the kitchen. The cats eyed Felipe with suspicion. Teresa scooped them up and shut them in the lounge, then returned past Felipe.

"If you need the bathroom, it's through here," she said as she stopped in the door-less doorway to her bedroom and pointed to the bathroom door on the other side of the room. "If you want to have a shower, I'll give you a towel."

"Thanks," he said without moving.

"You can sleep in my bed," she continued. "I'll get you clean sheets."

"No, I'll sleep on the sofa." he protested.

"No, you won't. That's the only room with a lock on the door, so I'll be sleeping in there. "Would you like some water?"

"I'm fine, thanks."

"Fine. Okay. Well, here's your towel," Teresa opened a cupboard, took out a folded towel and handed it to Felipe. "Why don't you have your shower while I change the sheets?"

"There's no need to change the sheets," he said.

"I'd rather," she said, not relishing the thought of a strange man spending the night sniffing her body odour off her used sheets. There was the possibility that he would rifle through her underwear drawer, but it was a risk she would have to take.

He thanked her, took the towel, crossed the room to the bathroom, and closed the door behind him. As she changed the sheets, she could hear the shower running and pictured him taking his shower. She took some clean sheets for herself and took them into the living room where her sofa, being a mattress on two piles of pallets, was easy to convert into a single bed.

Felipe emerged from the shower dressed in pyjamas.

"You brought pyjamas?" She said.

"Yes," said Felipe, finding nothing strange about the concept of travelling with a clean pair of pyjamas.

"OK... well, I'm having my shower now. If you want water, there's a large bottle of filtered water next to the kitchen sink."

She grabbed her towel and went into the bathroom, locking the door behind her. She undressed and stood naked for a while in front of the mirror. Did Felipe mean what he said about her being beautiful, or was it another load of bullshit?

"A load of bullshit," she told herself, and had her shower.

When she emerged from the bathroom in her robe, Felipe had already climbed into bed, but he was propped up on a pillow inspecting her.

"You know you are beautiful," he said.

"Night, night," she replied and walked through into the living room, joining the cats and locking the door behind her.

Sounds in the kitchen awoke her. At first, she didn't know where she was. Once she realised she was in the living room, it took a few moments to realise why she was there. The events of the previous night came flooding back to her, and she realised who it must be that was making all that noise in the kitchen. She listened, hearing Felipe placing a pan on the stove, the fridge door opening and, after a pause, closing again, the rustle of plastic, something that sounded like the toaster, water running, the sound of plastic parts fitting together, opening and closing of the fridge door again, the removal of a plastic lid, the refitting of a plastic lid and the fridge door opening and closing a third time.

Teresa got up to find out what he was doing, so put on her robe and unlocked the living room door, freeing the two curious moggies. Poking her head around the edge of the door, she saw him looking at her with a smile. The fact that anybody could be happy after they've just got up annoyed Teresa.

"Good morning," said Felipe. "Are you hungry? I thought I'd make you some breakfast. Did you sleep well?"

"I did until someone making noise in the kitchen woke me up," she said.

"Sorry. Why don't you go back to bed? I promise I'll be quiet until you get up. I think your fridge is broken."

"Doesn't matter. I'm up now." Teresa ignored the comment about the fridge and sat at the small white metal table and watched Felipe finish the breakfast. When the toast popped up in the toaster, he put the slices on a plate for her.

The cats brushed around his trousers.

"Looks like you've won them over," Teresa said, seeing the cats fuss over him like proper tarts.

"Ah, they think I'm going to feed them," Felipe said. Teresa thought he was right and considered how cats are such fickle creatures.

The coffee machine sounded as if it was choking on itself, so Felipe switched it off.

"How do you take your coffee?" He asked.

"Black."

He poured out two cups.

"Do you have any sugar?" he asked, handing Teresa a cup.

"Sorry." she shook her head.

"No matter," he said. "Would you like some butter on that toast?"

Teresa looked at the slices, getting cold, on the plate in front of her.

"Yes, please."

Felipe opened the fridge door again, took out a tub of low-fat spread and handed it to Teresa.

"When you've finished your toast, why don't you have a shower and get dressed and I'll take you for a proper breakfast?" Felipe suggested.

Teresa did not enjoy being told what to do, but she liked the suggestion.

"Okay." she consented and buttered her toast.

"Where should we go?" he asked when she was ready.

"There's a reasonable bakery on the way to Area Verde," she said. "We could go there and afterwards go straight to get the bus."

"Sounds like a plan," he said, following her out of the door while being careful to keep the inquisitive cats inside.

The bakery was like any other bakery in São Paulo. A counter in the centre surrounded the food preparation area around which customers could sit on stools to drink their coffee and eat their toast. Later in the day, the stools would be full of men drinking beer and watching football on the televisions which hung from the walls. Tables and chairs filled the edges of the establishment, and it was to one of these that Teresa sat, and Felipe followed.

At one end was a self-service buffet, and at the other end a small selection of groceries. The bakery was still quiet, and no sooner had they sat down than a member of staff delivered a menu to each of them.

"Do you know what you would like?" Felipe asked Teresa as the member of staff hovered.

"I'll have a coffee and some toast please," Teresa asked the staff member.

"Are you sure?" Felipe asked her. "It's my treat."

"OK, thanks," she said to Felipe, then turned back to the waiter. "I'll have a bauru and a fresh orange juice without ice or sugar."

"I'll have a cheeseburger and a beer please," said Felipe, then realised that Teresa was staring at him. "What? It's lunchtime already. And anyway, I'm on holiday."

"I said nothing." Teresa defended herself.

"You don't need to," said Felipe and already it felt to Teresa like they were an old couple who had been married for forty years arguing over the same old things.

The waitress brought Felipe's beer, and Felipe eyed it. The waitress left two glasses.

"It's okay," said Teresa. "But it's eleven thirty. Are you sure you don't have a drinking problem?"

"I don't have a drinking problem," he rebuffed. "I have no problem getting hold of a drink."

Teresa groaned. Felipe's smile dropped, and he looked her straight in the eyes.

"I promise that, after this one, I won't drink anymore."

Teresa protested.

"Or any less than I usually do," he continued, eliciting more groans from Teresa.

"Are all your jokes as bad as this?" She asked.

"Of course not," he protested. "Some of them are even worse. Would you like some beer?"

Teresa smiled, and he poured her a glass.

"You're beautiful when you smile," said Felipe, making her blush. "Why don't you do it more often?"

"Stop it," she warned him, as her orange juice arrived filled with ice.

"I asked for no ice and no sugar. Does it have sugar in it as well?"

"I... I don't know. I don't think so." said the embarrassed waitress.

"Could I have another, please?" Teresa demanded.

"Remind me not to get on the wrong side of you," Felipe told Teresa when the waitress had left.

"I was clear. Wasn't I?" Teresa checked.

"I heard you. No ice, no sugar." Felipe confirmed.

"Thank you," said Teresa. "At least I'm not going mad."

"As a medical professional, I can neither confirm nor deny that."

Teresa smiled.

"There's that smile again."

"Stop it," said Teresa, slapping his arm. "You're making me all self-conscious."

"Sorry," he said. But he wasn't.

When they'd finished their brunch, Felipe paid the bill, and the two of them walked up the hill to Area Verde and waited for the bus which would take them to the metro at Sacomã.

"Is everything uphill in this town?" asked Felipe.

"It feels like it," admitted Teresa

When they arrived at the bus stop, there was a man already there, waiting. He was skinny and between his newish looking trainers and sports socks and a pair of shorts, with more pockets than anyone could make use of, were a pair of the hairiest legs Teresa had ever seen. On his skeletal shoulders hung a T-shirt which, although small, was still too big for him, and a white and blue checked baseball cap which sat on his head unsupported on any side. The phone he held near his head spoke.

"Hello?" it said in a tinny voice.

"I'm on my way to the hospital," said the skinny man. Teresa was not surprised.

"You're at the hospital?" asked the phone.

"No!" corrected the man with a ferocity, which took Teresa by surprise. "I'm on my way to the hospital. I'm waiting for the bus."

"You're waiting at the hospital?" asked the phone, still unsure.

"No Pedro," the man said with frustration, now regretting that he had begun this courtesy call. "I am on my way to the hospital, waiting for a bus. I'll call you when I get there."

He pronounced each word with patronising slowness.

"Are you at the hospital?" he asked as an afterthought.

"You're at the hospital?" asked Pedro again, not grasping the gist of the conversation.

"No, Pedro, I am waiting for, for... look, the bus is here. I'll have to go," he hung up.

Teresa looked. He was right. There was the bus. The 152 to Sacomã. Felipe and Teresa jumped on it. Felipe had got change from the bakery so could pay his own fair for once.

Teresa and Felipe climbed onto the bus, delighted to find that there were many seats to choose from, as was usual on a Sunday morning. Ominous clouds were climbing over the horizon, threatening the possibility of rain, but were not yet preventing the blazing sun from streaming through the bus window.

At Sacomã metro station, there was an enormous queue of people waiting to buy tickets. They were all dressed in yellow, blue and green, the colours of the Brazilian flag, and were already chanting slogans deriding President Dilma and her predecessor, Lula.

Teresa had her travel card, but Felipe didn't, which meant they had to join the end of the huge queue.

"It's obvious that none of these people uses public transport," Teresa commented as she viewed the line of middle-class couples and families all wearing the Brazilian national team's football top and carrying assorted paraphernalia which they had bought the previous year during the World Cup.

Felipe apologised for not being a regular user of the metro, but Teresa said it didn't matter and anyway, the queue was moving.

The train was busy for a Sunday morning, but Teresa and Felipe still got seats among the cheering protesters in their patriotic colours. One worried looking young woman wearing red, the colour of the ruling Workers Party, PT, kept looking around at everyone at a loss to explain to herself why so many people had boarded the carriage wearing Brazilian colours and singing songs about Dilma. Either all the talk and the posters had passed her by or she was a fervent government supporter looking at disgust at the middle classes bad-mouthing her president with claims that they, the middle classes, shouldn't have to support the poor who have themselves to blame and have no real intention to work as long as the government are doling out handouts which they stole from the middle classes along with the oil money which was also stolen from the pockets of the middle classes and placed in the pockets of corrupt politicians, skiving plebs and Cuban dictators.

At every stop, more protesters got on and the carriage filled with cheers and more suggestions for which areas of her anatomy President Dilma should 'take it up'.

Teresa had agreed to meet Mariana at Trianon MASP metro station, the epicentre of the protest. It had seemed a good idea, but now Teresa thought the station would be so busy it would be impossible to find anyone, so she sent Mariana a text.

"She's already here," Teresa said, turning to Felipe and waving her phone at him as they ascended the escalators along with hordes of shouting protesters

"It'll be difficult to find her among all these people," he stated the obvious.

They emerged through the ticket barriers into the ticket hall where Mariana stood with her friends staring at Teresa and Felipe approach with a glare so fierce that Teresa wondered whether she had murdered Mariana's dog and had forgotten that she was wearing it as a hat.

"Hello," Teresa said as nice as she could as she and Felipe approached Mariana.

"Hello," Mariana replied. "Did you two bump into each other on the metro?"

"Well, that's a funny story," Felipe began. "Come on, let's go and I'll tell you all about it." Felipe took Mariana's arm, much to Mariana's delight, and with his characteristic limp, led her off, leaving Teresa to follow with Mariana's friends.

"Come on," Felipe turned and said to Teresa, with a wink she was sure he designed for Mariana to miss. "So, tell me all about what you got up to after I left," he asked Mariana.

Teresa wasn't sure why she should feel so put out that Felipe was now directing his attention to Mariana. She hadn't asked him to come up to São Paulo, to follow her home, to flirt with her. But somehow, now he had done all those things and given her such attention, she now missed that attention, the attention she hadn't felt since she first started seeing William, her now ex-husband, all those years earlier.

She viewed Felipe laugh and joke with Mariana, and she observed Mariana warm to him again as he complimented her and made her laugh. Teresa sighed and prepared herself for the return to her usual life of being ignored.

As they emerged from the entrance to the Metro, Teresa tried to follow Felipe, Mariana, and Mariana's friends as close as she could so as not to get lost among the crowds, which were now filling Avenida Paulista. The group tried to snake its way between the army of blue, green, and yellow and Teresa followed as best she could as it made its circuitous way towards the red pillars of the art museum, beneath which the centre of the protest gathered.

Parked at intervals along the road, open top buses had their top decks filled with protesters, some with microphones delivering impassioned speeches toward the yelling masses who cheered and applauded and joined in the chants the announcers bawled at them.

As she did her best to stay in touch with the group, she looked around her at the placard-waving, slogan shouting throng of people that were filling the road. Some were waving banners calling for military intervention. Another banner read 'runaway inflation' and another, 'get rid of the communists'. A drone buzzed over their heads.

Through the crowd, Teresa noticed a dirty-looking man with bedraggled hair, a blanket wrapped around his shoulders and an old pair of flip-flops on his feet. He was trying to cross Avenida Paulista, annoyed by the crowds of people who had invaded his Sunday afternoon.

'If anyone should be angry at the government,' thought Teresa. 'It is him, and yet he seemed the least interested in everything going on around him.'

Teresa looked up at the drone which hovered above their heads. They were almost level with the São Paulo Museum of Art, and the others stopped to listen to an announcer who stood on top of a truck with loudspeakers filling its bowels. He shouted about how corrupt the government was, how the country had had enough of the current leadership about how the people there believed in change.

Teresa observed.

"I know what you've been up to." Mariana appeared next to Teresa, accusing her.

"I'm sorry?"

"How could you do it?" Mariana asked.

"Do what?" she had surprised Teresa.

"He stayed at your place last night. How could you?"

"He had nowhere else to stay." Teresa had to shout over the crowd and the truck's loudspeaker system and over the buzz of the drone, which was now hovering above them, close to a tree Teresa noticed as she glanced up in annoyance.

"How could you do it?" Mariana continued. "You know I like him. How could you?"

"I swear nothing happened." Teresa pleaded, now becoming more and more worried about the proximity of the drone to the extremities of the tree under the margins of which they now stood.

"But you took him home." Mariana was unstoppable.

"Look, I think we should..." But before Teresa could say 'move', the drone clipped a branch and was now plummeting towards them. "Shit!" Exclaimed Teresa in time for Mariana to look up to see what Teresa was swearing at and catch one of the drone's blades square in the forehead,

Mariana and the drone fell to the ground in unison, thus proving Archimedes' theory. Mariana clutched her forehead; the drone lay in pieces.

Teresa rushed to her side.

"You okay?" she asked.

Mariana lay sprawled on the ground, hand against forehead, which she removed to check and saw the blood.

"Jesus!" Teresa exclaimed.

Felipe was there now, examining the wound in the epicentre of a circle of observers who had lost interest in the rest of the protest to watch the drama which was unfolding in front of them. A similar circle developed around the drone, which received similar prods with the same curiosity but less concern.

"Come on. Let's get you to the emergency room," said Felipe, helping Mariana to her feet. "Does your plan cover Santa Catarina?"

"It does," Mariana said with annoyance. And as the crowds parted to allow them to make slow progress towards the accident room, Teresa followed. For a moment, Felipe turned to look at her, and she couldn't be sure, but she thought a wry smile curled his mouth.

Teresa sat for what seemed forever on the uncomfortable plastic chairs of the hospital waiting room, watching television with pictures of what was happening outside. A million people, Globo News estimated, and Teresa noticed as they left the crowds behind on their way to the hospital, there were as many people still joining the demonstration as there were leaving.

Felipe returned to the waiting room.

"How is she?" Teresa asked.

"She'll be fine," said Felipe. "She'll have quite a bump, but it won't be as big as yours. She's had a few stitches, and she's waiting for some antibiotics, then she'll get a taxi to take her home."

"Good," said Teresa. "I mean, good that she's okay, not good that she's going home."

"Mariana is threatening to sue the owner of the drone. I think she will."

"I think she will too." agreed Teresa.

"Are you hungry?" Felipe asked.

"A bit," she said.

"When we've finished here, how about we get something to eat? There's a cafe nearby that invented the Bauru."

"Yes, but their Baurus are not as nice as the ones you get elsewhere."

"You've already been?" He asked.

She nodded.

"Let's go somewhere else," he suggested.

"No, it's fine. Have your Bauru. They're different, that's all. I prefer the other kind."

"We can go wherever you want, you choose."

"No, it's okay, let's go to the Bauru place." And she knew at that moment that she'd agreed to spend more time with him and she was pleased. "What about Mariana?"

"She'll be fine," he said. "I don't think she wants to spend more time with us. She's still upset about me staying at your place last night. Anyway, I better see how she is."

Felipe left Teresa alone in the waiting room once more and as she sat and watched the protests on Globo News, the thought that Felipe wanted to spend more time with her warmed her a little inside.

Chapter Twenty-Two - The Conversion – 15th February 2015

"What did you think of the protest?" Teresa asked as they sat in the restaurant and waited for their sandwiches.

"I understand that these are people who are pretty upset that their favoured candidate did not win the election. But to be willing, or even keen, to remove the elected Government, no matter how unpopular, and hand over power to an unelected group whose main role in society was to have lots of weapons and show them off whenever things seemed to get out of hand. I don't see how handing over the country to the military because you didn't get your way in an election is a solution of any kind. This is not the way to go about things. Not only 30 years after the country has wrestled power back off the dictators. What short memories these people have," he said. "They're talking about runaway inflation, but most of these protestors are enough to remember when Brazil had runaway inflation, not the 8% it has at the moment."

"Wow, I didn't know you felt that strongly," she said. "So, what are you doing here amongst so many angry right wing middle-class people?"

"I told you. I came to see you," he smiled, then got serious again. "And another thing, PT might be left wing, but they're not communist. They are as neoliberal as the next centre-left capitalist party. I have a lot of sympathy for the protesters. I'm also disgusted by the level of corruption. Corrupt politicians have stolen billions of dollars, some of whom are from the PT party. Billions of dollars which could have been better spent on hospitals, schools, adequate housing, clean water for all and filling in potholes."

Teresa raised her eyebrows. She had no idea Felipe had all this pent-up rage inside him.

"But I don't see how it would be a good idea to remove family allowance," Felipe continued. "That single benefit has lifted millions of low-income families out of poverty and guaranteed millions of Brazilian children an education. I'm also here because the Brazilian people have to show the corrupt politicians that they will not tolerate them robbing the country anymore. But mainly I'm here to see you."

The waiter arrived with their sandwiches.

Felipe bit into his Bauru.

"Yeah, I see what you mean," he said after a bit of chewing. "Still nice, though."

"I don't like them here," Teresa repeated.

"But they are the original recipe," argued Felipe.

"Original does not mean best."

He smiled. She hadn't noticed his smile before, but now she saw it, she liked what she saw.

"You have a nice smile," she said, cringing at hearing her thoughts spoken out loud.

"Thank you, so do you," he said, smiling even more. "You should do it more often."

"What's that supposed to mean?" she couldn't help herself. She was always on the defensive.

"Nothing, just that you look even more beautiful when you smile."

She blushed. She couldn't believe she was letting Felipe's cheap tricks fool her. It had been a while since anyone had paid her a compliment and she wasn't used to it. Her defences were low and his attack constant.

"What are you going to do?" she asked. "I'm working tomorrow."

"I'm not," he said with confidence that Teresa found almost irritating.

"It's a school night, so I need to get to bed." Teresa persisted

He nodded and took a sip of beer.

"Would you like some beer?" he asked, offering the bottle.

She laughed at his stubborn refusal to take the hint.

"OK, but I am working tomorrow."

"So you keep saying," he ignored the hint and poured some beer into her glass.

"You do not understand how difficult it is to deal with a classroom of small children," she protested.

"I can guess. Imagine working in an emergency room with a hangover."

"You wouldn't."

"I'm not working tomorrow."

"So you intend to get drunk," she assumed aloud. "How are you getting back to Praia Grande?"

"Bus," he attempted to say through a mouth full of Bauru.

"Were you hungry?" Teresa asked, amused.

"Yeah," he said, his mouth still stuffed. "Are you not?"

"No," she lied. "Anyway, I'm on a diet."

"You? On a diet?" He said. "Whatever for?"

It sounded like another of his tricks, but the possibility of Felipe being genuine, flattered Teresa. She didn't let this show and made sure that she fixed him with a stare, which let him know she could see right through his pathetic attempts at winning her over.

"No," he saw the sceptic in her eyes. "You're in great shape. I should know I'm a doctor."

She looked down at her beer.

"I'm not ready for this."

"Ready for what?" he asked.

"Ready for this?" she continued. "I haven't got over the last relationship."

Felipe said nothing for a moment. He refilled his glass with beer and took a sip.

"That's okay," he said. "We can still have fun together, can't we?"

"That all depends on what you mean by fun," she said.

"Well, this," he said, gesticulating at the table. "Eating a meal, having a drink, having a chat, laughing."

She looked at him. He looked at her.

"I enjoy being with you," he said. "I enjoy your company. And if you'd let me, I'd like to spend more time with you."

She looked down. Embarrassed. She never took compliments well.

"Can I spend more time with you?" he asked.

She looked up at his honest face, grinning back at her, and laughed.

"I guess so," she conceded.

"Come on. Let's do something before you have to go home to bed," Felipe said.

"Like what?" She asked.

"What do you suggest?"

Teresa wasn't sure what to suggest. She wanted to spend more time with this man whom she couldn't deny she found attractive and who flattered her with his attention. But she had to work the next day and wanted to go home and relax without being followed by a stalker. She thought about where they could go that required little effort, would satisfy his desire for more entertainment and yet would leave him on his way to the bus station.

"How about coffee?" she said at last.

"Here or somewhere else."

"Somewhere else."

"OK, where?" he asked.

"There's a good coffee shop in Shopping Santa Cruz," she suggested. "It's not far on the blue line, and it's on the way to Jabaquara for your bus."

"Sounds good. Let's get the bill," he mimed writing on his palm to the waiter, who brought a piece of paper with some scribbles on it. Teresa reached for her bag.

"I'll get this," said Felipe, pulling a card out of his wallet and handing it to the waiter. "Do you believe in God?" he asked Teresa as the waiter typed the amount into the portable payment machine.

"That's a big question," said Teresa, surprised, "My mother took me to church, so I've always believed in something, but I don't go to church anymore."

"I don't," said Felipe, handing the payment machine back to the waiter. "I believe that we just happen to be here and that when we die, we return to the soil and that's it. So we get one shot at life, so we need to be as happy as we can in the short time we have."

"Did you ever believe in a God?" Teresa asked.

"I grew up a Christian like you," he admitted, "but I thought about what the pastor was saying, and it sounded like a load of rubbish. Then one day someone gave me a book."

'Here we go,' thought Teresa.

"It was a book about superstring theory. It took me an entire year to read. The author had written it with the idea that the theories of modern science were not incompatible with belief in a creator. But the more I read, the more I decided that the idea of some supreme being creating us was much less likely than the idea that we were just here. In fact, being here is a kind of inevitability if you think about it."

Teresa didn't know how to begin thinking about it. They got up and left. Felipe followed Teresa as she led him through crowds still making their way towards the protest and joined the populous queues, leaving the protest until they arrived at Paraiso Metro.

Teresa felt tired. She hoped Felipe felt tired too because, although she was enjoying the attention, she wanted to go home, put her feet up, have a gin and tonic and stroke the cats.

Instead, they got off the train at Santa Cruz and ascended the stainless steel clad escalator into the shopping centre.

"Do you know where a coffee shop is?" he asked

"Of course," she answered, as if it was a stupid question.

He followed her up similar escalators until they reached a small coffee shop, which had a few tables and chairs arranged in front.

"What would you like? I'll get them while you save us a seat," he said, pointing to the only empty table.

"I'd like a chocolate cappuccino," she asked. She always had chocolate cappuccinos at this coffee shop and mocha lattes at the big chain from Seattle.

Moments later, Felipe returned with two cups. Teresa's cappuccino and an espresso for himself. Both had a tiny biscuit perched on the saucer.

"Here you go," he said, placing her drink in front of her.

"Thank you."

Some shoppers had been to Paulista. Teresa noticed their patriotic clothing and pointed it out to Felipe.

"Mmm," he nodded acknowledgement as he took a sip of his still too hot espresso. "I mean what I say, you know, about enjoying spending time with you."

It was Teresa's turn to nod, and she took a sip of her coffee. She felt a little embarrassed and didn't know what to do or say. She'd never been comfortable receiving compliments or attention of any sort.

"Is there a bowling alley here?" Felipe asked.

"I don't think so."

"Shame, I could have beaten you at...er...I mean, given you a game."

"What makes you think you would beat me?" she smiled.

"I don't know," he said. "But I'd have fun trying."

Teresa's heart was beating faster. Damn her heart. Her body was anticipating what her brain was trying to resist. Although there was nothing sexual for Teresa about a game of ten-pin bowling, Felipe had somehow, through the tone of his voice, loaded his sentence with innuendo.

"Okay," she said. "Any other sports you'd like to beat me at?"

"I can think of a few," he replied in such a way that her blood began pumping a little faster.

Teresa chastised herself for being so silly. Why did she feel like the heroine in a Bronte novel? She sipped at her coffee and tried to be more sensible. She had nothing in common with this man. He didn't even believe in God.

"Tell me more about yourself," Felipe asked. "Do you have any family here in São Paulo?"

"Yes," said Teresa. "But I have little to do with them anymore. Long story."

"I know how you feel," he said. "I haven't spoken to my family for ages. Long story."

Teresa looked at him with fresh interest.

Felipe nodded. He would not share any more of the story for the moment. Instead, he finished his espresso. Teresa looked at hers and took another sip too. She wondered whether she misjudged him and wondered why she was wondering this, why she cared? Teresa looked at him again, and he looked back, and she wondered whether he might be a kind, decent man. He was a doctor. He smiled at her, and this made her self-conscious, so she returned her attention to her coffee and sipped again, but as she removed the cup from her lips, she could see he was still watching her with a content smile. She put down her cup, and it clunked on the saucer.

"What do you see in me?" she asked. "I mean, why me? Why not Mariana?"

"Because you're interesting," he said. "You're different. You're not like Mariana."

"Yeah, I'm not like Mariana," Teresa laughed.

"I found you interesting."

"While you were sewing up my head?"

"And I wanted to see you again. I wanted to find out more about you."

"So you accepted Mariana's invitation, dumped her and stalked me."

Felipe thought about this for a moment.

"Yes," he admitted.

"I'm not an easy catch," Teresa warned.

"Okay," he said. "I can accept that. If you need time to fall in love with me, that's okay."

Teresa laughed.

"You're confident in yourself, aren't you?" she said.

"I try my best," he said, but Teresa noticed him give a nervous look downwards and wondered whether perhaps it was all an act to cover up his insecurities. He saw she was watching him, looked up again, and smiled.

"I'm also modest," he joked.

"I see," she smiled.

"What else are you good at?" she flirted.

He raised his eyebrows.

"Lots of things," he teased.

"Such as?"

"I'm a good doctor."

"I hope so," she pointed to the dressing covering her scar.

"You'll have to let me look at that."

"You want to give me a check-up, do you?"

"Yes, I do."

Teresa found she was becoming less embarrassed by his flirting and more excited.

"Shall we go?" she asked.

"Okay," he said, a trace of disappointment in his voice, mixed with a pinch of hope.

He paid the bill, and they descended the escalators all the way down into the metro station. They passed through the barriers.

"I can go via Jabaquara," said Teresa and so they both descended another escalator to the platform and waited for a train.

"Few people around now," Felipe commented and compared to the busy trains they'd taken at the start of the day, the one that now arrived was quiet as far as any metro train in São Paulo can be quiet.

They boarded the train and rode the half dozen stops to Jabaquara, not talking much, each not sure what to say. They arrived and exited into the concourse, which led to the local buses on one side and the long-distance buses to the coast on the other. Touts hung around the exit to the station, offering places on minibuses which sped their way to the coast as soon as they were full, but Felipe said he didn't trust their driving skills.

"The buses to the coast are through there," he pointed.

"My bus is that way," said Teresa, pointing in the opposite direction.

Felipe bent down to kiss her on the cheek, but as his face reached hers, he paused and kissed her on the lips. A long kiss, a kiss she reciprocated and which continued as he held her arms and her, his.

Teresa didn't know how long the kiss lasted, but it ended after a passer-by shouted: "Get a room".

She pulled her head away and looked at Felipe, the pair of them in a post-kiss daze, then they kissed again, this time more certain than the first. As they kissed, Felipe passed his hands over her back, feeling the contours under her blouse and she felt the muscles in his arms.

After a few moments, they pulled away again and their eyes connected like the opposite poles of two magnets.

"Would you like to stay at mine tonight?" Teresa asked so softly that Felipe wasn't confident that she'd said what he'd thought he heard amongst the noise of the station entrance.

"Yes please," he said, assuming that what he'd thought he'd heard was what he wanted to be true.

"Come on," she said, taking his hand and confirming his hopes.

She led him through a corridor and up another. They followed the long strip of bumpy blue plastic on the floor, designed for the visually impaired. Past a row of closed food stalls. There was a spring in Teresa's step as she now pulled him with enthusiasm up a flight of concrete steps and onto a platform at the other end of which a large electric bendy bus sat with its doors open. At the ticket barrier, Felipe paused and looked around.

"I don't have a ticket," he said.

"Don't worry," Teresa said, producing a card from her wallet and ushering Felipe towards one barrier. She placed her card on the reader, and the barrier swung open. Felipe walked through, and it swung closed behind him. She placed her card on the reader a second time and walked through to join him on the platform where he took her hand as if they had been parted for an age.

Teresa took up the lead again and led Felipe onto the bus, where they sat in the back row of seats and resumed their kissing. Felipe was caressing the belly which lay under her blouse, under her breasts and Teresa allowing her hand to pass over his thigh higher and higher.

The kissing continued until Teresa realised it was time to get off and pressed the bell. The driver slammed on the brakes so late that momentum carried them down the bus to the door.

"Obrigada!" Teresa shouted as they leapt from the bus.

Felipe looked around. This looked nothing like the place they'd got off the bus the night before.

"Come on," said Teresa, grabbing his hand.

She pulled him across a dual carriageway and up a side street which climbed a steep hill. They were both panting when they reached the top, but Teresa pulled Felipe with a vigour alien to her daily activities. Businesses lined the street, a wide variety of graffiti decorating their closed shutters. The only business open was a petrol station where a man was refilling a tatty old blue Volkswagen Beetle.

"Blue Beetle!" Teresa exclaimed and slapped Felipe on the arm.

"Ow, what was that for?" he complained, rubbing his sore arm.

"Have you never played that game?" Teresa asked, surprised.

"What game?" He asked, a little grumpy at being beaten.

"We used to play it all the time when we were little," Teresa explained. "Every time you see a blue Volkswagen Beetle, you slap the other person and say 'blue beetle' before they slap you."

"Huh, nice game," laughed Felipe.

The street descended towards a junction on the corner of which stood an enormous construction site where mud and water spewed from under its wooden fences. Felipe and Teresa took a detour onto the road to avoid the filth. They followed the bend of the road, which led them under a bridge, over which cars and trucks trundled.

"Anchieta," Teresa explained, meaning the highway which started in São Paulo and finished near Santos on the coast. They walked underneath the twin bridges supporting the southbound and northbound carriageways, negotiating the slip roads on either side. There was a little more life on the road now. Another petrol station with a shop which had a few cars refilling.

"Hospital Assunção," said Teresa, pointing to the enormous building on the opposite side of the road. The hospital car park seemed busy with cars queuing to get in and out. Outside a police station sat a wreck of what used to be a car, crumpled in every direction. Teresa shuddered at the thought that during the event which transformed the car into its current state, there would have been someone inside.

"This police station must handle the accidents on Anchieta," Teresa explained. "There's always a wreck outside."

As they walked past, Teresa noticed several people hanging around the waiting area. It was always busy.

On the corner of the next junction, a small army of motorcyclists waited outside a pizza delivery company, ready to take the next orders at breakneck speed through the backstreets to the waiting customers.

"Fancy a pizza?" asked Teresa.

"I'm fine, thanks," said Felipe. "But would you like one?"

"No, I'm okay," she said.

"Are you sure?" he asked. "I'll get you one if you want one."

"No, I'm okay," she repeated. "I've got other things I want to do when we get home."

They exchanged smiles and Teresa led him quicker, up to a side street, around a corner, into another side street, around another corner. Each time they turned a corner, the street would get smaller and quieter and filthier. As they walked, cockroaches scurried down drains.

"They come out to escape the heat," Teresa explained.

"Nice," commented Felipe.

The street turned again, and it looked like a dead end, but right at the end, there appeared a hidden exit, which Teresa led them around. They could now hear the sounds of funky music emanating from around the corner, and when they emerged from the alleyway into the next street, Felipe could see the same group of youths they had seen the night before, and he realised they were close.

"It's quite a mission to get to your house, isn't it?" Felipe commented.

"We're here now," said Teresa, taking her keys from her bag and leading Felipe to a gate he recognised.

He followed her through the gate and door and into her flat, where she herded the cats inside and locked the door behind them. Once inside, she dropped her bag and he his. She put her arms around his neck, and pulling him close, they kissed. A long, long kiss, which their tongues explored.

She led him through to the bedroom and pulled off her shirt, giving Felipe the opportunity to observe how well her bra contained her breasts.

"I'm going to have a shower," she said, kicking off her shoes.

"Let's have one together," he suggested, touching her bare arms.

"OK," she agreed and undressed Felipe, pulling off his T-shirt and unbuckling his belt.

He pushed her onto the bed and pulled off her trousers. As he removed his own, Teresa could see that beneath his boxer shorts his penis was already erect and, following the descent of his trousers to the floor, she saw one leg stopped below the knee where an artificial leg took over.

She froze in a stare that Felipe appeared to have been expecting.

"Is everything okay?" he said with a cheeky grin.

"When were you going to tell me you had one leg?" she asked.

"Now?" he answered. "Anyway, I've got more than one leg. I've got at least one and a half. Look, this one goes down below the knee. Is it a problem?"

Teresa looked at the artificial leg, then at the rest of Felipe's body, which otherwise seemed okay. In fact, it seemed more than okay.

"No, it's not a problem," she said, pulling him down on top of her. "As long as there's nothing else missing."

"I can assure you that it is in perfect working order," he said.

He got on top of her and, as they kissed, he ran his hands over the exposed areas of her body.

"What about that shower?" She asked.

"Let's go," he said, getting up and removing his boxer shorts so he now, save for his artificial leg, stood naked before her.

Teresa got up and removed her bra, but before the bra could hit the floor, Felipe was on her.

"The shower," she tried to say, pushing him away and removing her knickers.

Now they both stood naked. They embraced and kissed again. She felt his artificial leg against her's and tried not to think about it. He ran his hand down her back and grabbed a handful of buttock.

"Come on," she said, barely able to catch a breath, and dragged him into the shower where he detached the artificial part of his leg.

Under the running water, they kissed and caressed their wet skin tight to the touch. Felipe wanted to fuck her right there, but she fended him off. He pressed Teresa against the wall of the shower, and it impressed her how well he could balance with one leg. She grabbed the bar of soap and began washing him.

"I want to fuck you," she whispered in his ear, and he kissed her neck, supporting her as she almost collapsed in his arms.

"I want to fuck you," he said.

"Wash me," she demanded, and handed him the soap. He lathered his palms and rubbed soap lather all over her body, paying special attention to her breasts and vagina. He grabbed her buttocks and pulled her soapy body towards him, rubbing his body against hers. She gasped, feeling his chest against her breasts and his penis against the base of her stomach. Teresa tried not to flinch when his stump touched her leg. She wanted him inside her.

She pushed his body away, conscious that she did not want to push him off balance, and rinsed them both. He kissed her on the lips, and their tongues met. She reached for one towel hung over the shower box and thrust it into his face. He took the towel with a smile. Teresa grabbed another, and they both made a poor attempt at drying themselves before he dragged her hopping to the bed. Felipe threw her down on the bed and climbed on top of her. He kissed his way down to her navel and lower to the hair she wished she'd waxed. She pulled on his hair, and he climbed back on top of her, kissing her.

He rolled off her and reached over the side of the bed to pull his wallet out of his trousers. She propped herself up on her elbows and lay there, catching her breath as she watched him fishing about in his wallet until he produced a single wrapped condom.

"Come prepared?" she commented as he tore the plastic wrapping off with his teeth and lifted out what looked like a small rubber nipple and observed it in the light. He flipped it upside down, examined it for a moment, and turned it the other way again. Satisfied, he placed the condom on the end of his penis like a tiny hat and unrolled it until he was happy that it would not come off.

He climbed on top of her again, and she lay back in anticipation. As they fucked, he kissed her on the lips; she ran her hands over his back. He grabbed her arms and pulled them over her head, holding them there. He releases her arms, but she left them above her head as he ran his hand down her body to grab her buttock and pull it to the side. The sensation was more intense now, and Teresa pushed her head back into the pillow and closed her eyes. His rhythm became more frantic and his breathing heavier and more rapid. His breath whistled around her earlobe. She moved her pelvis in time to his in a crescendo of flesh and rhythm and sensation.

Her body tingled all over with her orgasm. She was light-headed, and her vision became blurred. She felt an incredible lightness in her body, and Felipe's movements became frantic. Her head was spinning, her body shaking, like she might black out.

Felipe let out a scream so loud that her heart almost leapt out of her body.

"Jesus Christ!" he yelled, pulling out of her and examining his genitals.

"What is it?" she cried in a panic, seeing a black flash shoot into the kitchen followed by the sound of empty plastic bottles scattering across the kitchen tiles.

"The little shit!" Felipe cursed, rubbing his sore testicles.

When Teresa realised what had happened, she couldn't stop herself from laughing much to the annoyance of the wounded Felipe.

"I'm sorry," she said, trying to stifle her giggles. "He wanted to play."

Teresa lost control and burst into hysterics.

"It's not funny," he protested, but her laughter was so addictive that he couldn't stop himself from chuckling.

She fell back on the pillow and sighed as the laughter began to subside. Soon her tight muscles began to relax, and she noticed now that she was sweating and she felt both peckish and sleepy. She lay there like a wet noodle, and when enough energy returned, she grabbed Felipe and held him. He kissed her again, small pecks on her neck and face and mouth. She let him go, and he lay on his side, facing her. Turning to him, they embraced. She wrapped her legs around his, and his stump felt strange against her skin.

Felipe checked the condom was still there, removed it, tied it in a knot and dropped it on the tile floor beside the bed, before turning back to her to embrace and kiss her once more.

"Are you hungry?" Teresa asked.

"I'm peckish," Felipe admitted.

"Would you like some popcorn?"

"Sure," he said. "I could do with a drink."

"Some water?"

"OK."

"Or something stronger?"

"Now you're talking."

Teresa rolled over him and out of bed. Slung over the back of her chair was her dressing gown. She grabbed it and put it on, found her crocks and slipped them on, taking a last look at the man in her bed before she shuffled into the kitchen.

The naked male in her bed got up hopped after her. Grabbing her from behind, Felipe wrapped his arms around her middle as she reached up into the cupboard to get the corn.

"Would you like to borrow a robe?" she asked.

"I'm OK," he said and hugged her closer.

With an extra appendage on her back, she tipped the corn and oil in the pan, waited for the minor symphony of popping to subside, and transferred the popped corn into a bowl.

"Have you ever eaten it with vinegar?" she asked. It was a taste she had picked up from her time in England.

"No, but I'll give it a go," he replied with a smile, which Teresa couldn't see because he was nibbling her neck.

They sat on the makeshift pallet sofa, sipping on gin and tonics, picking popcorn out of the bowl and crunching it as they watched Teresa's old TV.

"Do you like it?" Teresa asked about the popcorn.

"It's okay, but I prefer the other channel," Felipe said, misunderstanding on purpose.

"Not the TV. The popcorn," she said, chiding his deliberate awkwardness. Then she noticed it, under his hair. She'd always assumed he just had messy hair, but now she saw it there behind his hairline. An enormous scar.

"Can I ask you a question?" she asked. "How did you lose your leg?"

"Car accident."

"And the scar?"

"Oh, this," he said, reaching up to touch it. "Yes, same thing."

"My God, it's huge. I don't feel so bad about mine now."

"My hair hides mine," he said, reaching over and kissing her dressing. "Have you been using that bio oil?"

Teresa looked sheepish.

The last of the edible popcorn was gone, just salty smears and a selection of corn that refused to pop were left. Felipe took the bowl from her, and as he hopped into the kitchen, Teresa got a good look at the tightness of his naked bum.

Felipe opened the filter on the tap, but just the sound of rushing air came out.

"There's water in the fridge," Teresa shouted.

He turned off the hissing tap and, opening the fridge, found a plastic bottle that Teresa filled the day before.

The adaptations Teresa made regarding her water usage seemed strange to Felipe, who lived in Praia Grande, which, though only 40km away, had an abundance of water.

Fantastico finished. Teresa pushed the button on the remote and the picture compressed into a dot, then vanished. She led Felipe into the bedroom, flicking off the light switch as she passed.

"Would you mind locking the cats in the living room?" Felipe asked.

Teresa chuckled but agreed and ushered Ramsey and Oliver into the room, closing the door on their confused faces.

Teresa and Felipe collapsed onto the bed and embraced. They made love again, but this time, when Teresa enjoyed her climax, Felipe did not stop until she climaxed a second time. He ejaculated into another condom he had brought with him.

He let a moment pass before he pulled out, removed and knotted the condom. They rested in an embrace and soon fell asleep. Teresa dropped off first, and Felipe noted how she snored. He found it a beautiful snore as lovers, sleeping together for the first time, might.

Chapter Twenty-Three - The investigation – 30th January 2016

It was a Saturday morning when Selma knocked on the door. Teresa saw how much Selma relied on her stick as she hobbled through to the living room and sat on the sofa, looking at the patch on the floor which, despite being cleaned, was still a different tone to the rest of the floor.

"Can I get you a coffee?" Teresa shouted from the kitchen.

"No thanks," said Selma. "Come and sit down. I need to talk to you."

Teresa did as she was told and sat next to Selma, wondering what on Earth might happen next.

"I had a tip-off," Selma began. "From the officer in charge of the investigation into Felipe's disappearance."

Teresa prepared herself to listen.

Selma sighed.

"Why did you delete those messages, Teresa?"

"What?" Teresa wondered how they found out.

"Felipe's phone backed up his messages to his cloud," Selma explained. "While I was in hospital, one of the other detectives had the bright idea of comparing the records and discovered a load of messages to and from you that had been deleted. I've read those messages and didn't like what I read. I've seen conversations like this before."

Teresa felt small beads of sweat collecting on her brow and her neck.

"Why did you try to hide it?" Selma continued. "It seems from these texts that you might have been a victim of emotional abuse."

Teresa was silent.

"The problem is," said Selma. "That my colleagues think you might have been in an abusive relationship. And that gives you a motive."

"A motive?" Teresa asked.

"A reason to get rid of Felipe," Selma explained. "Teresa. If there's anything you haven't told me, now would be a good time to tell me."

"But this is ridiculous," Teresa protested. "I was in the hospital. I've got the invoice."

"You discharged yourself from the hospital without permission from the doctors and before the police interviewed you about the death of the dentist. You're now a suspect not only for the murder of Felipe but for the death of the dentist as well. They're probably on their way over here now to pick you up. The problem is," Selma was calm and patient. "You first reported Felipe's disappearance on the Tuesday and yet Felipe didn't turn up for work on the Friday. What happened that day, Teresa? What is it you're not telling me?"

"Nothing happened that day," Teresa was incredulous. "We'd argued the night before. He went to work. He came home, and we patched things up."

Selma gave Teresa a searching look.

"Most of the weekend was fine," Teresa continued. "On Sunday night, he got upset again and left. That was the last time I saw him. I went to work on Monday, went straight to the dentist and woke up in the hospital. When I got home on Tuesday, I found the note and called you."

"The trouble is," began Selma. "That while I was being patched up, my colleagues came up with a different theory. That you argued on Thursday night, that things got out of hand and something bad happened. You called in sick on Friday to drive down to the beach and dump the body."

"What? This is ridiculous. I don't even have a car."

"The thing is Teresa, that there are other details which would corroborate this theory."

Teresa leant forward.

"There is CCTV footage of your car on its way to and from the coast on the Friday."

"But I sold my car. I don't have one anymore."

"It's registered under your name."

Teresa cursed the second-hand car dealer.

"You remember the clothes they found on the beach?" Selma continued.

Teresa nodded.

"They found them on Saturday morning, not on Wednesday morning, as I thought."

"Well, what about the text messages he sent me on Monday?" Teresa argued.

"If you had his phone, which seems to be the case, you could have sent those yourself."

Teresa sighed in desperation.

"The lavender plant!" Teresa exclaimed, leaping off the sofa.

Selma watched Teresa with amusement as she ran into the kitchen and searched the window sill.

"It was here! It was here!" Teresa said, searching the kitchen.

"What was?"

"The lavender plant that Felipe bought me on the Sunday. You can check it out. The garden centre might have CCTV."

"Where did he buy it?" Selma asked.

"This garden centre down the road. The one near Anchieta."

"OK, I'll check it out," said Selma. "Prepare yourself for some awkward questions. My colleagues will want to speak to you. They have a dead dentist and a missing person and no answers. I'm not one for assisting fugitives, but come with me until we can find some answers."

Selma pushed herself off the sofa with obvious discomfort.

"Let's go to the garden centre and see if they've got footage of Felipe," Selma walked to the door and stopped. "Oh, and there's one other thing. Felipe's note."

"Yes? What about it?" Teresa asked.

"It doesn't match other samples of his handwriting."

Teresa stood and stared. She didn't know how to take in all this information.

"Come on, let's go," Selma insisted.

"OK, thank you," said Teresa as she followed Selma through the door, still trying to assimilate all this information.

She sat in the car in the garden centre car park, while Selma talked to the owner and tried to take it all in.

About half an hour later, Selma returned.

"No CCTV and the owner doesn't remember seeing Felipe. Sorry, Teresa."

"Thanks, Selma," a thought occurred to her. "Selma?"

"Why are the police so interested in Felipe's disappearance? Black men go missing in São Paulo all the time."

"The family is putting pressure on the department," answered Selma. "Look Teresa. Do you want to stay with us tonight? Give us time to find some answers."

"Thanks, Selma. That's kind."

Chapter Twenty-Four - Back to reality – 16th February 2015

The noise of a strumming guitar woke Teresa. She pressed the snooze button, silencing the alarm for a while.

"What time is it?" Felipe asked.

"Quarter to five."

"Jesus Christ!" he said. "Why do you set your alarm so early?"

"Cause I have to get up and go to work," she said and hugged him.

"Oh my God," he muttered to himself.

At ten to five, the guitar started strumming again. The cats were calling her from their exile, but she pressed snooze again and again at five to five. At five o'clock she turned off the alarm and dragged herself out of bed, freed the cats from the living room and wandered into the bathroom where she ran the shower and stood under the water for a soak. When she emerged wrapped in towels, Felipe had disappeared from the bed. She found him in the kitchen pouring fresh coffee into cups and being fussed over by Oliver and Ramsey.

"Would you like some toast?" he asked.

"No thanks," she said and gave him a big kiss. "The bathroom's free. Have a shower while I get dressed, then I'll dry my hair."

He did as he was told and after ten minutes emerged clean, naked, and still a little wet. They kissed again, and Teresa returned to the bathroom to dry her hair. Another ten minutes later, they downed their coffee and headed out of the door.

The streets were quiet, and it still wasn't light, yet so it surprised them at how many people were already at the bus stop when they arrived.

"Why do people get up so early?" Felipe wondered aloud.

"I take two hours to get to work. It's the same for these people," Teresa said.

"Two hours?"

"On a good day."

"But why don't you live closer to the school?"

"Can't afford it," she said. "The rent would be double what I pay here just to live near the metro."

"Well, why don't you get a job nearer where you live?"

"That's a possibility, now that...," she hesitated. "I need to get around to looking for another job."

For Felipe, living by the beach in Praia Grande, spending four hours of his day on buses and trains seemed ridiculous, but that was the norm for millions of people in São Paulo. Felipe had a ten-minute walk from his apartment to work, and he couldn't imagine needing to take public transport to work, let alone the return journey taking four hours.

A bus arrived, and Teresa and Felipe climbed on board. They stood in the aisle because other passengers had already taken all the seats.

"I used to drive to the Metro," Teresa explained. "I used to leave at six. It would take me an hour and a half rather than two hours."

"Why don't you drive anymore?" Felipe asked.

"I had to sell the car. I couldn't afford to run it anymore. Everything is getting so expensive. Don't you drive?" She asked. Anyone with money in São Paulo drove.

"I used to, but after the accident..." he trailed off. Teresa gave him an understanding cuddle.

"Did you have any other problems because of your accident?" She asked.

"Other problems?"

"Well, apart from not wanting to drive, have you experienced any other problems?"

"I used to suffer from depression," he admitted. "But I haven't had an episode for a long time."

She gave him another squeeze.

Because the bus had its own lane, it bypassed the queues of traffic which were already clogging the streets of São Bernardo and Diadema.

After a long, bumpy journey, the now packed bus arrived at Jabaquara bus station where it terminated and everyone got off. The passengers filed into an even more crowded metro station.

Teresa and Felipe halted in the same area of the entrance hall where their lips had first met the night before.

"Have a nice day," Felipe suggested.

"And you."

They hugged and kissed once more.

"Your number," Felipe remembered in a panic and retrieved his phone from his pocket to take it down. "I'll text you."

Panic over, they embraced and kissed again, and Teresa wiped her lipstick from his lips.

"Thank you for an amazing weekend," he said.

"Thank you," she said, knowing that she was in danger of being late for work, but not wanting to separate from him yet. "I'd better go."

He smiled, they kissed once more, and he let go of her hand. She turned and walked away, not daring to look back while he stood, watching her until she was through the barriers and had disappeared down the escalator.

Teresa glanced at her watch. It was already past seven. It would be touch and go whether she would arrive by 07:45.

Chapter Twenty-Five - Back to the Beach - 16th February 2015

Teresa wondered how long she could maintain her routine of two-hour commute, work, two-hour commute. Felipe's surprised reaction to her lifestyle made her question her work, travel, life balance. She considered the time she had spent with Felipe over the weekend and the fact that there was someone who wanted her, made her feel good in a way she hadn't felt for a long, long time. She thought about how lucky Felipe was not to have to work today, and she wished she didn't have to work either.

People packed the platform and, as usual, many of them failed to see why it was necessary to let passengers off the train before they tried to board, and a bout of pushing and shoving ensued. Teresa tried to distance herself from this behaviour when boarding, but when she was seeking to alight, she would keep her elbows pointing outward so she could give anyone attempting to push past her into the train a good shove. A torrent of indignation often followed this and sometimes abuse, but by that time, Teresa had shuffled away along the platform with the herds of other penguin-like commuters.

On this occasion, by the time Teresa entered the carriage, all the seats had been taken and so she found a place to stand, away from the doors where she would impede no-one's entrance or exit. She saw a group huddled in front of the doors through which they would need to exit, but their exit was no doubt many stops away and in the intervening time other passengers would have to negotiate this human obstruction. Over the course of the next six stops, Teresa watched her prophecy come true as the ranks of the obstructive passengers swelled, and everyone else had to squeeze around them.

Teresa tried to pass the time on metro journeys by listening to music or reading a book, but on this morning she day-dreamed about Felipe until her thoughts turned to Mariana. She hadn't given a second thought to Mariana since she'd left her at the hospital the day before, and now she felt a little guilty for not asking how she was. Teresa sent her a text.

'I'm still alive,' came the curt reply

'Will you be at school today?' Teresa asked.

'No,' came the simple answer, and Teresa was relieved that she would not have to face Mariana in the flesh.

The train arrived at Ana Rosa, and Teresa got off with a crowd of passengers and stood with them on the escalator, too full to walk up. At the top, she navigated through streams of people walking in all directions, some to the exit, some from the exit, some from the blue line to the green line, some from the green line to the blue line. There seemed to be no obvious path through the bustle and Teresa attempted to calculate where those approaching her were likely to be when they met to avoid a collision. Everyone else seemed to be walking in the direction they desired with little concern for those around them, secure in the knowledge that everyone else would avoid them as they carried on their journey, regardless. Teresa didn't know how they had the courage to walk, assuming everyone else would move out of the way. Teresa navigated her way down the steps to the green line as a train pulled to a halt by the platform. She jumped on as the door sounded, its alarm warning imminent closure. Teresa calculated she would just about make it to work in time, but that breakfast would be out of the question.

Her calculations proved accurate, and she arrived in her classroom at a quarter to eight.

"Good weekend?" Big Brenda asked as soon as Teresa walked through the door. "How was the protest?"

"Yes, thanks," replied Teresa with a smile, which betrayed all.

"Oh yes? I expect you to tell me everything."

"OK, maybe later," said Teresa. "It's complicated."

The children seemed more tolerable that Monday, and Teresa's work was a little less monotonous and demoralising. The day passed, and Teresa had to admit to herself that she'd enjoyed parts of it. It was made more bearable by the receipt of texts throughout the day from Felipe, who expressed how much he'd enjoyed himself and what he'd like to do with Teresa if he had her alone.

The journey home was as long as the journey to school, but Teresa was much more aware of being alone on the Metro and bus and of travelling towards a flat which was empty save for two fussy feline inhabitants. The occasional filthy text from Felipe made her feel less alone and interrupted the journey. She had someone who cared for her, though felt more alone because that person was far away.

By coincidence, in fact by the power of shuffle, *If you find yourself caught in love* by Belle and Sebastian started playing through her headphones advising her to 'say a prayer to the man above' and she wondered whether Felipe might chide her for thanking God for bringing them together.

As soon as she arrived home, tired from the long uncomfortable journey, she was pounced on as usual by Oliver and Ramsey, not so much kittens now as small cats. "With claws which needed cutting," she chuckled to herself.

Teresa topped up the kettle from one bottle she had filled at the weekend, the water supply having already been cut off for the evening. She was glad this gave her an excuse not to do the washing-up, although she stared at the plates and cups piling up, which had already attracted a reasonable number of fruit flies.

While she waited for the kettle to boil, Teresa texted Mariana to find out how she was doing.

'Fine,' was all she received in reply. Teresa wondered how, if Mariana were reacting like this now, she would react when she discovered Teresa had slept with Felipe, although it wasn't the sleeping part with which Mariana would have a problem.

Teresa was exhausted after a weekend of insufficient sleep. She flopped down on the sofa with a gin and tonic and the cats and turned on the TV to watch the usual diet of tea-time crime programmes which recounted a catalogue of murders, robberies, road accidents, car chases and arrests that had happened in and around São Paulo in the previous 24 hours. It was depressing stuff. No wonder people in the city were afraid to leave their houses and lived behind security bars and high fences.

Her phone rang. The display told her it was Felipe.

"Hello?" she said as she picked up.

"It's me," he said.

"I know."

"How was your day?"

"Good thanks. And yours?"

"Oh, you know. Bus journey. Lunch. Snooze. Snack. Another snooze."

"I hate you," she joked. "How was the journey?"

"Ordinary. No incidents."

"Okay."

Silence.

"Listen, it's just a quick call," he said. "I'm on the night shift tonight. I wanted to call you and thank you again for a great weekend."

"Thank you."

"Why don't you, if you're not doing anything, that is. Why don't you come down and spend next weekend here in Praia Grande with me?"

"That's kind of you. Thanks for the invite."

"Yes, well, think about it. No pressure."

"It sounds nice," she said, conscious of the fact that she would have to cancel the appointments to fix the roof and the fridge. This must be serious.

"Yes, well, okay. I'll call you again tomorrow. I wanted to hear your voice."

"Thanks for the call."

"Okay, speak to you tomorrow."

"Okay."

"Bye."

"Bye."

"Okay, bye."

"Bye."

He hung up. Teresa looked at her phone, feeling awkward. She hated the start of a relationship, the period when neither partner feels they know the other well enough to tell the other they love them and thought maybe at least she could have blown him a kiss, but then he didn't blow her any kisses.

Teresa went to the kitchen and made herself a drink and sent Mariana another futile text. Mariana texted she would go to work the next day and Teresa dreaded the inevitable confrontation over the fact that Teresa had stolen her object of desire.

Teresa resolved not to think about it and made her drink a large one to make sure. She soon nodded off and awoke to find a documentary about rescued cats and dogs on Animal Planet still fizzing away on the TV. She fumbled for the remote, turned it off and wandered to bed, waking again when the cats began prodding her a minute before her alarm was due to go off.

Teresa was exhausted, and perhaps a little hung over as she dragged herself out of bed, fed the cats and trundled into the bathroom. The cats followed her in sometime later and sat on the side of the sink while she finished her shower.

She felt a certain amount of guilt enjoying herself with Felipe when she felt she should be focussed on her daughter and getting back to England to see her.

It was getting cold and, without and heating or closing windows, Teresa dressed in a hurry, drank her not cooled enough coffee and left the house into the morning.

As she walked down the street, she admired the beauty the dawn was painting on the few clouds which dotted the sky. She tried to ignore the ugliness of São Bernardo silhouetted against it.

She walked through the back streets to catch the 152 to Sacoma and it surprised Teresa to find the bus arrive almost as soon as she reached the stop. She got a seat on the bus and, once at Sacoma, took the metro two stops in the opposite direction to ensure she got a seat. By the time the train returned to Sacoma, it was full with standing passengers occupying all the space in the corridor between the seats and the doors, and yet three more passengers squeezed in. At the next stop, Alto do Ipiranga; another four somehow forced their way into what Teresa had imagined was a full carriage.

In the seats next to and in front of Teresa, Women read *50 Shades of Grey*. The woman in front tried to disguise the fact by inserting her book into an attractive fabric book cover. The popularity of these reading accessories had grown in parallel with the popularity of *50 Shades of Grey* and the parallel rise in embarrassment that women experienced reading the volume in public. Teresa remembered going to see the film with Mariana. Giggling women packed the cinema. Two or three men had accompanied their partners and suffered the roars of laughter, and occasional heckles which punctuated the film. A cheer and a round of applause greeted the end titles. Teresa had never had such a strange cinema experience.

The reminiscence brought her mind back to Mariana and the dreadful encounter that would occur, eventually. Teresa wondered whether to avoid Mariana and delay the inevitable or seek her out and get it over with. Teresa's quandary was soon resolved because no sooner had Teresa taken ten paces through the school reception than she bumped into Mariana coming the other way.

"Mariana," Teresa said in surprise. "How are you feeling? How's the ...er... head?"

"I'd rather not talk to you at the moment if you don't mind," Mariana replied

"Look, Mariana, I didn't mean to..."

"No, but you did though didn't you?" Mariana interrupted.

Teresa couldn't deny it. She had. She stood there looking at Mariana, helpless as to what to say.

"Excuse me," said Mariana and pushed past her. Teresa watched her go for a moment, then turned and headed to the classroom.

The rest of the day, she found it difficult to focus on her duties. Even the occasional message from Felipe did little to cheer her up. Felipe was now in the habit of sending her filthy texts, describing all the things he would like to do with her in bed. Under normal circumstances, she would be thrilled at these and pour over the details, becoming moist as she imagined them in her head and asking him what more he would like to do? But today his texts made her feel even guiltier, and so she explained to him, by text, what had taken place that morning between Mariana and herself. Felipe's suggestion was 'screw Mariana', but Teresa said it was not her place to do such a thing and he should understand that Mariana would much rather be screwed by him. He texted a laugh.

The day dragged, and she was glad when it ended, and she could stop trying to avoid Mariana, go home and read Felipe's texts again.

The week dragged more and more as it progressed and she wasted no time after school on Friday but headed straight for the bus station at Jabaquara where she got on the next bus to Praia Grande.

It was already dark by the time the bus pulled away from the terminal and, as it was already starting to turn cold, there weren't as many people, as usual, going to the beach, and the road was much quieter

The bus itself wasn't full, and Teresa had a double seat to herself. She sent a text to Felipe to let him know she was on her way and felt guilty that she should be having a video chat with her daughter this weekend. Teresa hadn't spoken to her for a while, and she was nervous about asking Felipe if he minded her chatting with Annabel when she was in his flat.

At the bus station in Praia Grande, Teresa descended the steps of the bus together with the other alighting passengers and filed through the crowd of people waiting to board the bus into the waiting area where Felipe was waiting with a broad smile. They hugged.

"How was your week?" Felipe asked.

"Oh, you know," said Teresa. "I've had better. Glad it's over, and I'm here with you."

They hugged again and kissed, the kiss of reunited new lovers, a kiss which neither wanted to end.

"Come on," said Felipe, when the kiss ended. He took her bag and led her away from the bus station. "It's a short walk from here. Are you hungry?"

"For you," she said and gripped his hand.

They walked hand in hand with an elated bounce in their step, unique to new lovers. They passed an old couple coming the other way, dragging their heels in the way of people weary of a constant battle with life's assault.

"Do you think that'll be us in twenty years?" Teresa asked.

"I feel like that now," Felipe laughed.

It was a ten-minute brisk walk from the bus terminal to Felipe's flat, during which Felipe quizzed Teresa as to the kinds of things she would like to do over the weekend, and Teresa's answers involved staying in the bedroom.

They arrived at Felipe's apartment building. It was a small block. Not large enough for a security guard but large enough to have a tiny cabin next to the entrance gate which could house a security guard if the residents clubbed together to pay for one, which they didn't.

Felipe led Teresa through the entrance gate, across a small and badly maintained communal area and into the lobby of the building, which contained not much more than a tatty staircase and an old-looking lift.

"Let's take the stairs," Felipe suggested. "I don't trust the lift, and it's one flight."

Teresa assented, and they ascended the staircase to a grubby-looking corridor on the first floor. His front door looked as grubby as the corridor, but it relieved her to discover, when he opened his door, that the flat itself was cleaner than the rest of the building.

Felipe shut the door behind them, and they fell into an embrace, kissing. He began unbuttoning her blouse, and she began unbuttoning his shirt. Felipe tackled the fastening of her bra but, as he was struggling, Teresa lent a hand. He knelt down in front of her and, unfastening her trousers, pulled both the trousers and knickers round her ankles to leave her naked.

They made love. Or rather, he fucked her. Teresa liked rough stuff sometimes, but Felipe seemed aggressive. He held her arms, and when she said he was hurting her, he continued grabbing her hair to pull her head back. He waited for her to climax. She did. But when it was over, she couldn't dismiss the feeling she had. It was uncomfortable.

Chapter Twenty-Six - The First Disagreement - 20th February 2015

They lay in bed, catching their breath.

"Are you hungry?" Felipe said at last.

"I could eat something," Teresa admitted.

"Pasta?"

"Sure."

Felipe leant over and kissed her, slipped out of bed, attached his artificial leg and pulled on his boxer shorts and a T-shirt. Teresa followed him, slipping on her knickers and half buttoning her blouse. She followed him into the kitchen, which appeared to be new as it was of the type which boasted a breakfast bar and stools. She sat on one stool and mused whether Felipe would be her long-lost soul mate or whether their encounter would end in disaster like all her other relationships and that if it were to be the latter, what would be the nature of the disaster?

"You're quiet," Felipe commented.

"Sorry," said Teresa. "I was day-dreaming."

"Centavo for your thoughts?" he asked.

"Oh, I was wondering what will go wrong and ruin everything."

"My goodness," Felipe said in surprise. "You're optimistic, aren't you?"

"Sorry. It always seems to start out so perfect like this and something always appears to ruin everything."

"Can't you enjoy the moment?" he asked.

"Sorry."

"Would you like a drink? Red wine? Beer?"

"A red wine would be nice," Teresa said, feeling a little chastised for not enjoying the moment.

"Are you okay?" Felipe asked, sensing a change in her tone.

"Yes, fine."

She guessed Felipe knew this was a lie, but she knew there was little he could do to pursue it if she did not want to open up. He poured her drink and handed it to her with a kiss.

"Are you happy?" he asked as she took her first sip.

Teresa took far too long to respond.

"I'm happy here, with you, now," she said.

"And?"

"And what?"

"You don't seem convinced about your happiness," Felipe observed.

Teresa thought about this for a moment.

"I have a lot of baggage," she said at last.

"Don't we all?" Felipe laughed.

Teresa didn't join him in the joke, but smiled. Felipe kissed her again.

"Why don't you tell me all about it?" he said. "While I prepare the dinner."

So Teresa began her tale.

"I have a daughter," she began.

Felipe raised his eyebrows as he prepared to chop an onion.

"She lives in England with her father and his new wife."

"How old is she?"

"Seven. But I haven't seen her since she was three," Teresa said, looking down into her glass. "Apart from video calling her."

"Does she speak Portuguese?" Felipe asked.

"No. But I speak English; I lived there for eight years."

Felipe's eyebrows raised a second time.

"I was married to her father, but when the marriage broke down, he sued for custody and won. And I came back to Brazil, and now I don't have the money to go back and see her."

Felipe stopped chopping. There was too much information in one go for him to assimilate it all.

"Hold on a minute," he raised a palm. "You were married to this English guy and split up, and he got custody?"

Teresa nodded.

"Why?"

She knew this was a question she would have to answer eventually, so she bit the bullet

"I had a problem with alcohol when I was in England."

Felipe looked at her glass.

"I know," she said, seeing his glance. "I'm OK now. But at the time I was under a lot of pressure, and things didn't work out well."

"I'm not judging," he said. But Teresa knew he was, even if in a small way. She didn't mind. If he wanted to judge her and stopped liking her because of it, then that was his problem. She didn't want to be with someone who looked down on her. But if he knew all her horrible history and still wanted to be with her, then he was someone she might want to be with, too.

"Anyway, my husband," she stopped herself. "My ex-husband divorced me and claimed custody. I didn't have money to get myself a talented lawyer, and he shafted me. I came here, and now I can't afford to go back."

Emotion crept into her voice, and she stopped there before she broke down altogether.

"And it's been how many?"

"Four years."

"And you haven't been back?" Filipe scraped the onions off the wooden chopping board into a stainless steel pan where they crackled in the oil heating at the bottom. "How much is a flight to England? Could you not save enough?"

"It's not that," explained Teresa. "I've other expenses, and I'll need somewhere to stay, and the Real is so weak at the moment. It's ridiculous."

Felipe paused in thought for a moment and continued stirring the pan.

Teresa let the silence hang in the air and took a sip of wine.

"Would you like some music?" asked Felipe, becoming uncomfortable. "Turn the iPod on there."

He pointed to an iPod nestled in a docking station, which she turned on.

"Play anything you like."

She spooled through the artists.

"You have Belle and Sebastian," she said.

"Yeah, their new album is on there. Have you heard it?"

Teresa nodded.

"Shall I put it on now?" she asked.

"If you want," he said.

"What do you want?" she asked.

"I want whatever you want," he said, evading the question.

Teresa sighed and selected the first track of 'Girls in Peacetime', *Nobody's Empire,* letting it wash over her for a while.

"So what about you?" she said at last. "Don't you have any skeletons in the closet?"

"Plenty," he admitted.

"Come on, spill the beans."

Felipe frowned.

"Let's talk about nice things today," he said. "I'll tell you all the horrible stuff later. I promise."

He took a large gulp from his glass of wine. Teresa sipped hers and watched him cook.

"Do you enjoy working at the school?" he broke the silence.

"You've already asked me that."

"Have I? Well, what did you say?"

"You mean you weren't listening?"

"I was," Felipe protested. "I forgot what the answer was."

"Typical," Teresa muttered to herself.

"What's that?" Felipe asked.

"I said typical. You're like all the other men. You never listen."

"No, it's not that," he said. "I listen. It's just that I have a terrible memory. You have to tell me something two or three times before it sinks in. I have to write everything down."

She looked around the apartment. Every flat surface appeared to contain small piles of pieces of paper.

"How do you keep track of everything?" She asked.

"With great difficulty," he admitted. "But I get by."

"Doesn't it affect your work?"

"No," he said. "I make sure I write everything down."

She was lost in the rhythm of *The Book of You* for a moment.

Felipe seemed busy cooking the dinner.

Teresa snapped out of her daydream.

"How long have you lived here?" she asked, trying to make small talk.

"A few years now. Four?"

"What did you do before that?" she probed.

"I used to live with my parents. I moved out when I bought this place."

"In Praia Grande?"

"In Praia Grande."

"What are your parents like?"

He rolled his eyes.

"They're a lot like me," he said. "Just older."

Teresa wasn't happy with this and gave him a look which said as much.

"What do you want to know about them? They're old now. My father was a doctor and always insisted I follow him into the medical profession. My mum was a housewife until they retired and we moved out. Now she's a shopper."

"We?" said Teresa.

"My sister," he said. "She left home when she married some poor sod prepared to keep her in the manner to which she wanted to be accustomed."

"I see," Teresa pondered his story. "And you don't see them much?"

"No," he said. "I've got my own place now. It's nice not to be watched all the time. I can have you over for the weekend, for example."

"Are you going to introduce me to your parents?"

"There's plenty of time for that. Let's enjoy ourselves for now."

"Of course," said Teresa. She was always trying to rush into things.

There was a pause during which Teresa found her mind straying back to her two kittens, which she'd left home alone with piles of food and trays of water.

"I wonder how my cats are doing," she said, breaking the silence.

"Would you rather be with them than me?" Felipe joked, but Teresa sensed there was an element of truth in his humour.

"Of course not," she said, a little annoyed that she should even have to answer such a question and glad that she didn't mention the fact that all she wanted to do was call her daughter.

"Do you like pepper?" Felipe asked, holding the mill over the pan.

Teresa nodded, and he twisted the wooden cylinder, sending flakes of pepper cascading into the pot.

"How spicy?" He asked.

"Up to you."

"No, up to you," he persisted.

"I don't mind," she said. "However, you like it."

He sighed.

Teresa couldn't believe it. They were already getting annoyed with each other, like an old couple that have to endure the annoying habits of their partner for years and yet somehow stay together. Teresa and Felipe had slept together a few times and were already finding fault with each other. Or was it her imagination? Was she already looking for holes in the relationship, never satisfied with what she had? She looked at him as he cooked her meal. She found him attractive. He'd done nothing except ask her how spicy she liked her food. She got up and went over to him and kissed him on the cheek. He turned to her, smiled, and kissed her on the lips.

"It'll be ready in a moment," he said.

"Good, because I'm starving," she smiled.

Chapter Twenty-Seven - Ways to Die - 22nd February 2015

Teresa and Felipe lay still, both staring at the ceiling. Teresa spotted a patch of mould which had forced its way through the paint. Felipe wasn't staring at the ceiling at all but at a place in the middle distance, at a point in mid-air between his face and the ceiling.

They spent almost all day in bed finding a new excuse to return there every time it looked as if they should get up and do something.

Teresa was feeling a little guilty for spending the entire day in bed; she liked to leave the house at least once a day, even if it were to pop to the shop for a loaf of bread. She felt doubly guilty that she was not confident to ask whether she could have a video chat with Annabel.

"Let's go out," she said.

"Okay."

They didn't shower, having already spent some time in the shower that morning, but pulled on the clothes which they had discarded on the floor.

"Where would you like to go?" Felipe asked.

"To the beach?"

By the time they reached the sand, a ten-minute walk from Felipe's building. The sun was low in the sky, and kiosks, palm trees and tall buildings threw long shadows across the sand to the sea.

They sat on the sand together, and Felipe put his arm around her shoulder.

"It's beautiful," Teresa said, looking out at the stillness of the Atlantic Ocean, tipping its waves onto the beach.

Felipe nodded.

"Tell me you'll never leave me," Teresa asked him.

He looked at her for a moment.

"I'll never leave you," he said.

They watched the waves crashing on the shore till the sun descended behind them, and the stars rose over the ocean.

"If I was going to commit suicide," Felipe began.

"What?" Teresa interrupted him, incredulous at the sudden shift in conversation.

"I'm just saying," he continued. "That if I were going to commit suicide, that drowning would be the best way to do it."

"What are you talking about?"

"It would be unpleasant. But it would be a lot less messy, wouldn't it? I've seen a few attempted suicides in the emergency room and the effect it has on those left to clean up the mess. This way," he gesticulated towards the sea. "You become fish food."

Teresa winced.

"If you jump in front of a bus or off a tall building, someone has to come along and clean up."

"I see what you mean," said Teresa.

"I'm not thinking of committing suicide," said Felipe, seeing the concern on Teresa's face. "It's a hypothetical question."

"I see," said Teresa. "Can we talk about something a little less morbid?"

Felipe smiled and leant over to kiss her.

"Of course," he said.

There was a long, comfortable silence.

"Do you often think about suicide?" Teresa said at last.

"I thought you wanted to change the subject."

She glared at him.

"Rarely," he answered the question. "I did when I was suffering from depression."

Chapter Twenty-Eight - Learning to live together - 24th April 2015

It all happened quickly. Felipe made some comment about wouldn't it be easier if they were living in the same place and wondered if there were any jobs in São Paulo. Teresa said there might be jobs for her in Praia Grande but, before she got round to looking for anything, Felipe had already found a job in São Paulo and the next thing she realised, he rented out his flat and was moving in with her.

However, Felipe wasn't suited to life in São Paulo. He hated the commuting and Teresa's flat was a step down from what he was used to in Praia Grande. It wasn't long before he bought a car and they would have moved out of the flat as well had Teresa not had a year to run on her contract. Teresa would have preferred to move to Praia Grande but the whole thing happened so quickly, and so she found herself with a flatmate and was getting used to the small piles of paper that appeared around the flat.

They hadn't spoken to each other all day. None of the usual texts with the 'I love you's and all the 'X's. She didn't ask him if he had finished work yet or when he would come home. It was late already late, and she'd expected him long ago. She wondered what he might be doing, whether there might be another woman, what they might be doing and whether he would be home at all.

"Where have you been?" Teresa asked as Felipe walked through the door.

He paused and looked at her in annoyance.

"It's late," she continued. "Have you eaten? I didn't know whether to cook something, what time you would be home, whether you'd have eaten."

"I'm okay," he said, taking off his bag and coat and dropping them on a chair.

"Are you going to leave those there?" she asked.

He sighed, picked up the bag and coat, took them through into the living room and dropped them on top of a cardboard box that sat among many similar boxes at one end of the room.

"What are you going to do with all this?" he asked with obvious annoyance, gesticulating at the collection.

"We talked about that. Did you forget?" she replied, suddenly regretting her words. "We need more storage. Are you going to buy me more cupboards?"

"How much is that going to cost?" He complained.

"I sent you some websites. Did you not look at them?"

"I..," he said, remembering. "I haven't had time and can't sit around looking at websites at work and when do I ever look at them here? You know, I get up at the crack of dawn and don't get back till late."

Teresa scrutinised him for a moment and relented.

"Are you hungry?" she said at last.

"I'm okay," he said.

"Shall I make you a sandwich?"

"Don't worry."

"I'll make you one. What would you like? Ham and cheese?"

"It's okay, don't worry."

"Ham and cheese," she said. "And would you like a beer?"

At this, he turned and looked at her. The corners of his mouth were already turning upwards. She perceived his change in mood and smiled herself.

"A beer and a ham and cheese sandwich it is."

She opened the fridge and took out a bottle of beer, and gave it to Felipe.

"Thank you," he said and kissed her. "I love you."

"You love me when I'm giving you a beer," she said.

"I love you even when you're not bringing me a beer," he corrected. "I love you more when you are bringing me a beer."

She snorted her disapproval and assembled the ingredients for his sandwich.

"Be careful. I have a knife," she warned.

"And I have a bottle," he said.

"Well, I have two cats, and I'm not afraid to set them on you."

"Ooh, I'm scared," it was Felipe's turn with the sarcasm.

"Go get him!" She ordered the cats, who sat staring at the ham in her hand, moving their heads from side to side in a synchronised dance with the meat.

Chapter Twenty-Nine - The Family – 2nd May 2015

Teresa didn't want to visit her brother any more than Felipe, but it was her brother's birthday, so she felt an obligation. It wasn't her brother she minded so much as her brother's wife, Selma. Teresa always considered her brother to be a little androgynous, but when he married Selma, big butch Selma, Teresa thought they looked like two lesbians. Selma was a police officer and spoke with everyone she met, as if she was commanding them to put their hands in the air and step away from the weapon.

"So this is Felipe," Selma said, ushering Teresa past her and into the flat so she could give Felipe a handshake so firm that it would cement his opinion that she was just as much a man as he.

"Pleased to meet you," Felipe said.

"Selma," she informed him, inviting him to join Teresa inside the flat.

"This is my husband, Geraldo," Selma announced, gesturing to a soggy lump of flesh in the kitchen, acknowledging his own existence. "Offer them a beer."

Geraldo pulled two bottles out of the fridge, opened them, passed one to Teresa and the other to Felipe. Selma already had one on the go and raised it in the air.

"Good health," she toasted and downed the rest of the bottle. "He doesn't drink," she gestured to Geraldo as if this was further evidence of his inadequacy.

Geraldo grinned an embarrassed grin and offered Felipe a bowl of wasabi nuts.

"So what do you do?" Felipe made conversation.

"I'm a lawyer," Geraldo said.

Felipe raised his eyebrows to feign interest but couldn't think of anything else to say, and that was the end of the conversation.

"Teresa tells me you're a police officer," Felipe turned his efforts to Selma.

"For my sins. Who's hungry?"

Everyone nodded except Geraldo, who watched Selma in the manner a dog watches his master when he is expecting a beating.

"We have some news," Teresa announced. "Felipe has asked me to marry him."

"Oh, that's fantastic," exclaimed Selma.

"Congratulations, sis," said Geraldo, pleased.

"So, what's the date?" asked Selma. "Sit, sit. The food will get cold."

"Oh, we haven't got a date yet. Felipe has just started his new job, so he needs to find out when he can get time off for our honeymoon."

"Where are you working now?" Selma asked Felipe.

"Hospital Assunção."

"Hmm, handy."

"So it won't be for at least a year because we have to wait for Felipe's holiday."

"Well, if you need us to be witnesses," Selma offered when Teresa felt she should have waited to be asked.

"Of course," said Teresa, sitting at the table. "We still need to tell Felipe's family.

"Shall we pray?" asked Selma.

Felipe rolled his eyes.

Chapter Thirty - The in-laws – 9th May 2015

"Aren't you hungry Carlos?" Felipe's sister-in-law asked of Felipe's nephew who was sitting opposite at the large glass dining table, ignoring a full plate of meat and instead focusing on a game he was playing on his phone. "Get him to eat something, Horacio."

Horacio, her husband, Felipe's brother, sighed. He understood he had lost the battle between food and Carlos' phone a long time ago.

"Come on Carlos, put that down and eat your food," Horacio was going through the motions. He had no intention of attempting to separate Carlos from his phone. Not when they had guests.

Felipe's sister-in-law, Izadora, had the habit of closing her eyes as she spoke, which gave the impression that she viewed everyone with disdain. This was convenient because, in reality, she considered almost everyone she met with disdain.

"So how did you two meet?" asked Felipe's mother, Lucretia, passing Teresa a plastic plate loaded with meat that her husband, Jose, had filled from the barbeque.

"Through a friend." Teresa tried to be diplomatic.

"That's not true," Felipe corrected. "I met her in the emergency room when I was sewing up her head."

"Ooh," said Felipe's sister, Patricia, leaning forward to get a good look at the sizable scar on Teresa's forehead. "How unfortunate. I can give you some makeup that will hide that."

Patricia ran a beauty salon in the centre of São Paulo and had a makeup tip for every occasion.

"How did that happen?" asked Lucretia.

"Somebody threw a rock at my head."

The faces of Lucretia and Patricia winced in unison.

"Whatever for?" asked Lucretia.

"I think they were trying to rob us," Teresa explained. "But my friend had the prescience of mind to keep driving so they didn't have the chance to rob us."

"How awful," said Lucretia, while a contorted wince still adorned Patricia's face.

"I asked Teresa to marry me," Felipe announced.

A lump of meat fell from the plastic fork Izadora was about to put in her mouth. The chins of Lucretia and Patricia descended as one. Even Jose turned from his barbeque to witness the reaction and Horacio stopped opening the beer in his hand. Carlos continued tapping away with his thumbs, oblivious to the hush that descended on the gathering.

Nine eyes turned to examine Teresa. Jose's glass eye was the only dissenter.

"Marriage?" said Lucretia, scrutinising Teresa and letting the news sink in.

Patricia examined her mother, waiting for a sign.

Izadora and Horacio observed Lucretia and Patricia. It was Jose who broke the silence.

"Well, congratulations my boy," he said, offering Felipe his hand and ignoring the stares of Lucretia and Patricia.

"Thank you, Dad."

"Well," Lucretia exhaled. "There will be lots to prepare."

"Yes," chipped in Patricia, never one to turn down the opportunity to organise the wedding of someone else without being asked or wanted.

"Teresa already has some ideas about what she would like," Felipe tried to interject.

"I'm sure she does," said Lucretia. "Tell us all about them, Teresa."

Lucretia pretended to listen for a moment before continuing with her own ideas punctuated by interjections from Izadora who, almost closing her eyes, recounted the 'only way' of arranging a wedding.

As Lucretia and Izadora listed the best ways to organise a wedding, Patricia chipped in at regular intervals with suggestions of how she could be involved, most of which included ideas for decorations or food which horrified Teresa.

Horacio, feeling off the hook with this distraction, sidled over to Jose and started talking about football. Felipe apologised to Teresa, told her not to worry, and joined Horacio in their discussion about a sport in which he held no interest but which still seemed preferable to discussions of wedding preparations.

When they got home, Felipe apologised again while Teresa made a large gin.

"The latest research shows that drinking gin may cause depression," Felipe pointed out, opening a beer.

"I don't care," said Teresa as she dropped ice into the glass.

"I'm serious," he said. "I suffered from depression, so I know how terrible it is."

Teresa paused her drink making ritual and looked at Felipe.

"I know you did," she said. "I'm sorry about that, but I've had a tough afternoon listening to your family try to plan my wedding. Can't I have at least one drink?"

"Of course."

She turned back to her drink but paused in thought for a moment.

"Would you like one?" she asked.

"Yes, please."

Teresa rolled her eyes and started making a second gin and tonic while Felipe pressed the on-button on the stereo. Simple Minds *Promised you a Miracle* filled the room and Felipe slumped on the makeshift sofa.

"Are you going to promise me a miracle?" Teresa asked as she handed him his drink.

"What sort of miracle?" he asked.

"The kind that will pluck me from this life, make me a doctor's wife, transport me to a nice house with a nice car and nice holidays in England where we can visit my daughter and maybe bring her over to Brazil on holiday."

"I don't see why not," said Felipe, emboldened by his first mouthful of alcohol.

Teresa smiled and hugged him.

Chapter Thirty-One - Settling into a routine – 18th May 2015

When Felipe came out of the bathroom, she took his place and looked at the words he had written in the steam on the mirror. Good. He remembered. Some days he forgot.

"Where's my message?" She would say if there were no words etched in the steam.

"Messages of affection should be an act of spontaneity, not an obligation, a chore, expected and appraised," Felipe would complain. "My life is now scattered with these routines. You should not demand acts of affection as a matter of course."

But today he was a good boy. He kissed her before he left for work and a short time later; she received a text message, which he must have typed as he walked to work. She read the message; it had enough 'X's. If there are too few, she worries he is neglecting her. Over the course of their relationship, he has added more Xs to the end of his messages. If the number of Xs reduced, she worried his love for her was also on the decline. The night before, Felipe drank what must have been a quarter of a bottle of vodka while they discussed the wedding and the honeymoon. He said he needed to do it to get himself through it all. Teresa's head was a little thick, and the odds were even that a full-blown headache would ensue unless she got some liquid into herself.

She switched on the radio. It was an interview with an Irish Catholic priest who counselled a Brazilian who was shot in Indonesia for drug trafficking. The priest explained how the boy, Rodrigo, had schizophrenia and heard voices louder than the real voices around him and that right up to the morning of his death, he could not understand that he was about to be executed. Voices kept telling him that everything would be okay and he believed them. The priest recounted how he sang hymns and prayed while the boy was being tied to a post out of their sight. When a single volley of shots rang out, they began praying harder because they knew Rodrigo would groan in pain until the moment he died. Teresa listened in horror to Rodrigo's story, which somehow made her feel a little better about everything that was going on in her own life.

Her phone beeped. It was from Felipe again. She copied and pasted the message and sent it back to him before climbing out of bed and going to the bathroom, where the fading outline of 'I Love You' was still visible in the mirror. Reassured by these signs that there was someone who wanted her, she sat on the toilet and had a wee. When she was about to flush, she noticed spots in the water. She recalled the date. Not her period. She tried to remember whether she had eaten beetroot and couldn't remember the last occasion, so she went back into the bedroom, picked up her phone and set a reminder for her to make an appointment with the doctor. Teresa knew Felipe was a doctor, but she didn't want to trouble him with something that might be trivial. He seemed stressed. Perhaps it was his work that was a burden for him or perhaps he, like Teresa, was concerned that all the plans for the wedding should be right. He had frowned a great deal the previous night when Teresa explained all the preparations she was making and excused himself for bed earlier than usual, but not before having at least three large vodka and tonics.

She knew, because she had drunk the same. Her cold was moving through its usual progression of phases. The current phase was the one which involved a blocked nose, a cough which seemed incapable of dislodging any phlegm kept her and Felipe awake for most of the night, and she now possessed tingling fatigue that would make everything she attempted today more difficult.

Teresa dwelt on the idea that she and her daughter would soon be together. If only for a brief time. Felipe had not questioned the suggestion of a honeymoon in England. He too often considered the possibility of travel and always wanted to see the sights of London. The Queen's Palace, Big Ben, and the house where Sherlock Holmes lived. He told her he always dreamt of visiting these places, and now he would have the opportunity. Once Felipe had warmed to the idea of a honeymoon in England, Teresa revealed her ulterior motive, to visit, and to spend time with, her daughter. Felipe was not opposed to the idea, and so she contacted her daughter's father by email and suggested the visit. This reply was also positive and, for the first time in a long time, Teresa was optimistic that things were on the up.

As usual, she caught the metro the wrong way so she could get a seat. A train had pulled into the station as she descended the stairs to the platform, so she rushed to the open doors, dodging the passengers emerging from the train, including a woman carrying a sleeping baby. She leapt through the closing doors and searched for her preferred seat. One by a window, away from the aisle so she couldn't be made to feel guilty by someone needier than her. These people did not understand that Teresa had travelled two stops in the opposite direction for her seat and that she was not about to give it up.

Chapter Thirty-Two - the calm before the storm – 15th October 2015

Teresa waved Felipe over as soon as he rushed inside to escape the torrential rain. The video call was already dialling on the laptop in front of her, punctuated by bursts of thunder from outside.

"Come here. Would you like to see my daughter?" she beckoned and gave him a short kiss on the lips, peck would be a better description. Felipe looked at the screen, but all he could see was a grey cartoon silhouette and some numbers.

The screen burst into life, and a kind-looking man with dark hair, starting to grey, filled the screen, though not looking at it but at a slight angle towards the side.

"Hello," said Teresa, excitement bubbling in her voice.

A bright flash and a loud crack, after which all the lights went off and the image on the screen of the laptop froze.

"Jesus!" Teresa clutched her hand to her heart, which was beating faster with genuine fear.

"That was close," said Felipe.

After a moment, the lights came back on, and the TV digital box began rebooting itself. However, the Internet router remained lifeless and Teresa's screen frozen.

"What's happened? Why isn't it working?" Teresa was panicking.

Felipe fiddled with the box, plugging it into different sockets and turned the switches on and off, but it was dead.

"The lightning must have fried it," he said, showing Teresa the now useless lump of plastic.

Teresa burst into tears.

"Now what?"

"We'll have to get them to come out and give us another," said Felipe.

"But I was chatting with Annabel," Teresa protested.

"I'm sorry darling."

Teresa went into a sulk.

"What can I do? It's not my fault," said Felipe, but this did not placate Teresa, who was now determined to remain in a bad mood.

Felipe sighed a long, deep sigh, got up and walked through to the bedroom.

"Where are you going?" Teresa shouted after him. Felipe didn't answer.

Teresa contemplated how Felipe seemed moody. Teresa felt she had to be careful not to upset him. She heard him shut the bathroom door with a bang and then bang the shower door and turn the water on.

Felipe seemed to be working longer and longer shifts, taking more opportunities for overtime. He said that they needed the money for the wedding and honeymoon, but Teresa felt like she hardly ever saw him. She wondered what she was doing wrong to make him not want to be with her.

She went into the bedroom, sat on the bed, and waited for him to emerge from the bathroom. When he appeared, he was wearing his robe and hopped to the end of the bed.

"What is it, darling?" Teresa asked, trying to sound as concerned as possible.

"It's not my fault the lightning fried the Internet," he said, still upset.

"It's not your fault," she said. "I was upset that I didn't get to speak to my daughter. That was all."

She rested her hand on his shoulder and smiled. He turned to look at her.

"I love you," she said.

He pulled her down onto the bed, and they kissed.

Chapter Thirty-Three – The wine – 7th January 2016

"Did you get it?" Teresa asked as soon as Felipe walked through the door.

"Here you go," he said, pulling a bottle from his bag.

"That's not the one I wanted?" Teresa exclaimed.

Felipe sighed and dumped the bottle on the kitchen table.

"It doesn't matter," she said. "It'll have to do."

"Well, it does matter, doesn't it?" Felipe complained. "Why are they coming again?"

"They're coming to have pizza. We don't see them often."

Felipe exhaled a deep sigh.

"Come on," Teresa tried to reason. "We never have company. We never go out. Let's be sociable for a change."

"It's not my fault you don't have any friends," he said.

"That's not a nice thing to say," Teresa protested.

"I'm joking."

"Ha, ha, hilarious."

"What are we going to talk about? We've got nothing in common," Felipe protested.

Felipe looked like a little boy who had been told he had to do his homework.

"Do it for me, please," Teresa pleaded.

"Okay, but you owe me," Felipe warned, going into the bedroom to get changed.

Teresa breathed a sigh of relief and continued tidying the kitchen, feeling guilty for putting Felipe through this evening with her brother and sister-in-law. She heard a bird singing outside and stopped to listen.

"Oh no," she said aloud.

"What's wrong?" Felipe asked from the bedroom.

"Nothing. I heard a striped cuckoo."

"What?" Felipe asked, appearing at the bedroom door.

"A striped cuckoo. You know what they say about the striped cuckoo being Saci."

"What?"

"My mother always used to say that if you hear a striped cuckoo that something bad is about to happen. I think there must be a family of them nesting on our roof."

"What a load of rubbish," Felipe said. "You shouldn't believe in all this mumbo-jumbo. Why don't you ask your dear Lord to protect you?"

"You don't have to agree with my beliefs. But you should at least respect my rights to have them."

"Fine, you believe in your imaginary friends if you want to."

"Please don't get into an argument with Selma about God again."

"So I can't believe what I want in my own house?"

"You can believe whatever you want, just don't start an argument with her about what she believes. You know how much she loves a good argument."

"She better not start praying," Felipe warned.

"And if she does?" Teresa argued. "Leave her."

"In my house."

"I believe in God as well," Teresa reminded him.

"Yes, but you don't pray over your food."

Teresa sighed.

"Please," she begged.

"OK," Felipe consented. "But only because it's you."

Felipe opened the fridge and got out a beer.

"Are you going to offer me one?" Teresa asked.

Felipe sighed, re-opened the fridge door, pulled out a beer, and set it down on the table in front of Teresa.

"Thank you," she said.

"I'm not your servant."

"No, but a little consideration once in a while wouldn't be a bad thing."

"Yeah, cause I'm such a bastard, aren't I?" he said, taking his beer and stomping into the living room, where he turned on the TV.

"Aren't you going to give me a hand?"

Felipe delivered another large sigh.

"What do you want me to do?" he asked.

"Would you set the table, please?"

Another sigh as Felipe pushed himself up and returned to the kitchen.

"Thank you," said Teresa.

"I've had a hard day," Felipe protested.

"We can't all be doctors saving the world."

"I'm not devaluing what you do."

"Oh, no?"

"No, I'm just saying that I can't believe your day was as difficult as mine, you're on holiday, and I'm tired, and I want to sit down for five minutes and have a rest before your bloody family turns up."

"OK, I'll do it," Teresa said, trying to take the knives and forks out of Felipe's hand.

"No, I'll do it," said Felipe, holding onto the cutlery so that a small tug-of-war contest ensued.

Felipe wrenched the cutlery out of Teresa's hand, cutting her.

"You've cut me," Teresa exclaimed as they both stare at her hand in horror.

"You should have let go," Felipe protested.

"You cut me," Teresa repeated in disbelief.

"It's nothing," he said, looking at the small cut in Teresa's palm.

"But you cut me."

"Arrghh, I can't do anything right, can I?" Felipe shouted. "Fuck this!"

He threw the cutlery across the kitchen, causing Teresa to flinch.

"Fuck everything! Fuck your fucking family and fuck their fucking pizza."

He grabbed the small metal table and threw it to the floor with an enormous crash that made Teresa back up to the kitchen sink, then Felipe stormed off to the living room, slammed the door behind him as loudly as he could and locked it.

Teresa stood alone in the silence and cried.

She slumped into the metal kitchen chair still standing, took out her phone and texted Selma to cancel.

Chapter Thirty-Four - The Morning After – 8th January 2016

When Teresa awoke, she wondered where Felipe was for a while until he remembered that he'd slept in the living room and then all the horrible recollections of the previous evening came flooding back to her. She raised herself to a seated position, and her hand hurt.

At that point, the memory of Felipe grabbing the cutlery from her hand returned. She could see the contents of the kitchen table still scattered across the floor and heard Felipe get up, unlock and open the door of the living room. Teresa pretended to be asleep as she heard him walk into the kitchen, which she had not bothered to tidy, and across to the bedroom as quietly as he could. The bedroom had never had a door, so Teresa imagined Felipe thought it was easy to slip into the bedroom without waking her.

Teresa lay with her back to the door, so it was impossible for him to determine whether she was sleeping. Felipe crept across the room to the bathroom, closed the door behind him quietly, and turned on the shower. Teresa imagined the warm water felt good. When he had gone, she would have a hot shower and let the water run over her as if it could cleanse her of everything that had happened. But she knew it would be no use. At the end of the shower, all the memories would still be there. It was impossible now to go back and change the past. Everything that had happened, had happened and would always have happened, and there was nothing she could do to change that fact.

Teresa heard Felipe turn off the shower, towel himself dry and take his bathrobe from the back of the door.

"So you're going to sneak off, are you?" Teresa said as he emerged from the bathroom.

"No, I er..." he hesitated.

"Are we not going to talk?"

"Of course," he said. "But I need to get to work."

"OK, so that's it, is it?"

"No, but..," he didn't have a 'but'. He sat down on the edge of the bed. "Okay, you want to talk, so let's talk."

They sat in silence for a moment. Felipe looked tired. Teresa thought he didn't look like he could complete his shift. Teresa did not need to work. It was the school holidays. For a few moments, neither of them spoke. Felipe looked like he did not know what to say, and Teresa felt it was not her who should need to start the conversation.

"Are you not going to say anything?" She asked when her patience ran out, which was not long.

"I'm sorry about last night," he said.

"Sorry will change nothing."

"I know," he said.

There was another awkward pause.

"Look, I have to go to work. Can I talk about this when I get back?"

"You don't care about me, is that it?" She accused.

"I do," he protested.

"Funny way to show it."

"I know."

"So what are we going to do?" she asked.

He shrugged.

"What do you want to do?"

He shrugged again.

"You don't know much, do you?"

He shook his head.

Another pause.

"Look..."

"You need to go to work."

"We'll talk when I get back," he suggested.

"Maybe," her response was a kind of warning, but Felipe just sighed.

"OK, I'll see you later," he said, getting up to leave.

"Maybe," she repeated. But her threat had no teeth. Where was she supposed to go? He was in a much better position to not return than she was to leave, and she knew he knew this.

He looked at her once more and left. She buried her head in her pillow and cried. What had she done to deserve this luck? The one man she thought might be different had also turned out to be a bastard.

Teresa's flaw in relationships was that she had a belief that she could change the man into the man she wanted him to be. She had never converted a man into the individual she desired and spent many years, many unsuccessful relationships, many tearful nights trying, but to no avail.

There was no evidence to suggest that this relationship would differ from any of the others, but she did not want to fail again. She was getting too old, she felt, to keep starting again and she would like, if she could, to have another child. The clock was ticking; time was running out. If there was a chance to make it work, she had to try. But Felipe had displayed behaviour that was unacceptable. That no-one should have to tolerate. Perhaps this was Karma for her betrayal of Mariana, whom she had barely spoken to since her relationship with Felipe had begun.

She couldn't help feeling, however, that Felipe was different and that she could help him change in a way that she had failed with the others. Part of her told her she was deluding herself, but another part argued that she had to try. This internal argument went backwards and forwards for a while, with one voice telling her she should get as far away from this man as soon as she could and the other seeing a future, a happy life. It was school holidays, so she tried to get some sleep, but neither her agitated mind nor two excited cats, delighted at the fact she hadn't left for work again, would let her slumber.

She gave up altogether and got up to make herself some breakfast.

Teresa fed the cats and made some coffee, feeling more bullish by the minute. She should confess everything to Mariana and try to patch things up. Explain what a bastard Felipe had turned out to be and tell Felipe to get out.

She sent Mariana a text which read 'Hello?' but Marina apparently ignored it.

Felipe arrived home early. His arrival surprised Teresa.

"Hello," he said as he entered the kitchen, his face looking as ashamed as it had the moment he had left.

"Hello?" she said, pretending to be surprised, even though she heard him opening the entrance gates moments earlier. "You're back early."

"Yes, I called in a favour," he said, taking off his coat and bag and putting them in the place where Teresa, during a previous argument, had requested he leave them. She noted his obedience. The cats entered the kitchen to investigate the arrival.

"I'm baking a cake," Teresa explained. "Would you like some coffee?"

"Yes please," he said, seating himself in a chair where he could see her work.

She poured some cold coffee from the percolator jug into a cup and put it in the microwave, where the ballerina printed on the side whirred around in its tiny spotlight.

"How was your day?" Teresa asked in her polite making conversation voice. Felipe shrugged.

"Same old shit," he said in a tired voice.

It annoyed Teresa that Felipe never talked about the details of his day. He'd tried to pass his secrecy off as doctor-patient confidentiality, but it wasn't that. He didn't want to talk about it. She always flourished him with all the details of her day when he asked her how it had gone - a question that she'd insisted he asks as soon as he walked through the door. When she asked him how his day had been his answers were always brief and vague. He insisted he wasn't trying to cover anything up, that he was tired and didn't want to talk about work, but this left Teresa frustrated that he wouldn't open up to her the way she opened up to him.

"I trust you," she said. "Why wouldn't I?"

"I don't know," he admitted. "It feels like you think I'm an idiot."

"Why would I think you're an idiot? You're a doctor."

"Why don't you listen to me? Why do you have to question everything I do? You don't trust me to do anything. Nothing is ever right."

"I do."

"Why do you need to criticise everything? What about the wine?"

Teresa looked at him.

"I'm sorry," she said.

"No, I'm sorry," he corrected. "My behaviour was unacceptable."

"Yes. It was."

He stood up. Walked over to Teresa and they embraced. Teresa wept.

"What is it?" he asked.

She knew she should walk away. Get as far away from Felipe as she could. But her capacity for an optimistic belief in change, despite the pessimism which ruled the rest of her life, told her he was a good man. A man she could help. She believed him when he asked for forgiveness, that he was willing to solve these problems and also thought that here was a man who would make it possible for her to see her daughter again.

Teresa forgave him, and they carried on with their lives as best they could, like a broken cup that had been glued back together. From a distance, it looked like the same cup, but on closer inspection, the cracks become visible, given away by the dried glue tracing their path.

Felipe sat and looked grumpy. Perhaps it was embarrassment. A man of his profession was not supposed to behave the way he had.

"I have a problem," he began, this much Teresa already knew. "I have an issue with people who question me. It's like you are questioning me as a person. Like you don't trust me."

"I must be crazy," said Teresa.

Felipe said nothing.

Chapter Thirty-Five - Same old story – 10th January 2016

Felipe had the weekend off for a change, so, in response to Teresa's complaints that he did not spend enough quality time with her, on Sunday they went for a walk. They looked around the garden centre, and Felipe bought her a small lavender plant, which she placed on the windowsill above the kitchen sink.

Felipe made them both a cup of tea. She had almost converted him to tea, though he preferred green tea, and the pair of them slipped off their shoes and slumped on top of the bed, each staring at their mobile phones.

"Who's Joaquim?" Felipe asked without looking up from his phone.

"Who?" Teresa asked.

"Joaquim. He's liked your photo on Facebook."

"Oh, he works at the school."

"Oh, yes?"

"What's that supposed to mean?" Teresa demanded.

"Nothing, just saying. I don't know what you get up to while I'm at work."

"Oh God," Teresa sighed. "There's loads of women you work with I know nothing about."

"Yes, but they don't like my photo on Facebook, do they?"

"So what? God knows what you could get up to on these long night shifts that you do."

"Are you accusing me of having an affair?" Felipe asked.

"No, of course not. But you could get up to all sorts, and I wouldn't know anything about it," Teresa reasoned.

"I can't believe you don't trust me."

"What? Who said anything about not trusting you?"

"You did," he said.

"No, I didn't. You're twisting my words."

"Oh, now it's my fault, is it?"

"What do you mean? Who said anything about fault?" she asked.

"You did. You said I was having an affair."

"No, I didn't."

Silence.

"Are you grumpy now?" Teresa asked.

"You don't trust me," he said.

"Where did this come from?" It bemused Teresa.

"You tell me," he said. "You started it."

"How?"

"By accusing me of having an affair?"

"I did not," Teresa protested. "You started it by asking me who Joaquim was."

Silence

"Because he liked your bloody post on Facebook. There's no need to overreact."

Teresa sighed.

"I'm sorry," she said and leant over to kiss him.

"You get too stressed out," he said. "You should learn to relax. How about doing some meditation or some yoga? It'll help you get in shape too."

"What are you saying? That I'm fat?"

"No, it's not that. With the wedding coming up and everything," Felipe tried to avoid Teresa's gaze. "You don't exercise, do you? And you're not getting any younger either. You need to think about your health."

Teresa did not like this assessment of her physical condition. Felipe realised he had done nothing to improve her mood and had made the situation much worse.

"I'm just saying that it might do you good getting some exercise. It might help you stop getting so stressed."

Teresa contemplated this advice in silence.

"Are you grumpy now?" he asked her.

"Are you sure you want to marry me?" she asked.

"Of course," he said after a brief pause. "Why?"

"What do you see in me?" she asked.

There was a long pause while Felipe considered his response.

"You're beautiful, funny, and intelligent."

"But why do you want to marry me?"

"Why not?"

"That's not a good enough reason."

"Why do you want to marry me?" Felipe asked.

"Because I love you," Teresa answered. "I know I shouldn't, and I don't know why I do, but I do."

Felipe looked at her in silence.

"But my love is like a flower," she continued. "Every time you hurt me, my love loses a petal until one day there'll be no petals left."

"Oh great. Now I'm getting told off," Felipe complained.

"I'm not telling you off."

"Oh no? Well, what do you call this?"

Teresa sighed.

"I'm telling you how I feel," she explained. "Can't we have a conversation where we share our feelings?"

"You mean where you have a go at me?"

"God! I'm not having a go at you."

"Sounded like it to me. You're always complaining about me. About everything I do. Nothing I do is ever good enough, is it?"

"I'm trying to talk," Teresa persisted.

"Well, can't you say something nice?"

"I told you I loved you," said Teresa.

"Yes, and reminded me what a bastard I am," he said.

Teresa knew there was no winning this argument.

"Maybe we shouldn't get married," Felipe suggested.

"Is that what you want?"

"No, but if it'll be this much effort."

"Well, if you think it's too much effort."

"This is what I'm talking about," Felipe shouted

"What?" asked a shocked Teresa.

"This constant prodding," shouted Felipe, getting out of bed.

"What are you talking about?"

"You can't leave it, can you?" Felipe looked agitated, as if tormented by a persistent yet invisible swarm of bees. "You keep on pushing, pushing until you drive me to this."

He picked up a pillow and threw it across the room.

"Felipe. Stop it. You're scaring me."

"I can't take it," he shouted. "I can't take this anymore."

He picked up another pillow and threw it after the last one, but the second took a different trajectory and cleared all Teresa's perfume and jewellery off the dresser and sent it all crashing to the floor in a cacophony of broken bottles.

Felipe slipped on his shoes, limped out, across the kitchen and into the living room, slamming the door behind him so hard that it rattled the bedroom window next to Teresa who sat frozen in fear and astonishment.

When Felipe slammed the door behind him, he saw that one of the stupid cats had sneaked into the room with him. Felipe grabbed the cat and threw it at the wall. The small, black furry body slammed against the plaster-covered brick with a crunch and fell, limp, to the floor.

He glanced at the closed door and rushed over to the pile of fur laying on the floor. It was lifeless.

He scanned the room and found a plastic bag. Mumbling to himself, he lifted the limp feline and dropped it into the empty bag and wrapped the bag around the cat to disguise its contents.

Felipe listened at the door.

He turned the handle and slipped into the kitchen. Hiding the bag behind his body, he tried to open the door as quietly as possible. He had it open and was already walking through it when he heard Teresa call his name. He ignored her, closed the door behind himself and locked it, running into the street.

Chapter Thirty-Six - Another morning after – 11th January 2016

It was a long, sleepless night for Teresa, and when she got up the next morning, Felipe was still not home. Tears welled up in her eyes once more and cascaded down her cheeks. She forced herself to get up and have a shower. Ramsey sat on the sink, watching her, wondering what to make of this confusing human. Teresa thought he was wondering what he should play with next or whether she would feed him. She looked everywhere for Oliver but could not find him. Now she was even angrier with Felipe, whom she assumed must have let Oliver escape from the house when he left last night. Taking care not to lose Ramsey too, she opened the door and called Oliver, but he did not come.

Teresa tried phoning Felipe, but there was no answer. He never answered his phone during the day; he was probably already working.

She got ready to go out for her dental appointment, fed the remaining cat, and left the house.

The bus was full, so when she arrived at the Metro, she was glad she travelled in the opposite direction first so she could get a seat as usual. Passengers crammed onto the train. Commuters were stranded on the platform, unable to get on. It was later than usual, and Teresa wondered whether she would arrive at her appointment on time. There was nothing she could do about it now, so she just tried to avoid the glances of the standing passengers in the same way she was trying to ignore her rumbling stomach.

Most seated passengers pretended to be asleep, and Teresa nodded off as well. Perhaps it was the warmth. All those people crammed in a small area generating all that heat.

The large numbers of people on the metro distracted Teresa, as did the minutiae of her daily tasks. She had a dental appointment, so she would have to wait before she could resolve her issues with Felipe and the missing cat.

Chapter Thirty-Seven - Life after Felipe – 27th January 2016

She endured the nightmares, endured her sessions with her psychologist, endured work, endured home, endured her family, endured the distance from her daughter and endured the blood which trickled into the toilet mixed in with her piss.

Chapter Thirty-Eight - The examination – 28th January 2016

Teresa reclined on the chair; naked save for a surgical gown made from some type of paper. She lay with her knees bent and apart and her feet flat and together like she'd been told to do the last time she went for a smear test. One nurse held Teresa's hand while another swabbed her private area down, then inserted a local anaesthetic. Teresa flinched with the cold but felt relieved it was not more uncomfortable or painful. The doctor inserted the camera, and it surprised Teresa to find it didn't hurt either.

"It's in," said the nurse, holding Teresa's hand. "You can watch on the monitor."

The doctor filled Teresa's bladder with water, which made her want to go to the toilet. She winced as the biopsy tool pinched the inner wall of her bladder and removed a sample. The tube's journey back out of Teresa was more uncomfortable and, though she didn't admit it to the kind nurse holding her hand, a little painful.

The whole procedure was over within twenty minutes, and before long Teresa was in a private room sipping on juice, the kind nurse had given her when she had come into the room to tell her that, as soon as she did a wee, she could go home.

Chapter Thirty-Nine – The Chip Shop – 6th December 2013

Teresa had been drinking all day. She had drunk a few the night before, too. She'd already taken time off work because she felt things were getting too much, but she was more stressed than usual.

It was Annabel's 5th birthday the next day, and she spent hours preparing everything for the party which they were having at the house because William said they couldn't afford to hire anywhere to do a buffet the Brazilian way. William assured her that English families always had their birthday parties at home.

Annabel complained she was hungry and Teresa was so tired, having spent the entire day making Brazilian and sweets and savouries, much less baking the most ambitious cake she ever attempted. Everything had an ice princess theme, and she made different shades of blue icing. She could have given Annabel one or two of the savouries, but she was nervous as it was that there would not be enough for tomorrow.

Teresa looked through the cupboards; there was nothing easy to make. She could go to the chip shop, but it was cold outside, and Annabel was too annoying to make her walk all the way. She looked out the window at the car parked in the driveway. It wouldn't take five minutes by car. Just there and back, what could go wrong?

"Fish and chips?" Teresa suggested to her daughter, who began clapping her hands together at the prospect.

Teresa was careful to wrap up Annabel warm against the cold, and it was only when she bundled her into the back seat she remembered she had left her daughter's safety seat having only just finished cleaning it from the time Annabel threw up on the way back from dropping William at the train station. She looked back at the house, and at her daughter in the back seat.

'It's only five minutes,' she thought.

"Here you go darling, put on your seatbelt, tuck this part under your arm, so it doesn't rub on your neck," she said as she fastened in her daughter.

"Here we go," she said, jumping into the front seat. "Let's get some chips."

*

Teresa did not recognise where she was. Her head hurt. She touched it with her hand. It seemed wet. She looked at her fingers. Blood. Where was she? What had happened? She was in the car. A man was shouting at her through the driver's window. She heard crying. She turned to see Annabel in the back seat in tears.

"It's okay darling," she said. "Everything will be okay."

There was a tapping on the window. It was a police officer. Teresa stepped out of the car.

"Are you able to tell me what happened?" asked the police officer. Teresa could see an angry-looking man behind him talking to another police officer and pointing towards her.

Teresa said nothing. She could not say anything. She had no recollection of what had happened.

"I'll have to ask you to give me a breath test," said the police officer, producing a breathalyser.

Teresa panicked. If she took the breath test, they would find out she had been drinking.

"What are you accuthing me of?" she slurred.

"I assure you it is the normal procedure in these situations, madam," said the policeman.

"I am not blowing into that thing!" she shouted. "My daughter ith in the car. Do you think I would drive and drink?"

The policeman raised his eyebrows at her slurred speech.

"If you do not provide a sample of breath," the policeman continued. "I shall have to arrest you and take you to the station."

"This ith outrageous," Teresa began waving her arms in the air. "Fucking outrageous."

*

"Would you come this way, please?" A police officer led Teresa through the station to the entrance where William was waiting with an expression which caused a shiver of fear to run down her spine.

"You refused to give a bloody breath test?" were the first words he uttered.

"Where is she?" Teresa asked after Annabel.

"With mother," William said as if irritated at being side-tracked. "You realise you will have to go to court. You might have killed yourself, or worse, you could have killed Annabel."

Chapter Forty - The Results – 25th February 2016

Teresa stared at the doctor, not believing what he had told her. Her head raced with questions, but she had no idea which one to ask first. She felt overwhelmed and scared.

"There are a few more tests we must do to find out more about your cancer, to help us treat it better," the doctor said as if he hadn't uttered the C word and everything was fine.

But everything wasn't fine. Teresa could see the doctor talking, but none of his words seemed to register in her brain, which was struggling to deal with the maelstrom of emotions swirling around inside her head. She felt she was being carried along by something out of her control. She was angry. Why did all this stupid shit have to happen to her? What had she done to God to piss him off so much?

The doctor asked Teresa if she was still seeing her psychologist and Teresa said that she was.

"Good," he said. "You should talk to your psychologist and your family. The more support, the better."

The support Teresa wanted was a large gin and tonic, but she thought that was what got her into this mess.

Chapter Forty-One - The Cuckoo – 26th February 2016

The school had given Teresa compassionate sick leave, or something like that, and she went to the beach to stare at the same ocean she had stared at with Felipe.

She felt empty. There seemed nothing for her to do. She had no interest in her job. Her chances of visiting her daughter had disappeared. The thought of her cancer treatment filled her with horror. And now the police were after her, not only about Felipe's disappearance but also regarding the death of the dentist.

She heard a noise and turned to see a striped cuckoo perched on a bush a couple of metres away.

"Oh, it's you," she said to the cuckoo. "Haven't you got me into enough trouble already?"

She watched the waves crashing onto the shore. The sea seemed calm, broken by the waves themselves as they took it in turns to dash themselves against the sands. It was a clear day, and she could see the island. The tide was out, and it looked so close. It looked so reachable. Teresa knew how strong the currents were and knew she would never reach the island. She remembered her conversation with Felipe. Such a neat way to die. Eaten by fish. The drowning part must be horrible, she thought, but it wouldn't last for long and then she would be free. Free from pain, free from guilt, free from responsibility, free from debt.

She lay down and closed her eyes.

"Hello there."

She woke with a start and sat up to see Felipe stood by the bush where the cuckoo had been, with his arms folded across his chest.

"You! You bastard," she said, getting to her feet. "Where the fuck have you been? Your family is going berserk. The police have been questioning me. They think I killed you."

"That's a shame isn't it," said Felipe.

"You need to tell everyone that you're still alive," she said.

"Now why would I want to do a thing like that?" said Felipe. His tone sounding a little sinister.

"People are worried about you. You need to show the police I didn't kill you."

"And spoil all the fun?"

"Fun? What the fuck are you talking about? These last few weeks have been anything but fun."

"For you maybe," said Felipe. "But it's been interesting to me seeing how you deal with it all."

"Are you mad? Why did you come down here that Friday and plant your clothes on the beach?"

"Is that what happened?" asked Felipe. "I thought you killed me. Drove me down here and dragged me into the sea. Isn't that what the police think?"

"That's what they think, and you have to tell them it's not true, you crazy fuck."

"Isn't it?" said Felipe, unfolding his arms to reveal a deep red bloodstain on his chest. "How do you explain this?"

Teresa rubbed her eyes. When she looked back again, Felipe had gone, but the small striped cuckoo was standing there in the bush, staring at her.

"Felipe?" she asked the cuckoo, before deciding how crazy her idea was.

The cuckoo continued to stare at her for a moment before disappearing into the sky.

Teresa turned to watch the sea. She watched its relentless movement. Imagined a moon pulling it with invisible power. How easy it would be to swim. Swim until she could swim no more. Succumb to fatigue. Too far out to return.

Teresa looked along the beach. It was almost deserted despite being not long after Carnival.

She kicked off her flip-flops and walked to the water's edge. A wave arrived and bathed her feet in cold water.

She took a deep breath and stepped forward.

Teresa panicked and inhaled. Water flooded into her lungs and she felt the fight slipping out of her. She succumbed to the dark water which enveloped her.

Chapter Forty-Two – Taking control – 29th February 2016

Teresa reported the recurring dream about drowning to her psychologist during her next visit. She felt her appointment had helped her to deal with her feelings about the prospect of her cancer treatment.

She told the psychologist how she had contemplated suicide that day on the beach before she fell asleep on the sand and since then, she had often reflected on her decision not to perish below the foamy brine. A victim of circumstances unable to cope any more with the obstacles which life continued to throw her way, but to have done so would have been a disservice to herself. Teresa admitted she had made lots of mistakes in her life. Who hadn't? She recounted how she had often felt like a passive observer of events as they had happened to her, but for Teresa to have given up at that moment would, in her opinion, have let her daughter down. Her daughter who, one day, would want to get to know her biological mother and the circumstances which tore them apart. Teresa said she was also well aware there were millions of Brazilian women whose lives were tougher than hers.

Teresa knew she had enough and realised what she needed to do. She would not lie down and take it anymore but would take control of her life and fight. She would get back to her daughter, whatever it took.

Chapter Forty-Three - The Fight Back – 1st March 2016

Teresa thanked Selma for putting her up and said that she was returning to her flat. She sat down on a kitchen chair and sent a text to the school explaining that she would return to work. She also sent a text to the police detective who had left some voicemails trying to contact her about Felipe's disappearance. The phone rang almost straight away. It was the detective. He asked where she was and she told him she was at home and that she had no intention of leaving again. The detective asked her when she could go to the station and she said she could go right away.

A tall, fair-haired man greeted Teresa at the police station.

"Teresa? Please come this way," he said in what seemed to Teresa a kind voice.

"Of course," she said and followed him into a small office littered with paperwork.

"Have a seat. Would you like a coffee?" the detective asked.

"No, I'm fine, thanks," she said.

"It's been difficult getting hold of you."

"Yes, I'm sorry about that," said Teresa. "It's been a difficult time."

"I understand, but it makes our job harder if you're not available to answer our questions."

Teresa looked down in embarrassment.

"Why did you leave the hospital without being discharged?"

"I didn't realise that I needed to be discharged," Teresa explained. "They gave me a bunch of forms, and I thought that was it."

"When our officers arrived at the hospital to interview you about the incident at the dental surgery, they found some confused doctors and nurses wondering where you had gone. We got your details from the dentist's records, but your sister-in-law told us about your fiancé's disappearance and convinced us to put off questioning you for a bit. I stupidly agreed, and your sister-in-law shot herself. I visited her in the hospital before I contacted you, as a courtesy to an old friend. We go to the same church. But then you disappeared, didn't return my calls. You can forgive me for thinking you might have been hiding from something."

Teresa offered an apologetic smile.

"I've been diagnosed with cancer," Teresa went the sympathy route.

"I'm sorry to hear that," said the detective. "It must be difficult, on top of your fiancé's disappearance, and the incident with the dentist. A stressful time."

The detective's words did not sound sincere.

"Sometimes stress makes people do strange things," he continued. "I expect Selma has already filled you in on the theory that has been floating around at the station."

Teresa nodded.

"It's an understandable scenario. A stressful situation. Things reach a head. We say or even do things we regret. But then it's too late, isn't it? Some things we can't take back, things we've said, or things we've done."

"What are you insinuating?"

"I know you deleted those text messages."

Teresa sighed.

"I thought they might give someone the wrong idea," she tried to explain.

"Or maybe they would give someone the right idea. You had plenty of time to go to the beach and back."

"To do what?"

"To dispose of the evidence. I'm sure it was an accident. But who would believe you with all those incriminating text messages? Maybe the neighbours heard shouting?"

"Speak to the neighbours."

"I already have. Illuminating."

"So why don't you arrest me if you think I did it?"

"I thought it only fair to give you the chance to tell your side of the story first."

"You already know my side of the story."

"I wanted to hear it from the horse's mouth, so to speak."

"And now you've heard it. I came home and found the note. That's all there is to it."

"So you didn't argue?"

"Yes, we argued. He left. I went to the dentist, woke up in the hospital, and when I came home, I found the note."

"And his phone."

"And his phone," she confirmed.

The detective sighed.

"Teresa, if there is anything you want to tell me, now would be a good time."

Teresa looks the detective straight in the eyes.

"I did not kill Felipe."

"Okay. Well, in the absence of a body or a murder weapon, I'm not in a position to disagree with you. But if you think of anything you would like to share, then here's my card. I'll show you out."

The detective got up and walked to the door, then stopped and turned.

"Oh, one more thing," he said. "At the dentist, you didn't get a look at the man who attacked you, did you?"

"No," said Teresa. "He was wearing a mask."

The detective laughed.

"They always are," he said, and showed her out.

Chapter Forty-Four - The cancer treatment – 15th March 2016

They caught the cancer early; they said. Teresa was lucky, the doctors said. Lucky to have only her cervix removed. Teresa didn't want to think what would have happened had she been unlucky. A radical trachelectomy, they had called it. Teresa had taken the time to learn how to pronounce it. She was lucky; they had said her plan would cover it, but she didn't feel lucky, not in the slightest bit lucky.

They told her it was common to feel anxious. That was good because she felt very anxious. More anxious than usual and she was a woman used to feeling anxious. They would remove her cervix and the upper third part of her vagina. Teresa had little experience of being 'lucky', but she was sure that this was not what it felt like. They would also remove some tissue she couldn't remember the name of and some lymph nodes or something, but this just seemed like icing on the cake compared to the loss of her cervix and a third of her vagina.

At least she would have a general anaesthetic and would sleep through the whole thing. She'd had to take more time off work having only just gone back, but the school had been sympathetic. Well, most people, the few people who knew the truth. She'd told Mariana. Mariana had approached her, in fact. She had heard about Felipe's disappearance and the whole dentist thing, probably through the head teacher, and she had sat next to Teresa in the lunchroom one break time and offered to make up. Teresa, not in a position to turn away friends, had accepted, and she was glad she had. Mariana turned out to be one of her greatest supports when it came time to have some of her innards removed.

They said it was only early stage cervical cancer. Only. The doctors said Teresa should still be able to get pregnant if she wished. Yeah, right? Like anyone other than a complete fucking psychopath was willing to take her to bed. She didn't say this to the doctors, of course. She was very polite and nodded at all the right moments. They had offered her a full hysterectomy, which seemed very kind of them. This would have ended any hope of ever having another child. Not that she wanted another child, it was just that she always thought it best to keep her options open. Maybe she should have been impregnated by Felipe while she had the chance. Then she would have raised her own little psychopath. Maybe with half her genes, it would have only turned out half, or two-thirds, psychotic.

They had mentioned the possibility of removing some eggs before the hysterectomy, which could be frozen in case she ever met someone who wanted to fertilise them in which case she could have them placed in a surrogate mother, something she did not feel like wishing on anyone.

They also offered her radiotherapy with the bonus of chemotherapy for added effectiveness, but the long-time side effects were worse, and it would prevent the possibility of her ever breeding a little psychopath.

There was a knock on the door.

"Enter," said Teresa, feeling important.

A doctor, with a small entourage of nurses, entered, brandishing some forms. He smiled a kind smile.

"Is everything okay?" he asked.

"Yes, fine," Teresa lied.

"I just need you to sign these, then you'll need to get changed, and we'll get you down to the theatre," he handed her the forms.

"What are these?" she asked.

"Just standard procedure," he reassured her. "Your permission for us to operate and to take any measures that might be necessary when you are under general anaesthetic. During which time you won't be in any state to give any permissions."

He laughed to himself, some kind of personal joke.

"What measures?"

"Well, there is a small risk of bleeding either during or after the operation so it may be necessary to give you a blood transfusion."

Teresa raised her eyebrows.

"There is the risk of infection," the doctor continued. "So you need to permit us to give you antibiotics both during and after."

Teresa thought this seemed reasonable.

"There is the risk of cutting the bowel or bladder, but if this occurs we will repair it during the surgery."

"That's nice."

"And there's the usual stuff related to having a general anaesthetic."

"Of course."

"Oh, and you'll need to wear these," the doctor handed her a pair of stockings.

"What are these?"

"Stockings to help prevent deep vein thrombosis. You must wear them after the operation and have anticoagulant injections to prevent clotting. It just thins your blood."

"Are there any other risks I should know?"

"There are lots of potential complications," said the doctor, quite matter of fact. "But let's not worry about those unless we have to."

Teresa didn't look very comfortable. The doctor sat beside her.

"Don't worry," he said. "As I explained before, the procedure is simple. We will remove the cervix and the parametrial tissue, the supporting tissue around the cervix, through the vagina. We will also remove the pelvic lymph nodes through an opening made in the abdomen. It will only take three or four small incisions, and you'll have a small scar, but nothing to worry about."

Teresa tried to force a smile.

"We will insert a large permanent stitch through the opening of the uterus. This will hold the opening of the uterus together, but it still allows you to have your period and to conceive. So don't worry about that."

Teresa thought maybe the hysterectomy would have been the better option, if only for the sake of not having her period. The doctor touched her arm.

"Don't worry," he said. "Get changed, and the anaesthetist will be back in a jiffy to take you down."

Teresa hoped that meant to the operating theatre and was not some wrestling reference.

*

When she awoke, Teresa realised an oxygen mask was covering her mouth. Then she realised there was also something in her arm and saw that they had connected a drip to her arm. She lifted her hand. It looked like someone had attached a clothes peg to her finger. She felt sleepy, and she felt uncomfortable down below. She tried to look, but someone was preventing her from sitting up.

"You've had a catheter fitted," explained a female voice. "You'll not be able to get out of bed to pee for a while. Plus, it helps us keep track of how much you're peeing."

This was too much information for Teresa, who wasn't really awake yet. There seemed to be tubes everywhere, and she ached in all kinds of places.

"There's also a temporary drain in your abdomen," the nurse continued. "It will drain any excess fluid or blood that might be present,"

Teresa felt shit.

"This is your pump for pain relief," the nurse explained. "You can press this button any time you feel the pain is getting too much."

Teresa remembered the anaesthetist explaining something about this before the operation. Above all, Teresa felt exhausted. She did not want to talk to the nurse or talk to anyone, she just wanted to rest.

Once she was back in the ward, the nurse told Teresa she had to get out of bed and sit in the chair. Teresa was not at all happy about it, but she did as she was told because it was something to do with her lungs working properly or something. Something to do with not getting a chest infection, which she did not like the sound of, so she obeyed. They also told her to move about, but that was a step too far for Teresa. She had their fucking stockings on. What more did they want?

Then the injections started. Teresa hated injections at the best of times, but they said that she would have to have daily injections to stop her blood from clotting. This was her idea of purgatory.

The next day, they made her move around even more, and a physiotherapist visited to educate her all about pelvic floor exercises. This seemed to comprise sitting as comfortably as she could and then clenching her muscles, you know, the ones down there, and then holding them for 10 to 15 seconds. This was very embarrassing for Teresa, but she didn't want to disappoint, so she tried her best.

A nurse came and told her she had been drinking a satisfactory quantity of fluids and removed the drip. One less tube to worry about. They also took away her pain pump and started giving her suppositories. She joked that, for all the good they did her, she might as well have shoved them up her arse. After five days, they removed the catheter.

Teresa felt very down. She just wanted to cry all the time. The nurses were so matter of fact and business-as-usual. She missed someone to chat to, so sent a 'hello' text to Mariana and got a 'hello' text back. This was a major step forward, but then Teresa realised she didn't know what to say to her. A few moments later, she received another text:

'how are things?'

'Lousy,' Teresa replied.

'Where are you?' Mariana asked.

'Still, in the hospital, they're letting me go home tomorrow.'

'Do you need a lift?' Mariana offered.

Teresa was taken aback by the offer.

'That's very kind,' she texted. 'But Selma is coming to collect me.'

'No problem,' texted Mariana. 'Anything you need, just let me know.'

'Thanks,' Teresa replied, and that was the end of the conversation. Still, it was a step in the right direction.

At home, Teresa continued to practise the pelvic floor exercises they had shown her. After about a week, the amount of pinkish/brown fluid that had been coming out of her vagina since the operation suddenly increased and she panicked and called the doctor. The nurse who took her call reassured her that this was normal, that it would only last a few days, and that it was part of the healing process.

They had given Teresa a detailed list of things that she could and couldn't do at home. She couldn't lift anything heavier than a full kettle or do any physical exercise. This was fine for her as it gave her another excuse not to go to the gym. They had prohibited her from having sex, chance would be a fine thing, or sticking anything inside her vagina but seeing as though she'd never got into that kind of thing anyway, it didn't matter. She wasn't allowed to drive, which made her feel less bad about selling her car. The cost of the panty liners she needed to buy to soak up the continual vaginal discharge outweighed any money she saved on petrol.

After four weeks, she had to return to work to face the barrage of sympathy. Teresa tried to avoid people, but that was impossible in a school. On the first day back, during the morning break, she tried to sit by herself, but Mariana came and sat opposite her.

"I'm sorry," Teresa began.

"Don't be," said Mariana. "I heard about what happened with Felipe and all the medical stuff you've had to deal with. It was selfish of me; I should have never reacted in the way I did. I'm sorry."

Teresa forced a smile which was returned by Mariana in a way that seemed genuine.

"How are you feeling?" asked Mariana.

"Scared, angry, depressed, anxious, confused," said Teresa, seeing no reason she shouldn't be blunt. "I've got no appetite, am constipated, have the occasional panic attack, and I can't sleep. Apart from that, I'm fine. How are you?"

Mariana smiled.

"Have you spoken to anyone about this?" she said.

"Oh yes. My doctor. My psychologist. They all say it's normal."

Teresa left out the bit about the terrible flatulence she was experiencing.

"I feel like I've done a million sit-ups," she said, trying to be nice. "I'm drinking loads of water. That seems to help."

"Teresa, you once told me you were trying to save up to visit your daughter in England."

"That's right."

"Have you saved up anything yet?"

"No," Teresa laughed. "Every time I get any money in my savings account, something happens, and I have to use it."

"How much is a ticket?"

"About R\$4,000 but then I would need to pay accommodation and living expenses. Why? Are you going to buy me a ticket?"

"No," Mariana laughed. "But I might help you save up."

"How do you mean?"

"I have some private lessons that I give after school. I have four students who I help with literacy and numeracy, and I also have some English language students I teach in nearby offices. Teresa, I'll hand all my students over to you."

"What?"

"I don't need the money, Teresa, and I could do with a break. You'd be doing me a favour. The students are straight after school, and the English language students are after. You'd be finished by 7 pm every night and I can even give you materials for the English lessons. You'd be earning an extra R$800 a week."

"What? Are you sure?"

"I'm sure. You get paid in cash, in advance, so that if the students cancel, you don't lose any money."

"I couldn't," said Teresa.

"You can. And you will. We'll get you to see your daughter in no time."

"Oh, Ma... I don't know what to say," Teresa was crying.

"Say nothing. Just say you'll do it."

"OK, I'll do it."

"I don't need the money," said Mariana. "I've only been doing it because I've been considering setting up my own language school. I get so many offers to teach that if you take my current clients, I'll have another full set of students in a few months, anyway."

Teresa didn't know whether to be envious or grateful, but she was very grateful.

Chapter Forty-Five - A visit from Lucretia – 11th April 2016

When Teresa arrived home, she looked in the kitchen cupboard at the bottle of cheap gin, three-quarters empty. She closed the cupboard door again, her hand resting on the handle, undecided.

The sound of clapping snapped her out of her trance. She opened the door and it surprised her to see none other than Felipe's mother stood at the other side of the gate.

"Lucretia!" Teresa said with surprise. "Come in."

She unlocked the gate, being careful not to allow her remaining cat to escape.

"Can I offer you a drink? Coffee? Something stronger?"

"No thank you, Teresa," Lucretia said, upset about something. Something more, Teresa suspected, than her son's disappearance. "Some water please."

Teresa offered her almost-mother-in-law a kitchen chair, which she accepted gratefully and then took a glass from the cupboard and filled it with filtered water.

"What a surprise," Teresa admitted. "Is everything okay?"

"Yes, I'm sorry I never visited before. You must have thought me rude."

"Not at all," Teresa lied.

"I expect a lot of things must have seemed strange," Lucretia continued. "Like our initial reaction to the news that you and Felipe decided to get married."

"I expect it was a shock."

"Yes, it was. But not for the reasons you might expect."

Teresa was thinking about the gin again and wished Lucretia had accepted something stronger so she would have an excuse to pour one for herself.

"You know Felipe had an accident?" Lucretia asked.

"Yes, he told me."

"Did he tell you the consequences of his accident? I mean, the way it affected him?"

"He said it affected his memory; he was always leaving little piles of notes around the place. I'm surprised it didn't affect his work."

"Hmm, yes. There was that. Felipe seemed to have devised some kind of system which seemed to work. No, I'm not talking about that. Did you ever notice any mood swings? Anything of that kind?"

"He could be moody sometimes, yes, but..."

"But never violent?"

"Well..."

"Did he ever hit you, Teresa?"

"Not as such, no."

"What do you mean, not as such?"

"Well, he never hit me, but he threw things around and sometimes broke things."

"Did he ever threaten you?"

"No, not really. I mean, Felipe would threaten to leave but never threaten me with violence."

"Good."

"Why? Why do you ask?"

Lucretia sighed.

"Teresa. What I am about to say is difficult for me. You weren't the first."

"I didn't think I was."

"Not like that. You weren't the first girl he abused."

"Who said he abused me?"

"Oh, come on, Teresa. I know my son better than you. I know what he's like."

"Do you think he's still alive?" Teresa asked.

"Who knows? The point I'm trying to make is this. And you must promise me that what I am about to tell you stays between us."

Lucretia waited for Teresa to nod her affirmation that what she was about to hear would go no further.

"The point is, Teresa, that you were not the first. This incident was not the first. After the accident, he amazed us at the speed of his recovery. As you know, my husband was a surgeon, so he knows about these things and he said he'd seen nothing like it. Felipe returned to work, and he seemed to be getting on with his life once more. His fiancé at the time stuck with him through the whole affair, poor girl, but we noticed slight changes. We noticed he treated her differently, and this had been going on for quite some time. He was more short-tempered. Spoke curtly. It was around this time that we noticed the problems he was having with his memory. He's been clever at hiding it from us. Well, to cut a long story short, we think he was unkind to her at home, if you know what I mean."

Teresa gave Lucretia a puzzled look.

"We think he was hitting her. Once I noticed she had bruises and she seemed very embarrassed to talk about them, said she just bumped herself or something. I asked Felipe about it, but he told me to mind my own business. We were concerned, but there wasn't much we could do about it because not long after, the poor girl disappeared."

"Disappeared?"

"Without a trace. There was an investigation. The police were involved and were asking some awkward questions. My husband is influential in our little corner of the world, and he used his influence to make it all go away. Oh my goodness, if he knew I was here now."

Lucretia took a sip of her water.

"Are you sure you wouldn't like something stronger?" suggests Teresa, getting up from her chair.

"No, I'm fine thanks, dear," said Lucretia and Teresa sat back down again.

"You see, the thing is," Lucretia continued. "That we suspected foul play. That Felipe was involved somehow in the disappearance of the poor girl. We had no proof, and we could not draw Felipe on the subject, but I know my son, and I know that something happened. And....well... the thing is that when you arrived on the scene, we were a bit weary, but when you announced that you were getting married. I'm sure you must have thought we were rude it was just that the memories of what happened before were still fresh in our minds and after what has happened. It might seem a terrible thing to say because he is my son, but the thing is dear that I'm glad that he disappeared this time because I don't know what we would do if another girl went missing."

Teresa wasn't sure how to react.

"Look, Teresa," Lucretia continued. "I came to say that well..."

Teresa realised how difficult this was for the woman she thought so little of until today.

"What is it?" Teresa asked.

"If he comes back," Lucretia seemed uncomfortable with what she was forcing herself to say. "If he comes back, Teresa. Have nothing to do with him."

Teresa was taken aback.

"He's unpredictable," Lucretia continued. "If he comes back, don't let him in. Call me. No, better still. Call the police."

Chapter Forty-Six - The Detective Returns – 11th April 2016

Teresa was sitting on the bed, watching TV and peeling an orange with a knife, when the doorbell rang again. She turned off the TV and dragged herself off the bed and to the front door, where she straightened when she saw the detective at the other side of the security gate. She invited him in, offered him a coffee or water. He declined both. He accepted the seat she offered; then he waited until she was settled before he spoke.

"Teresa," he said. "I have some news. About the incident at the dentist."

Teresa sat up.

"We got the CCTV footage," he continued. "The computer was fire damaged, but we got some footage, and there's something you should know."

Teresa leant forward.

"We got quite a clear view of the individual who broke into the practice. They covered their head with a mask, and the footage is low resolution but, we've been looking at it in some detail, and there is something about him we are fairly sure about but might come as a surprise. I've got a still here to show you."

The detective pulled a piece of paper from his coat pocket, unfolded it, and handed it to Teresa. It was a colour image of a man dressed in black, wearing a mask. Teresa recognised him as the man who punched her in the face.

"Is there anything familiar about him?" the detective asked.

"He's the man who robbed me," said Teresa.

"Anything else?" asked the detective.

Teresa looked at the picture again, shrugged, and shook her head. The detective seemed to scrutinise her. She looked at the picture a third time.

"What?" she asked.

"There's nothing familiar about the photo?" the detective asked again.

Teresa shook her head.

"When we were analysing the video," the detective explained. "There was something strange about the way he moves. I thought nothing about it myself, but I have a colleague, João. João is mad about motorcycles. He has a Harley Davidson. You know, one of those big bikes?"

Teresa nodded.

"João watched the video only once, and he spotted something straight away. Something none of us would have spotted. The thing is that João has a cousin who is also mad about motorcycles. They used to drive down to the beach together for the day on a Sunday. Get up early, drive down to the beach, go for a swim, have something to eat and come back the same day. The thing is that they used to have a few beers too. João used to have a couple, but his cousin was a big drinker, and João warned him that something would happen, but his cousin wouldn't listen. Anyway, one day, they'd been to the beach, and late in the afternoon, it rained. They had dinner in a bar, as usual, João had a few beers, and his cousin had a few beers more. On the way back, in the rain, João and his cousin were riding between the traffic when some idiot changed lanes without looking in their mirrors and slammed straight into João's cousin. The car crushed his leg into his bike and shattered the bone. They rushed him to the hospital and pinned his leg. The problem was that João's cousin, who was a heavy drinker, as I think I've explained... the thing was that unbeknown to him, he had developed diabetes, and that affected his circulation. The leg didn't heal properly, and they had to amputate it above the knee."

"This is all fascinating," interrupted Teresa. "But what has it got to do with me?"

"The thing is that João is observant. He's probably the most observant person I know. I mean he can walk in and out of a room in a few seconds and describe the entire contents in real detail. I think he might be on the autistic spectrum, but I can't be sure."

Teresa gives the detective an impatient stare.

"Yes, well, the thing is that as soon as João watched this video, it reminded him of his cousin. I asked him why but he couldn't place it at first, but then it came to him. He said that this guy in the video walked the same way as his cousin. The thing is that he has noticed that amputees have a certain way of walking and apparently the guy in this video walks in this way, the same as his cousin."

Teresa stared at the photo again.

"We think the guy in this video was an amputee. Felipe was an amputee, wasn't he?"

Teresa nodded.

"Teresa," the detective spoke with gravity. "Do you think the man in the photo is Felipe?"

"I don't know," said Teresa. "It's possible. But why?"

"Good question. According to Felipe's family, it sounds like he's volatile. Worst case scenario, if this man is Felipe, it means that he is probably still alive and, what's worse, he's a murderer. My advice to you, Teresa, would be not to answer the door to anyone unless you are sure you know who they are. Until we can locate Felipe."

Teresa sat in silence for a moment, processing the information.

"Why would he do this?" she asked.

"We think he might have psychological issues."

Chapter Forty-Seven - Felipe returns – 11th April 2016

When the detective left, Teresa locked the gate and used both locks on the door before turning off the lights and going to bed. She dreamt that Felipe was sitting on the edge of the bed and that he was speaking to her.

"Teresa. Teresa."

She turned over, hoping the dream would go away. But it didn't.

"Teresa. Teresa."

She tried to wake herself up to make the dream go away and then realised it wasn't a dream. She sat up and saw that Felipe was there. He was wearing black again, like in the photo from the dentist's CCTV. She filled her lungs with air, ready to scream, but before she could exhale, Felipe grabbed her head and covered her mouth with his hand. She screamed anyway, and he struggled to stifle the noise, so he grabbed a pillow and pressed it over her face.

She tried to pull him off, but he was too strong and she was struggling to breathe, trying to move her head to get air, but Felipe was pushing the pillow down onto her head with such force that she could not move it. She tried pushing him away, but he had his full weight on her. She reached out to grab something to hit him with, but all her fingers found were orange peel.

Felipe increased the pressure, and Teresa could not draw breath. She stretched out as far as she could, hoping to find something, anything, she might find to hit him. Her fingertips touched steel as she used all of her strength to extend her arm and, grabbing the knife, stabbed Felipe as hard as she could. He released the pressure, and she pushed him off, removing the pillow from her face and taking a deep breath. She watched as Felipe staggered backwards; the knife sticking out of his temple, blood dripping down the side of his face and onto her floor.

Teresa jumped out of bed and backed away from Felipe, grabbing her phone and backing into the kitchen where the door and gate were wide open. She thought of Ramsey and pulled the gate shut as she dialled 190, keeping Felipe in her sight in case he made any sudden moves. She looked at the knife protruding from his head and doubted he would push himself off the floor where he slumped, staring at her, his eyes betraying the disbelief of what happened.

Chapter Forty-Eight - Teresa returns – 7th October 2016

Teresa pushed the trolley out into the arrivals area, past all the expectant faces and raised notices. She could see the sun streaming through the terminal windows, though she knew when she got outside she would barely feel its effects on her skin.

Six months of twelve-hour days had taken its toll. She was tired to the core, but she also felt exhilarated. In moments, she would see her daughter in person for the first time in years, and that eclipsed everything else. Even the day the doctor had given her the all-clear did not feel this good. She searched the faces lined up on the other side of the barrier, wondering whether she would recognise them. None of them were familiar. She looked back to see whether she had missed them, but she hadn't.

She pushed her trolley clear of the barriers and found herself in the middle of the terminal where she looked around, but she could not see them anywhere. Her heart sank. And then, from the end of the terminal, she saw William. He saw her. She looked around; she could not see her girl. William turned, beckoning to someone. She followed his gaze and then she saw her.

She was so big. Annabel ran to her father, and he hugged her. Teresa watched as William explained something to her daughter and then led the child towards her. Teresa made eye contact with William. Something distracted Annabel, looking elsewhere. As they drew closer, William tried to draw Annabel's attention to Teresa. As they were about to meet, Teresa crouched down and reached out her arms. Annabel noticed her and shrank away in fear. William tried to reassure her, but Annabel did not recognise this woman trying to grab her.

"Don't worry princess," said William, gathering his daughter up into his arms and lifting her up. "This is your Mummy, darling."

"Hello," said Teresa.

Annabel buried her head in her father's shoulder.

"She's shy," William reasoned.

Teresa smiled. She knew it might be difficult to win back her daughter's affection after so long. Being this close to her was enough. For now.

*

Enjoy this book? You can make a big difference.

Reviews are the most powerful tools in my arsenal when it comes to getting attention for my books. Much as I'd like to, I don't have the financial muscle of a large publisher. I can't take out take out full page ads in the newspaper or put posters on the subway.

(Not yet anyway),

But I have something much more powerful and effective than that, and it's something those publishers would kill to get their hands on.

A committed and loyal bunch of readers.

Honest reviews of my books help bring them to the attention of other readers.

If you've enjoyed this book, I would be very grateful if you could spend just five minutes leaving a review (it can be as short as you like).

Thank you very much.

Not ready to leave Teresa?

Read on for an extract of the next book in the series…
LEAVE TO REMAIN
(previously released as Living with the Headless Mule)

Chapter One - Teresa returns - 8th October 2016

"It's OK," said Teresa. "She needs time to get used to this stranger."

"She'll be fine," said William. "The car is this way."

Teresa looked around the airport terminal. It looked different from the last time she had been here. On that occasion, she had been fleeing England and abandoning her daughter. It had taken her two and a half years before she could accumulate the money to return and, in that time, despite frequent conversations on Skype, her daughter had almost forgotten who she was.

"It's just shyness," said William, aware of Teresa's disappointment.

"How's your wife?" Teresa asked about William's second wife, Jennifer, the bitch whom he chose over her.

"She just popped to the shop to get something for Annabel. She's getting hungry. We were waiting longer than we expected."

"Yes, sorry about that," said Teresa. But she felt she was not responsible for a delayed flight. She wasn't flying the plane. "Thanks for picking me up."

"That's OK. The tube, with luggage, can be a nightmare. Are you OK with that?"

William saw Teresa was struggling with her bag.

"Yes, I'm fine," she lied. "The wheels have a mind of their own."

"Ah, there she is."

Teresa followed William's gaze to where Jennifer, his wife, was exiting from a shop with a carrier bag, which looked like it was crammed to the limit with sandwiches, crisps and drinks.

"Ah, so she's here," Jennifer said as she approached. "They have nothing healthy in there. I got sandwiches and orange juice. And if you don't like the flavour of sandwiches, then you'll have to lump it."

Jennifer directed this last comment towards Annabel, who just buried her head deeper in her father's neck.

"Put her down," said Jennifer. "She's not a baby."

Teresa tried to smile, but Jennifer had reminded Teresa of every reason she hated this woman who stole her husband and her daughter.

"Well? Shall we go?"

"Yes, the car is this way," said William, putting Annabel down and taking her hand.

*

Teresa was pleased that for the drive from the airport, she was could sit in the back seat with Annabel. At first, her daughter eyed her with suspicion but warmed to her.

"Look at the sheep," said Teresa, pointing to the side of a reservoir where there were many of the white woolly creatures grazing on the green grass. Teresa had forgotten how green England was.

"There is a farm near where we live where Daddy took me to see some sheep," Annabel said with enthusiasm.

"Oh yes? Tell me about it."

"They have lots of different animals, and they have a riding school. Daddy says that if I'm good when I'm old enough, he might get me riding lessons. Would you like to see it?"

Teresa nodded.

"Daddy, can we take her to see the horses at the farm? Can we please?"

"We'll have to see," came the answer. But not from William. The answer came from his new wife in the passenger seat.

Annabel offered Teresa a look as if to say that this was par for the course.

"They let you feed the animals," Annabel continued. "I fed some... they look like sheep... but they have long necks."

"Llamas?" Teresa suggested.

"I'm not sure," said Annabel.

"Alpacas," William confirmed from the driving seat.

"Keep your eyes on the road," warned his new wife.

"Yes, that's right. Alpacas. They look like sheep, but they have long necks," said Annabel.

"I've seen some in photos," said Teresa.

"Well, you can feed them at this place. You have to go there."

Annabel offered a nervous glance towards the passenger seat to see whether there would be another interjection. There wasn't, and she relaxed a little.

"When we get home, I'll show you my bedroom," Annabel continued. "I have lots of toys."

"And clothes," came the voice on the passenger seat.

Teresa wondered whether this was another dig at her. She always sent Annabel clothes for Christmas and birthdays. They were easier to post. And she always bought clothes on the larger side, Annabel would grow into them. Looking at Annabel now, she was not on the large side. Teresa imagined her ex-husband's new wife struggling to stuff all these clothes into a cupboard, waiting for years before Annabel was large enough to wear them.

William divorced Teresa and sued for custody of Annabel a year after Teresa's drunk driving incident. However, the speed with which he remarried suggested to Teresa that he already was seeing the bitch even when he and Teresa had been together. She had no proof, though.

"You're growing up," Teresa said to Annabel and then cringed. That was what an elderly aunt would say. Annabel just smiled.

"I'll be eight in December," Annabel announced with confidence.

"Yes," said Teresa. "We should visit Hamleys while I am here, and you can choose a birthday present."

"What's Ham...?"

"Hamleys? It's the largest toy shop in London, possibly in the world."

Annabel wriggled with excitement.

"Can she Daddy? Can she take me to Ham... can she take me to the toy shop?"

"We'll see," came the answer from the passenger seat.

"Let's see," said Teresa. "If we have time, we'll go. But either way, I'll let you choose your birthday present."

"But it's only October."

"But I won't see you again before January, and it will save me posting more clothes from Brazil. "

Teresa smiled.

"Yay," Annabel made a fist and pulled her arm back in a victorious gesture. "I'm on holiday next week. It's half term."

"Any idea what you might like for your birthday?"

Annabel sank deep into contemplation.

*

As William pulled up outside his house, Teresa's heart sank to see that his mother, her ex-mother-in-law, was waiting for them on the doorstep. It was October, didn't the old witch feel any cold?

As soon as Teresa let her out of the car, Annabel ran up to greet her grandmother, who whisked her inside out of the cold to the central heating.

Jennifer left William to help Teresa get her bag out of the car while she swept along the front path to the house. She was wearing a long skirt, and Teresa wondered whether her feet touched the ground or whether she just hovered like a spirit.

Teresa was self-conscious of the noise the wheels of her bag made on the stone path as she pulled it behind, following William up to the house, a much bigger house than they lived in when they got married. He must have been doing much better now as a climate change consultant for a large company than he had been working at the Gaia environmental charity when they met.

The inside of the house confirmed that this was true unless Jennifer bought for the plush interior. Teresa tried to remember what Jennifer did. It might have been something to do with law. That would explain the expensive interior decorating. And the fact that she seemed to be the one wearing the metaphorical trousers in the relationship. It might be something to do with management consulting. They seemed to be just as well paid and were just as arrogant.

"Come on, I'll show you to your room," said William, having closed the door behind her. He then led her across the varnished floorboards of the hall to the varnished staircase.

"Thanks for... for this," she said.

"That's okay. It's only for a week. It's good for Annabel. Just don't make a habit of it."

He turned, offering her a weak smile as he climbed the stairs ahead of her. Teresa picked up her case by the handle and lifted it so as not to scratch the pristine woodwork.

"Maria made up one of the guest bedrooms," he said.

"Maria?"

"She's our cleaner. She's a Brazilian too. I must introduce her to you."

A cleaner? Things were looking up for William.

"How many bedrooms do you have?"

"Four."

"Is your mother staying?"

"Yes, she's in the other guest bedroom."

Teresa's heart deflated once more. The last thing she wanted for her week with Annabel was to have that old witch hanging around, sticking her nose in all the time. No matter. She had no option and would have to make the most of it. At least she was lucky that William had given her somewhere to stay. Beggars couldn't be choosers.

"Just one more flight," said William, leading her across the landing to more varnished stairs. "Are you OK with that bag?"

"Yes, fine, thanks," she lied, worried that at any moment she would break out in a sweat.

"Not far now."

He led her onto a second landing.

"This is our loft conversion. We got two more rooms out of it. The walls are a little thin, so be careful. My mother will hear your every move. She's next door."

Teresa smiled at his little joke, but what she wanted to do was curse the woman who brought William into the world. The irony was that without William and his evil mother, there would not have been an Annabel. Half of her genes came from her father's side.

"I'll leave you to freshen up. Dinner will be ready soon."

Teresa walked into the room. It was on the small side but still accommodated a double bed, a chest of drawers, a small wardrobe, and there was a door in the corner which Teresa discovered contained a small bathroom with a shower cubicle, toilet, washbasin, and mirror.

Someone had folded two plush towels on the bed, and there was another matching towel for the bathroom. She opened her case and took out her toiletries, which she intended to augment this week with big economy bottles which she could buy in England at half the price she could buy them in Brazil. She stripped off and headed for the shower. On the way, she caught sight of her naked self, reflected in the mirror on the wardrobe. She stopped to look at herself. It hadn't been that long ago that she hadn't been able to stand the sight of her own naked body. Since Felipe, she had been trying to take more care of herself, doing more exercise and, as she looked at herself, she felt much better, less saggy, and she looked less saggy. Teresa was even happier about her breasts, which were always a source of self-conscious disappointment. Feeling pleased, she stood under a warm shower and let the water wash the residue of her journey from Brazil off her skin and down the drain.

Wrapping a towel around her, she padded over to her case to choose some clean clothes. There was a knock at the door, and then, to her surprise, it opened, and William popped his head through the opening.

"Oh, sorry," he said, embarrassed at discovering her wearing nothing but a towel. But he did not retreat.

Teresa checked that the towel was secured.

"Can I help you?" she asked.

"Oh Yes," he awoke from his trance. "Dinner is ready. I'll see you downstairs."

"Ok. I'll be five minutes."

"Right then. Sorry."

William backed out of the doorway and closed the door. Teresa breathed out a sigh of relief and then let out a little giggle before letting her towel fall to the floor as she selected a clean pair of knickers.

*

When she arrived in the enormous kitchen dining area, the whole family was waiting for her.

"Sorry," said Teresa.

"That's OK," said William, who found himself on the receiving end of some spectacular evil stares from his new wife and his mother, Henrietta. Teresa remembered the old woman's name.

"Come on, let's get started before it gets any colder," Henrietta grumbled.

Teresa felt the four cold eyes of the women, laden with bad intentions, piercing her flesh and burrowing towards her soul. It was understandable, Teresa supposed, that there would be animosity towards her, as William's ex-wife, staying for a week.

"I can't thank you enough for letting me stay this week. It means a lot to me, to see Annabel."

"Oh, don't thank me," said William's current wife. "You have William to thank for that."

Teresa smiled in William's direction, but he seemed to be trying to avoid eye contact with all and sundry. Most of all, his mother who seemed to alternate her attempts to use her eyes to burn holes in Teresa's skull, with similar efforts on William.

"William told me about your terrible experience with that man in Brazil," Henrietta sounded sympathetic, but Teresa suspected she was revelling in the opportunity to dredge up terrible memories for her.

William offered Teresa a look of apology.

"What happened again?" Henrietta pursued the subject.

"Mother, I'm sure Teresa doesn't want you to remind her of that," William interceded.

"Oh?" His mother feigned surprise. "Is that right Teresa? Well, I suppose it must be a terrible experience when you…"

"Mother," William raised his voice. "Not in front of Annabel."

Henrietta held her peace. Annabel looked interested in whatever she wasn't supposed to know.

"Eat your dinner," William told his daughter.

Teresa focused on her plate, as if William had also directed his comment at her. His mother achieved her aim of filling Teresa's mind with the events of that terrible night. The struggle, police, trial, endless questions, nightmares which still haunted her sleep. She watched Annabel eating and tried to put the thoughts out of her head.

Then she noticed something. She looked at Annabel's plate, then at her own, then at William's, his wife's and mother's. Teresa looked once more at the chicken on her plate and then at the chicken on William's.

"I thought you were vegetarian," she said at last.

"We're flexitarian now," William said, with what Teresa thought might be a little embarrassment.

"Flexitarian? What's that?"

"It means I'm vegetarian most of the time, but sometimes I eat meat."

Teresa stared at him in amazement. He reminded her of all those traumatic moments spent trying to find something for William to eat, especially when he went through his vegan phase. The criticism she suffered if William found something in the cupboard which wasn't vegetarian, organic or fairtrade. Teresa barely touched the flesh of a dead animal in all the time she spent with him. One of the first things she did when she returned to Brazil was stuff her face with as much meat as possible, especially the delicious shredded pork sandwiches, *pernil*.

Everything seemed so good for Brazil back in 2014. They were about to host the World Cup, the Rio Olympics were on their way, 'pre sal' oil reserves would bring a lot of wealth and prosperity to the country. There was a general sense of optimism. Two years later, the Rio Olympics ended, and the mood changed. The politicians impeached the Brazilian president, Dilma Rousseff. The national oil company, Petrobras, posted terrible financial results because of a widespread system of corruption in which investigators identified $38bn in bribes and backhanders. Meanwhile, there was insufficient funding for public health, education and transport systems, and the mood of the nation changed to one of pessimism in what the media described as a national crisis.

Teresa hadn't found the quality of life for which she hoped when she fled England two and a half years earlier. This added to the bitterness she felt towards William, who had not stood by her during her year of rehabilitation, following her drunk driving conviction, but asked for a divorce and sued for custody of their daughter.

Now William appeared to have abandoned all of those ideals which he had clung to during their relationship and which made Teresa's life so difficult when they were together.

She watched William stuffing a piece of chicken into his mouth, and she wished he would choke on it. After everything, she had to swallow when they were married.

They finished their meals in silence and then, after a nudge from Jennifer, William asked Annabel to get ready for bed. Annabel was reluctant, but she didn't complain.

"I expect you'll be tired," Jennifer addressed Teresa.

"Yes, but perhaps I might do the dishes first."

"We have a dishwasher," said Jennifer, as if the fact was obvious.

"In that case, I will turn in. Thank you again for everything."

Jennifer's smile was insincere.

"Do you have everything you need?" William asked.

"Yes, I think so."

"Sleep in tomorrow. You can have breakfast whenever you want."

"Great. Thanks. Well, goodnight then everyone."

"Good night," William alone responded.

Teresa wasn't tired at all, and it was too early to go to bed, but she felt so awkward to be in the presence of William's wife and mother that she wanted to get away and have some time by herself to adjust to this strange situation.

As she reached the first landing, Annabel was rushing to the bathroom as if Teresa had caught her doing something other than getting ready for bed.

"Annabel. Wait."

The seven-year-old halted in the doorway.

"I'm going to bed too, darling, so I'll see you in the morning, Okay?"

"Okay."

"Perhaps tomorrow we can do something fun together. Would you like that?"

"Maybe Daddy will let us go to the farm, and I can show you the sheep with long necks."

"Alpaca."

"And the horses. I can show you the horses."

"That sounds good. Let's ask your father if we can do that tomorrow, then."

"Will you ask him?"

"We'll both ask him."

"Yes, because Jennifer might want to do something else."

"Let's see. Okay, night night darling and we'll see each other tomorrow, Okay?"

"Okay, night night," said Annabel and closed the bathroom door.

Teresa stared at the door, wishing Annabel had given her a goodnight hug and kiss. But, determined to give Annabel the time she needed, Teresa climbed the second set of stairs and entered her bedroom, closing the door behind her and noticing there was no lock on the door.

After changing into the pyjamas she bought for the trip, she got into bed with a book on Brazilian Folklore she bought before she left Sao Paulo. She'd bought the book because during her brief relationship with her ex-fiancé in which she had questioned her own sanity and had imagined that he might be a manifestation of the mischievous character from Brazilian folklore, Saci Perere.

She had already read the chapter on Saci and turned to the next chapter, which was about the legend of the headless mule. The legend was about the ghost of a woman who had been cursed by God for fornicating with a priest in a church. The curse turned her into a fire spewing headless mule which galloped through the countryside from Thursday sundown to Friday sunrise. Teresa's body clock was still two hours behind in Brazil. She put her book down, turned off the light, and rested her head on the pillow.

*

"Teresa, Teresa."

Teresa awoke in a panic, wondering whether she had locked the gate and both locks on the door. Had anyone got into the flat? Had he got into the flat? She's heard his voice. She sat up straight and looked around.

It was then that she realised where she was. She was hyperventilating, and on touching her face, she realised she was sweating.

If she closed her eyes, she could see the same black silhouette she had awoken to last April. A silhouette of her fiancé just before he tried to suffocate her with her pillow. The memory left her breathless, and she tried not to think about how it ended — the knife sticking out of his temple, blood dripping down the side of his face and onto the floor.

His eyes haunted her. The look of disbelief on his face as he slumped on the floor, with the knife protruding from his head, while Teresa called the police.

Find out what happens next

Get your copy [1]

Get a free novel

Building a relationship with my readers is the very best thing about writing. I occasionally send newsletters with details on new releases, special offers and other bits of news relating to my novels.

If you sign up to the mailing list, I'll send you a free copy of LEAVE TO REMAIN.

You can get the novel, **for free,** by signing up at:-
https://dl.bookfunnel.com/7spkpgc0at [2]

---

2.   https://dl.bookfunnel.com/7spkpgc0at

ABOUT THE AUTHOR

M J Dees is the author of Living with Saci and The Astonishing Anniversaries of James and David, Part One. He makes his online home at themichaeldees.com/[1]. You can connect with M J on Twitter at @themichaeldees[2], on Facebook[3] and send him an email at michael@themichaeldees.com if the mood strikes you.

---

1. http://www.themichaeldees.com/

2. http://www.twitter.com/themichaeldees

3. https://www.facebook.com/profile.php?id=100085345437884

DEDICATION

To Maria, Absolem and Raya.

ACKNOWLEDGEMENTS

I am indebted to my beta and advance review teams.

COPYRIGHT

---

1.   http://www.goon